SWEET CRAVINGS – BOOK 2

THOSE
Summer
NIGHTS

IVY SMOAK

This book is an original publication of Loft Troll Ink.

This book is a work of fiction. Names, characters, places, and incidents are fictitious. Any resemblance to actual persons, living or dead, events, or locales is purely coincidental.

Copyright © 2019 by Ivy Smoak
All rights reserved

ISBN: 9781086141443

Cover art copyright © 2020 by Ivy Smoak

2020 Edition

To all the summer nights I've spent with these characters. And all the summer nights I walked on Rehoboth boardwalk wishing I had a boyfriend.

PROLOGUE

"It's a little short, don't you think?" I asked as I stared at my reflection in the mirror. The sleek black fabric hugged every curve that I didn't even realize I had. It was almost suggestive. And I wasn't exactly trying to suggest anything. The stiletto heels that I could barely even stand in did nothing to help the situation. Why had I agreed to let Peyton help me get ready again? She was shorter than me and this dress would still be classified as inappropriate on her. I was suddenly itching for my jean shorts and Keds.

"Mila, that's kinda the point," Peyton said.

I laughed and turned toward her. "What do you mean?" I tucked a loose strand of hair behind my ear. I was about five seconds away from grabbing the clothes I came over in and sprinting out the door.

She swatted my hand away. "Stop, your hair is already perfect." She grabbed my shoulders and turned me back toward the mirror. "What I mean is that you're going to want to look your best. This is a *big* night."

Usually I could ignore the way she emphasized random words in sentences, but she was driving me particularly crazy today. It wasn't a big night. Yes, Aiden would be heading back home for spring break tomorrow and I would be stuck here by myself. But we'd only be apart for a week. Peyton was acting like it was the end of the world. I frowned at my reflection and reached for the zipper of the ridiculous dress she had forced on me. "Yeah…I'm going to change."

Peyton threw her hands up in the air. "God, you're impossible. I promised myself I wouldn't say anything, but clearly I was meant to overhear the guys at that party last night."

"Party? What party?" Aiden had told me he was studying all day yesterday.

"Wrong question, Mila. The important question is *what* were they discussing."

"Aiden said he was studying for an exam, so I hope they were discussing engineering things." Honestly everything about engineering was over my head. I couldn't even give a proper example of what he'd be reading.

"Mila, this had nothing to do with classes. Aiden said that the two of you really needed to talk. That he'd been planning on telling you for a while. He said it was important. That he couldn't wait any longer." She raised both her eyebrows and stared at me.

The talk. I'd seen so many romcoms that my mind instantly went to a terrible place. Aiden was going to break up with me? And I was supposed to dress up for him to do this why exactly? The borrowed dress suddenly felt even tighter. Why would Aiden do this? We were good. We were really good. The thought of having to live in Santa Monica without him made my whole body start to get all sweaty. My stomach churned. I was probably leaving embarrassing pit stains on Peyton's dress. "I…" my voice trailed off. "What exactly did you overhear?"

Peyton sighed. "Put it together, girl." She pointed to her ring finger on her left hand.

I just stared at her. And then I started laughing because it was completely ridiculous. "You think he's going to propose? I'm only a junior." The thought was even more preposterous than the idea of him breaking up with me. Just barely.

"Yeah, but he's a senior. He'll be done school in a few months and obviously he wants to put a ring on it before he leaves. Oh! Maybe he's going to surprise you and ask you to go to his parents for spring break!"

Aiden and I had been dating basically since I first stepped foot on campus. And not once had he wanted to introduce me to his parents. Apparently they were quite snooty. But the other part of her guess? The proposal part. It was starting to sink in. The dread in my stomach was slowly being replaced by excitement. Because he had asked me to a fancy restaurant for dinner. I thought it was just a "goodbye I'll see you after spring break" date. But what if it was more? Peyton and Aiden had been friends forever. She knew him better than anyone. If she thought Aiden was about to pop the question…he might be. "Do you really think he's going to propose?"

"Yes!" she squealed and clapped both her hands together. "Which is why you need to suck it up and wear that dress."

If Aiden was going to propose tonight, I wanted to be myself, not some version of Peyton. The girl staring back at me in the mirror was not me. I barely even recognized myself. "I should probably get going."

"Wait. Isn't he picking you up here?"

"Yeah, but I forgot something. I'll call you after, okay?"

"You better!"

I grabbed my bag and hobbled out the door as quickly as I could in Peyton's stilettos. Peyton could have easily misunderstood what she had overheard Aiden talking about. But had she said overheard? Or was she part of the conversation? I kicked off my heels so I could walk faster. Normally the campus at Santa Monica University could easily take my mind off any of my worries. Today the palm trees swaying in the wind did nothing for me.

Aiden's going to propose. Aiden's going to propose. Aiden's going to propose. I let the thought settle in and a smile spread across my face. It all made sense. The study session lie so he could get his friends' advice. He'd been a little distant recently, probably because he was nervous. I glanced down at my left hand, imagining an engagement ring there. Aiden and I made sense together. We fit. I was young, but that didn't mean I wasn't ready for the rest of my life to start.

And I wanted to do it by looking like myself. Which meant a cute spring dress, not some slutty number from Peyton's closet. I knew the perfect dress. It was hanging in Aiden's closet. I basically lived in his apartment even though we hadn't officially moved in together. I was going to miss him terribly when he was gone for spring break, but knowing that we were engaged would certainly make it more bearable.

I stopped outside his apartment building. The more I thought about it, the more it made sense. We'd be parting ways in a few months. I'd be staying on campus during the summer and he was starting his new job. Being engaged meant he wouldn't forget me while we were apart. I shook the thought away. That was ridiculous. He wasn't going to forget about me. And I certainly wasn't going to forget him. He was everything to me. We were building our future together.

It was impossible for me to remove the smile plastered to my face as I opened up the door to his building. I wasn't sure what I would have done without Aiden. I pretended I was a badass for moving here from a small town in Delaware. But honestly, when I stepped onto campus three falls ago, I was terrified. If I hadn't literally bumped into him on the second week of classes, I'd probably still be crying myself to sleep every night alone in my dorm. All his friends became my friends. And I couldn't imagine being any happier. I chose SMU for a fresh start. Aiden became my actual fresh start.

I pulled out the key to his apartment as I walked up the stairs. If I really thought about it, I should have known a proposal was coming. I loved him. I was absolutely sure of it. He was kind. And smart. And God was he sexy. I wanted him to know that he was my whole world.

I stopped outside his door. There had always been a little fear in the back of my mind that I wasn't good enough for him. That his parents didn't approve of me and that's why I hadn't met them. But tonight would change everything. I wanted to be enough for him. He was enough for me. He was *it* for me.

So why was I still all sweaty? *Stop being weird.* I took a deep breath as I slid the key into the lock and opened the door. "Aiden?" I stepped into his empty apartment. Of course he wasn't here. He was probably on his way to pick me up from Peyton's. I laughed and grabbed his t-shirt off the floor. He must have been in a hurry to get ready for our date. I folded it, draped it over my arm, and walked toward his bedroom. My comfy dress was calling to me. I couldn't wait to change.

Before I reached his room, I pulled out my cell phone and called him. Hopefully he wouldn't go in and talk to Peyton. Their friendship had always bothered me a little. And it bugged me that she knew about him proposing before even I did. I wanted to forget that the past half hour had even happened and enjoy our night. My stomach growled, reminding me of the fact that I was starving.

Aiden's ringtone sounded on the other side of the bedroom door. He never went anywhere without his phone. He was almost anal about it. Which meant he was home. *Crap*. I didn't want him to see me in this dress because I had a feeling he'd like it and I really wanted to change. "Aiden?" I said as I turned the door handle. "I need to grab my dress from..." The shirt I had folded fell silently to the ground.

"Mila? Shit." Aiden fell out of bed. Naked. Pulling the sheets off the bed with him to cover his junk.

The girl he left sheet-less screamed and covered herself with her hands.

What. The. Hell.

I felt like a deflated balloon. *The* talk. God, my first instinct was right. He was going to break up with me. I could hear Peyton's voice in my head: "Aiden said that the two of you really needed to talk. That he'd been planning on telling you for a while. He said it was important. That he couldn't wait any longer."

He'd been planning on breaking up with me for a while. Not proposing. And he couldn't wait any longer because I guess he was too excited to put his dick into this chick. He didn't love me. He was into the girl that was currently naked on my side of his bed. Where I had slept so many nights this semester. With Aiden's arms around me. I didn't even wait for him to say anything else. I threw the phone in my hand at his head.

He ducked and it made a horrible cracking noise against his wall before falling to the ground with a thud.

"Mila, you don't understand."

I blinked. *Don't understand?* "Are you kidding me?" Everything seemed pretty clear. He was naked in bed with someone who was not me. Perfectly clear. I lifted one of my high heels in the air.

"Whoa. Whoa." He put one hand out in front of him, keeping his other fist around the sheet that was covering his junk.

I threw it as hard as I could and it hit his shoulder as he tried to duck again.

"Jesus, Mila! Would you calm down?"

Calm down? "You said you loved me." I lifted my other heel.

"And I do."

"Excuse me?" the girl in the bed said. She was still sitting there naked, like she wasn't the one intruding.

"I mean...I did." Aiden stepped toward me.

Did. When had we become past tense? "How could you?" I was angry about how small my voice sounded.

He took another step toward me. And I hated that all I wanted was for his arms to be around me again. Because he was the only one that could ever comfort me. He knew my worries and my fears. He knew me. And he didn't want me.

"Mila, come on. What did you expect? It's not like I could ever keep dating you after graduation. This was inevitable."

Inevitable? Why? I thought the future I had just pictured with him was the inevitable thing. Not *this*. But the words didn't come out. They stayed stuck in my throat as big fat tears began to roll down my cheeks. I had a million things to say. A million questions running around in my mind. But all I could focus on was the hurt. The pain that was searing across my chest.

He took another step toward me. And I realized that he wasn't attempting to comfort me. He was trying to get me to leave. He was ushering me out of his life. He wanted *her* to stay. I felt so...used. And all I could do was shake my head. All those words stuck inside, rattling back and forth.

"We can talk about this later." His voice had dropped, like he didn't want the girl in his bed to hear.

There was nothing for us to talk about. But again, the words wouldn't come out. I didn't even realize that the other heel had slipped out of my hand until I heard it thud against the ground. I turned around and walked away from the boy who meant everything...and I wound up knee-deep in a bowl of ice cream.

The teenaged girl at the counter of the ice cream shop was staring at me like I was an alien. I looked down at my Keds. The combination with my stupid fancy dress was ridiculous, but they were the only shoes I had in my bag, and I couldn't exactly walk into this establishment barefoot. There was a sign and everything. Besides, didn't she see that I was in pain? Maybe she was just appalled by the mascara streaming down my cheeks. Instead of wiping underneath my eyes with one of the napkins on my table, I shoved another spoonful of ice cream into my mouth. That seemed to appall her even more. *Stop staring at me, you monster. Haven't you ever had your heart broken?*

I let my spoon drop into my bowl. *What am I doing?* I wasn't mad at the ice cream girl. I was mad at Aiden. And the naked girl I had never seen before. I put my face in my hand.

The girl at the counter cleared her throat, like she was trying to stop me from making a scene. All I was doing was sobbing in public. I wasn't hurting anyone. If I worked at an ice cream shop, I'd be a lot nicer than the girl who worked here. I'd be friendly. And offer someone a freaking tissue if they were crying.

It was now official. I hated Santa Monica. The adjustment here had been hard for a reason. I didn't belong. Everyone was so unfriendly. And fake. And so perfectly beautiful. No one was supposed to look this good in a beach town. It was supposed to be all cutoff jean shorts and bikini tops. Not designer clothes and fake eyelashes.

I lifted my face out of my hands. Maybe I didn't wear enough makeup. Or care about what brand of clothing I wore. But that didn't mean I was unworthy of love. It didn't mean I deserved to be feeling the way I was currently feeling.

I stared at the clock on the wall. I should have been sitting across from Aiden at some fancy restaurant right now. Holding his hand. Laughing. I had so easily pictured him getting down on one knee.

Stop. I stood up and threw out the rest of my ice cream. I wasn't at all surprised that the ice cream shop employee didn't tell me to have a "great rest of your day," as I walked back outside. I squinted at the brightness of the outdoors. It felt like I was walking out into the real world for the first time. I wasn't sure I was a fan of the real world. It seemed bleak and uninviting.

I needed a friendly face. A shoulder to cry on. I just needed to go somewhere that no one would be silently judging me. I whispered a curse when I got to Peyton's dorm. Normally I'd just call her so she could let me in, but I didn't have my cell phone. It was currently on the floor of Aiden's apartment. Besides, it was probably broken.

I stared up at the dorm building. *Ugh.* It was past dinnertime now. Students wouldn't be coming in or out as often. I sat down on the step outside of the door. I suddenly felt like crying again. I bit the inside of my cheek to prevent myself from shedding any more tears. My whole body felt cold. I had this odd feeling like none of this was really happening. Like I was having a bad dream.

A clicking noise brought me out of the dreamlike state. Someone was walking out of Peyton's dorm building. I quickly stood up and grabbed the handle of the door before it closed, ignoring the way the girl stared at me. It was the same look the ice cream shop girl had given me. Utter disgust. Did no one on this campus understand what I was going through? *Stop staring at me like that!* I slipped inside the building and sighed when the stranger didn't follow me. I half expected her to call the police and say a homeless prostitute was breaking into her dorm building.

I took the stairs two at a time, happy that I had abandoned the heels at Aiden's. Hopefully Peyton wouldn't be too angry. And hopefully she wouldn't ask me to get them back for her. I couldn't handle seeing Aiden. The thought of him ushering me out of his apartment made me feel queasy. Or maybe it was all the ice cream I had eaten.

I stopped outside Peyton's dorm room and knocked.

When she opened the door, her eyes scanned me from my head to my feet. "Um...hey." Her voice sounded cold and uninviting.

"Peyton." My tears were already threatening to spill out again. "He...Aiden..."

She pressed her lips together. "I know. He was just here. He wanted to make sure you had this." She outstretched her hand.

Suddenly I realized that her other hand was firmly holding the door in place. She hadn't opened it to invite me inside. I reached out and grabbed my phone. "Can I come in?"

"I'm a little busy right now, Mila. Packing for spring break and everything."

I swallowed hard. "Right." I blinked fast, trying to remove the tears forming in my eyes.

"I'll see you around." She started to close the door.

I put my hand out to stop her. "Peyton, he cheated on me."

She gave me a sympathetic look that didn't seem at all genuine. "Yeah, he told me the whole story. I'm sorry."

Even her "I'm sorry" didn't sound sincere. What was going on? "I don't even understand. Why was he taking me out to a nice restaurant if he was just planning on dumping me before the main course came?"

"Probably so you wouldn't make a scene. Which...it kinda sounds like you did."

Ouch. I tried to ignore her harsh words. "Can I come in? I really just need to talk. I don't understand what happened. I thought everything was going so well. You even thought he was going to propose. Not...this." I felt naive and stupid. It was mostly because of the expression on Peyton's face.

She lowered her eyebrows slightly. "Yeah, and I'm sorry about that. That was my bad. But we can't talk anymore. We're friends through association, Mila."

I just stared at her.

"Through Aiden," she added, like I was an idiot. "And honestly, I've always liked Rebecca."

Rebecca. "Is that the other girl's name?"

"Yeah. Look, I feel for you, I do. But I mean...I can't be friends with both you and Aiden. That would just be...awkward."

I laughed. It sounded strange in my throat. "So, you're breaking up with me too?"

"Don't be so dramatic. It's not like we were close."

Peyton was my best friend. Besides for Aiden. But I wasn't about to tell her that. "Right."

"I really do need to get back to packing."

I nodded.

"And you can keep the dress," she said casually as she closed the door in my face.

She didn't say it, but I imagined her adding, "it has failure all over it now."

CHAPTER 1
3 Months Later - Tuesday

I ran across the hot sand to my usual spot and quickly spread out my towel before my feet burned. I wasn't sure my soles would ever adjust to the scalding temperatures of the sand in the afternoon. But even that was a welcome sensation. I had felt numb when I left Santa Monica. Being back at the beach I had gone to when I was a kid was exactly what I needed. This was my fresh start. Or was I actually just reverting back to an old version of myself that no longer really existed? Searching for somewhere to call home because I was lost? *Stop overthinking everything.* All that mattered was that SMU and my ex were almost 3,000 glorious miles away.

A whistle blew and I looked up at the lifeguard, whose stand was only a few feet away from me. He was part of the reason I always picked this same spot. He was dreamy. His skin was tan and he had shaggy brown hair. He had six pack abs that made it hard for me to look away. The fact that he looked nothing like Aiden was a plus too.

The aviators he wore made it impossible to tell where he was looking, but I was almost certain it wasn't at me. I had sat here every Tuesday and Thursday for the past three weeks and he never glanced in my direction. And that made his presence even more comforting. It was nice that he was always there. I liked the idea of him. That was it. I didn't want to date anyone for a long time. Besides, this summer was about me. I needed to figure out what I wanted to do with my life. I only had one year left of college. I had changed my major five times, but I was still no closer to figuring it out.

After a few minutes, I realized I had been awkwardly staring at the lifeguard. I closed my eyes and took a deep breath. Listening to the waves crashing and the seagulls cawing was my new favorite thing. I hadn't felt this relaxed in a long time. The thought of going back to school in a few months completely ruined my vibe. Maybe I'd just stay here forever. I sighed and snuck another peek at the lifeguard.

The heat from the sun was already getting to me, because for just a second I thought he was staring back at me. But clearly I was hallucinating from mild heatstroke. I quickly turned away from my daydreams, pulled off my tank top, and unbuttoned my jean shorts. I swapped my clothes for a book out of my bag and lay down on my stomach. There had been so many books I had been wanting to read recently, and now I finally had time. I opened up my copy of Twisted Love. Just because my own love life had recently blown up in flames, it didn't mean I didn't still love a good romance. And this one had great reviews. Well, minus all those one stars voted up to the top because it apparently ends in a cliffy. But I had recently fallen from a figurative cliff, and I wasn't bitching about it. I'd give myself five stars every time for my notorious comeback. Well, soon to be comeback. I was sure I'd be fine eventually.

***

The sound of high-pitched laughter woke me from my nap. I yawned and sat up, brushing a few specks of sand off the side of my face. There were a few girls standing next to the lifeguard's stand chatting with him. He must have been funny, because the girls couldn't seem to stop laughing. I rolled my eyes and pulled my phone out of my bag to check the time.

It was almost five o'clock. I clicked on the lone text message from my friend, Kristen. I almost didn't look at it, because I had a feeling I knew what it said. She had texted me the same thing every day after that margarita night where I confessed that I partially came to the beach on my days off in order to watch the hot lifeguard. But maybe today was different. Maybe Kristen finally forgot my confession and decided to be nice. I clicked on the message.

"How's stalking the hot lifeguard? Come home soon, I'm hungry."

I never should have told her about the lifeguard. Margarita night was now officially banned from my weekly activities. Maybe I should also cancel my phone plan. I had recently only been using it as a clock and for receiving the same repetitive texts from Kristen. I could just buy a watch and save myself some money. Or I could pick up a few more shifts at Sweet Cravings, the ice cream shop I worked at. The owners, Rory and Keira, were freaking amazing and I knew they'd give me extra hours if I asked. But then when would I have time to sit here and stare at the hot lifeguard? I sighed. Maybe Kristen was right. Maybe I was a stalker.

"Stop complaining, I'll be home in a few minutes," I typed and pressed send.

My phone dinged almost immediately.

"Stop staring at his abs and feed me!"

I laughed and shoved my phone back into my bag. I wasn't staring at his abs. *Stupid margaritas.*

Since it was almost five o'clock, it was time to go into the ocean and cool off. It gave me just enough time to come out right before the lifeguards would leave for the day. I told myself I didn't want him to notice me. But maybe I did. I shook away the thought and made my way down to the water.

I never gracefully walked into the ocean. The water was freezing in June and if I didn't run, I could never force myself to go all the way in. I ran through the waves, held back the stupidly shrill scream that wanted to escape my throat, and dove into the water before the waves could knock me over. There was no better feeling than saltwater on my skin. And the sun reflecting off the top of the water, somehow warming me despite the frigid temperature. Complete and utter bliss. Screw Aiden. Screw SMU. Screw the whole freaking west coast. This was living.

A few minutes later whistles began to blow. The lifeguards up and down the shore signaled people to come out of the water. It was a rather silly game. They made everyone get out while they left. And as soon as they were out of sight, everyone always just went back in the water. I guess it gave the lifeguards peace of mind if something were to happen after their watch had ended. Which of course happened occasionally. After all, sharks came out at night. As well as skanks named Rebecca. *Stop thinking about*

Aiden. He's a life-sized dick hat. I awkwardly laughed out loud at my own thought. What the heck is a life-sized dick hat? Regardless, Aiden was absolutely one.

I held my breath and went under water once more. Saltwater was my new favorite hair product. And it was currently the only one I could afford. I wrung out my hair as I made my way out of the ocean.

The other lifeguards that I could see were all pushing their stands up to dryer sand. But my lifeguard was staring at me. *My lifeguard.* I laughed at myself. Well, it seemed like he was staring at me. He was looking in my general direction, but I couldn't see his eyes behind his aviators. He was probably just annoyed that I hadn't gotten out of the water yet.

While I was staring awkwardly at him, I felt something brush against my leg. Before I could move, a sharp pain seared the inside of my thigh. "Ow," I said way too loudly. *What the hell was that?* It burned way worse than my feet in the hot sand. And it seemed like it got worse every second. I looked around but the water was too cloudy to see anything. "Ow!" I almost yelled as I felt another sharp pain right below my ass. I tried to run out of the water, but the pain from the stings made it more of an adorable hobble. And by adorable I mean a hideous ogre hobble. When I finally made it to the shore, I looked down at the inside of my right thigh. There was already a red line. I turned my head to look at the matching red line right below my bathing suit bottom. Couldn't they have been in less awkward places?

I tried not to grimace as I ungracefully walked back to my towel. If the lifeguard hadn't been watching me before, he definitely was now. And now I was I certain that I had never wanted him to notice me in the first place. Especially not at this moment. I'd go home and google what to do. I silently willed him to just go home and ignore me.

As I walked toward my towel, he approached my towel from where he was. *He knows where I sit?* I quickly realized that my towel was one of the only ones left on the beach. *Of course he doesn't know where I sit.*

"Hey, are you okay?" he asked.

"Umm...yes," I said through a clenched jaw. I sat down on my towel and pressed my thighs together. *Ow, that makes it hurt more.*

"You don't seem okay. What happened?"

"I don't know. I felt something sting me. But it's fine. Really."

"Well let me see it. I can tell you what it was."

I laughed awkwardly. "Nope. That's okay. I don't need to know."

"Don't be ridiculous. I have stuff to help whatever it is. Where did it get you?"

"It's, well..." I sighed and looked down at my legs.

"Oh." He gave me a small smile. "You don't have to be embarrassed, it's my job." He shrugged his shoulders.

Right. I was making this so much more awkward than it needed to be. He was just trying to do his job. He probably had to deal with stuff like this all the time.

He knelt down in the sand in front of me. He put his hand on my right knee and pushed my thigh out to the side. He leaned forward and traced his index finger right underneath the sting. *Holy shit.* I suddenly forgot about the pain. I swallowed hard.

"It was a jellyfish. I actually have just the thing for that." He let go of my leg and stood up.

No. God, no. "Oh please don't. I can't..." I let my voice trail off. I knew what he was about to do.

"It'll just take a minute."

"No. I...please, I can't ask you to pee on me."

He laughed. "Um, golden showers aren't really my thing..."

"What?"

"That's what it's called when you pee on...you know what, never mind." He scratched the back of his neck and laughed. "I have a spray bottle of stuff. It's not my pee, I swear. I'll be right back."

Damn it. If I hadn't just seen that episode of Friends where they had to pee on Monica at the beach, I never would have said that. I could feel my face turning red. *What is wrong with me?*

When he came back he was smiling. "I can't believe you thought I was going to pee on you. I can only imagine if that was the protocol. I'm not sure I would have agreed to be a lifeguard if I had to go around peeing on people."

"I know, I'm sorry. I was watching this rerun of Friends last night and..."

"Oh, yeah." He laughed. "I've seen that episode." He knelt down in front of me. "Here, this is going to make it feel a lot better."

I moved my thigh to the side for him this time. He sprayed the solution on the sting. It started to feel better right away.

"Actually, if you blow on it, it feels even more sooth-ing."

I looked down at my thigh. "Thanks, but I can't really bend that way."

"Here, let me." He put his hand on my knee again and leaned forward. He lightly blew on the sting. It felt amazing, in more ways than one. This was the most physical contact I had experienced in months. I had to remind myself that he was just doing his job.

He leaned back on his heels. "Did it get you anywhere else?"

"Yes, well, my...tush." *Why the hell did I just say tush?*

He laughed. "Pretty sure you got stung in the most awkward places ever. That jellyfish must have liked you."

"I wish he hadn't."

"So...did you want to roll over so I can spray you?" He innocently held up the bottle.

I bit my lip. *He's just doing his job. This is just a normal day for him. Stop being weird!* I lay down on my blanket. "It's right..."

"I can see it," he said, cutting me off. "Spread your legs a bit for me. It kind of laces between your thighs again."

Oh my God. I followed his instructions. He put his hand on the back of my upper thigh and in a second I felt the soothing liquid.

"That feels so much better, thank you." I rested my head against my forearm. He was good at his job. My body tensed when I felt him blowing on the sting right below my ass. I couldn't help the sigh that escaped my lips. I tried to cover it up with a cough. I quickly rolled over and looked up at him. His hands were on either side of my legs and he was leaning over me slightly. He was definitely being flirtatious. He couldn't possibly act this way every time he did his job. *Or maybe he does.* I was so out of experience that I couldn't tell anymore.

He moved so that he was sitting on my blanket next to me.

Yes, he's flirting with me. Wouldn't he just leave otherwise? Or maybe I was wrong. Maybe he's terrible at his job. The absolute worst. Totally unprofessional.

"So do you live around here?" he asked. "Or are you just here for the summer?"

He knows I'm not just on vacation. He must have noticed me here before. Or maybe he just assumes people don't vacation alone. He didn't realize how weird I was. "I grew up like an hour from here. But I go to school in Santa Monica. I came back for the summer. I just needed a change."

"Well if you needed a break from constant sunshine, you shouldn't have come to the beach." He smiled at me. "What year are you?"

"I just finished my junior year."

"What are you studying?"

"Ugh. I don't know. I've changed my major so many times. It's hard to decide what I want to spend the rest of my life doing. I wish I could just stay here forever."

"Yeah, tell me about it." He looked out toward the water.

I was suddenly even more curious about him. What was he escaping from by being here? "What about you? Are you in school?"

"Yo!" someone called from behind us. I turned my head. There were a group of lifeguards standing by the small shack where they sold popsicles and drinks. "Let's go!" the same guy yelled.

"Sorry, I have to go." He stood up.

"Of course. Don't let me hold you up. And thanks for your help. You're a lifesaver." I laughed at my own joke. *What the hell is wrong with me?*

He laughed too. I wasn't sure if it was with me or at me. But I liked his laugh. "I guess I'll see you on Thursday, Jellyfish Girl."

He does know my schedule.

He smiled at me and walked over to his lifeguard stand. I watched him push it away from the water so it wouldn't be swept away in high tide. He joined his friends. A girl ran up to him and grabbed his arm, pulling him toward the others. She had long brunette hair and perfectly tanned skin. She was basically a female equivalent of him. I instantly disliked her.

He turned his head and looked back in my direction. I quickly looked away and out toward the ocean. My heart was racing. I had let myself get excited for a second. Not that I wanted to date anyone. Besides, guys like that were never available. That was probably his girlfriend. I shook my head and lay back down on my blanket. So much for that. I still wished I had asked him his name, though.

CHAPTER 2
Tuesday

"I'm dying of starvation!" Kristen said and pretended to faint, falling backward onto the worn couch.

"Stop being so dramatic." I closed the front door of our little condo behind me. Most of the apartments had already been filled by the time I arrived at the beginning of summer, but I had found a room for rent above someone's garage. It was quaint, small, quiet, and so much better than living in an apartment with a bunch of other people. I wanted to get away from college life, not immerse myself in the same situation just on the opposite side of the country. Plus, my place was only a block from the beach. The only downside was that I couldn't afford it on my own.

I had texted a few of my friends from high school, hoping to reconnect. But I quickly realized that I had completely lost touch with all of them. One of them was engaged to some billionaire in the big city. The exact opposite of me. Broke. Single. I tossed my bag on the floor and kicked off my flip flops, ignoring the fact that I desperately needed to sweep. The only downside of living at the beach was all the sand. Everywhere. Every. Where.

Thankfully, Kristen had answered my ad where I basically talked about being a loser and begged for a roommate. She never even made fun of me for it. And she wasn't around all that often. She liked to party. I liked to read. She liked to run several miles in the morning. I liked to eat ice cream for breakfast. In my defense, she was training to be part of the summer games next year, representing the U.S. women's volleyball team. So she was training to win a gold medal. And I was...well, still eating ice cream for breakfast.

But she was always here for dinner. Training left her famished. Which was great, because I loved trying out new recipes for more than just myself. Actually, she was the perfect roommate, and she was quickly becoming one of my best friends.

I thought about all the people I believed I had been friends with in Santa Monica. They had dropped me like a hot potato. And all the people I had originally left behind in Delaware? Gone. Not dead, but dead from my life I guess. Who was I kidding? Kristen wasn't becoming *one of* my best friends. She was my only friend.

"Feed me, you monster!" Kristen said.

I flopped down on the couch beside her and hit her with a throw pillow.

"Ow." She snatched it from me. "If you're not going to cook, do you want to go out for dinner? Drinks are on me."

This sounds like margarita night all over again. "No, I'll cook." I got up and tried to hide my wince. The spray that the lifeguard had used on my legs had initially helped. But it had quickly worn off.

"What took you so long at the beach today?" Kristen asked. "Usually you're back at 5:05. And by usually, I mean always."

I opened up the fridge. "Nothing."

She laughed. "You're lying."

"I'm not lying."

"You are. But it's okay. A few drinks in and I'll get the truth out of you. I made a pitcher of sangria!"

There was no way I was drinking with her tonight. Confessing that I was attracted to the lifeguard in the first place was bad enough. A confession about being turned on just from the lifeguard's touch was too much information. I barely knew Kristen, even if she was my bestie.

I ignored the pitcher of sangria and pulled out some broccoli, garlic, eggs, and cheddar cheese. "How does a quiche sound?"

"Not as good as tacos."

"You know, you could always feed yourself."

She stuck out her bottom lip. "But the food you make is always so amazing."

"Quiche it is then. Trust me, you'll like it. The secret ingredient to a great quiche is red pepper flakes. It's got that kick that you like."

"Mmm. Okay, I trust you, Chef Mila."

I laughed and started chopping the broccoli.

Less than an hour later, we were sitting on the couch, balancing plates precariously on our laps.

"What do you want to watch?" Kristen asked as she channel surfed.

Honestly, I didn't want to watch anything. I liked enjoying my food after I cooked it. But if we had a show on, Kristen was less likely to badger me about my lifeguard. "Want to watch the next season of Project Runway?"

"Yaasss!" She blew me a kiss, Tim Gunn style, and pulled it up on Hulu in two seconds flat. She had definitely already queued it up and was just waiting for my okay.

I smiled and took a bite of my masterpiece. We had been making our way through all the old seasons of Project Runway since we moved in together. We'd both never seen the show before and now we were totally hooked. Especially on Swatch. A Swatch sighting when the contestants were shopping for fabric was a jump-up-and-down moment. And I didn't even like dogs. If I ever lost my mind and decided to get a pet, it would probably be a Swatch dog. But clearly it wasn't meant to be, because I didn't even know what type of dog he was.

I shifted on the couch to get more comfortable and grimaced. Geez, who knew jellyfish bites stung so freaking much? It felt like I was doing an unconventional materials challenge on the show and got burned by a hot glue gun.

Kristen turned the volume down. "Okay...seriously, spill it. Clearly you got rammed and for some reason have decided not to tell me and I'm hurt." She put her hands over her heart to show her pain, almost dropping her quiche on the floor in the process.

"Rammed?" I was trying my best to focus on the show instead of her sad face.

"You know." She made a rude gesture of putting her index finger through an "O" shape she'd made with her other hand. "Boned. Laid. Stuffed like a Thanksgiving turkey. Hanky panky. Wham, bam, thank you, ma'am."

I laughed. "Gross, stop it." I slapped both her hands.

"Tell me."

"I promise I didn't get stuffed like a Thanksgiving turkey."

"So no anal…"

"That's not what getting stuffed like a Thanksgiving turkey means."

"Of course it is. Because you ram the stuffing up the turkey's ass for all that extra flavor."

Gross. "I meant I didn't have sex period." The thought of sex made me picture Aiden naked, trying to get me out of his bedroom so he could continue cheating on me. God I hated men. "I told you, no boys for me this summer. I'm focusing on me."

Kristen had the audacity to pause the show right in the middle of a Tim Gunn critique.

"Hey, I was watching that."

"Mila, I know you were hurt." She put her feet up on the couch so she could turn toward me. "But you can't just shut yourself off from love. And when did you say Aiden lost his mind? During spring break? That was like…in March. It's been three months."

"Three months is not that much time! I thought he was going to propose!"

"And we both know you would have said no."

"That's not…"

"He was not your person. He was an egotistical asshole. You would have said no. And even if you didn't, you would have changed your mind before you walked down the aisle and ruined your whole life. You're smarter than that. And you shouldn't let someone as stupid as Aiden ruin your whole summer. You're a junior. It's your last real summer break. You deserve to enjoy it."

Her words made me tear up. She was right. Why was I still letting Aiden dictate my happiness? Yup, Kristen was definitely my best friend. Before I could thank her for what she said, she started talking again.

"And the best way to enjoy this summer is by drinking sangria with your main squeeze and watching reruns of Project Runway!" She got up and quickly poured me a glass of sangria. "But getting rammed by aforementioned hot lifeguard would really be the cherry on top. I'm sure he'd make you forget all about Aiden."

I laughed and took the glass from her. She wasn't wrong. But nothing was going to happen with me and the lifeguard.

"So if you didn't do the dirty deed, what the hell happened? You can barely move without looking like you're going to keel over."

"Jellyfish sting."

"Oh ouch. Did you get someone to pee on you? That's really supposed to help."

I laughed. At least I wasn't the only one whose mind automatically went there. "Apparently there's a spray for it. So no pee necessary." *Thank God.*

"Nice." She just stared at me instead of restarting our TV show.

"What?"

"So how do you know about the spray? Did you look it up online? Or did someone give it to you?"

"A lifeguard sprayed me."

"Which lifeguard?"

We proceeded to have a staring contest for almost a minute before Kristen squealed.

"Hot lifeguard sprayed you with pee?!"

"That's not what I said. It's not pee spray. Just a normal jellyfish spray of some kind."

"Not important." She waved her hand through the air. "It was *him*?"

"Yeah, you know I always sit next to his stand."

"So you met him. What did he say? What was he like? Did you get a good whiff of him? He probably smells amazing. Did you touch his abs?"

I laughed. "No, I didn't sniff him or touch him." Although, he had touched me. I shook away the thought. "He was just really professional." *Kind of.* I remembered the feeling of him blowing on my ass and a chill ran down my spine. "And...nice."

"Nice? That is literally the worst way to describe someone. That's how you describe a stranger's grandmother. Give me more than that."

"He was really sweet. And he said he'd see me on Thursday. So I'm pretty sure he knows my schedule."

"That's big."

"It's not." I took a huge gulp of my sangria. Was it? I wasn't sure why I was even entertaining the idea. I was 100 percent not going to ever go on a date with my lifeguard. And even if I wanted to, which I didn't, I was pretty sure he had a girlfriend.

"It is." She lifted her glass in the air. "Here's to hooking up with sexy lifeguards all summer."

I wasn't going to argue with her anymore. Instead, I clinked my glass with hers and un-paused the show. The only man I needed in my life was Swatch. He was probably a really good snuggler.

CHAPTER 3
Wednesday

I wiped down the counter near the cash register. My shift ended soon and the ice cream shop was dead during dinner time. Everyone else wanted to work at night and on the weekends because they wanted good tips. But I didn't care. The thought of being behind this counter at night with the long lines didn't seem like a relaxing summer job at all. It sounded like a surefire way to lose my mind and end up locked in the freezer binge-eating all the stock. And I only needed to work Monday, Wednesday, and Friday during the day in order to afford my rent and groceries. My phone vibrated. I looked down and saw that my mother was trying to call me. There was one other girl in the shop right now and she was sitting in the back room talking to her boyfriend on the phone. She was always talking on the phone. I slipped my phone back in my pocket. I'd have to call my mom back later. Someone needed to man the counter.

I had originally wanted to come back home and stay with her for the summer to try and forget about everything, but my mother had a new boyfriend and it was only a matter of time before he officially moved in. That was how my mother operated. She loved hard and fast and fell out of love just as quickly. The last thing she needed was for her grownup daughter showing up on her doorstep and cramping her style. And even though her house was home to me, it felt like I was intruding on them.

I had also thought about staying with my father. But then I pictured his wife's face if I announced I was coming there for a whole summer. It was enough to make me abandon that idea too.

This was the next best thing. I had spent so much time here in the summer it almost felt like home. It was enough. And I was finally starting to feel whole again. I was in a good routine. I'd made a new friend. Was I doing great? No. But I was doing okay. And that was enough for right now.

There was a spot on the counter that just wouldn't get clean. I scrubbed it harder. I never would have thought an ice cream shop would be hot, but it was stifling in here. I wiped my forehead with the back of my hand.

"Hey, Jellyfish Girl."

I froze. *Oh my God.* I looked up at the lifeguard. He was in his red lifeguard swim trunks but he was wearing a t-shirt. He looked amazing even without his six pack showing. I realized I was staring awkwardly at him. "Hey...lifeguard."

He laughed and leaned on the counter. "I almost didn't recognize you with so many clothes on. How are your stings feeling?"

He was being so forward. I could feel my face blushing. "A lot better, thanks to you."

"I was just doing my job." He smiled at me. He had definitely just gotten off of work and was walking back to wherever he lived. But I had never seen him walk past the

IVY SMOAK

ice cream shop before. Maybe he was here to get some ice cream. His eyes were still hidden behind his aviators. I wished I could see what color they were. I was being ridiculous. He probably had a girlfriend.

"So this is where you work when you're not at the beach?" he asked.

"Yes, this is my glamorous summer job."

"Do you work weekends too? This place is always packed on the weekend. You must make insane tips."

"No, thank God. Just Monday, Wednesday, and Friday during the day. I do not want to deal with that many people."

He laughed. "Yeah, summer is supposed to be relaxing."

I found myself leaning forward, hoping to figure out what he smelled like so I could appease Kristen. That was definitely the only reason. But I couldn't get close enough without sprawling myself all over the counter. "I know. My bosses can't believe I don't want those hours, but I can't even imagine being here at night, let alone on the weekend."

"I couldn't agree more. That's why I chose not to work the weekend shifts."

"Yeah, I know. I mean, I didn't know that for sure. I just noticed that you weren't there on the weekends. Not like I always notice you or anything. I just meant in a normal spectator of the beach way. Like, I'm pretty sure every person that frequents the beach recognizes their normal lifeguard. That's a thing." *Oh my God, stop talking!*

"Sure. In a beach spectator way. Of course." He was smiling at me.

Kill me now. "So, did you want some ice cream or are you just stalking me?"

"Stalking you? If anything you're stalking me. You visit me at my place of work all the time. And you always sit right next to me like a really obvious, bad stalker." He raised his eyebrow at me.

Shit. "I'm not stalking you...I..."

"I know." He laughed again and leaned forward a little more. "So I have to ask, what is better than sex?"

"What?" My face was probably redder than it had ever been. All the euphemisms for sex Kristen mentioned last night started to roll around in my head. Especially that Thanksgiving turkey one, until all I could think to say was something about a Thanksgiving feast. Instead I bit the inside of my lip so I wouldn't accidentally start talking about anal.

He pointed to the wall that listed all the flavors. "The ice cream flavor. Better Than Sex." He flashed me another smile.

"Right, of course. I knew what you meant. Obviously. You're just here to get some." *No!* "I didn't mean that in a sexual way. I just meant get some ice cream. Not some of me." *What?* "Let me just go get you a sample." *Damn it, why does this place have to have such ridiculous names for their ice cream flavors?* I turned around and went to get him a sample. I took a deep breath as I filled up the little cup. He made me so nervous that I was acting even more awkward than I usually did. I went back to the counter and handed him the sample cup. He was tall and muscular, and he looked silly with the small cup and spoon. It helped calm my nerves.

"So have you sampled all these flavors?"

"It was part of orientation. That was probably the best part of getting this job." And the fact that my bosses were the nicest people ever.

He ate the small amount of ice cream I had given him. "You know, it's good, but it's definitely not better than sex."

No, it's not. If I could see his eyes I probably would have melted into the floor. I was suddenly grateful that he was still wearing his aviators.

He put the sample cup on the counter and scratched the back of his neck. "So, which kind is your favorite?"

"Hmm...probably the Pink Dream. It sounds super ridiculous, but it's raspberry with tons of dark chocolate chips in it and it's amazing. I guess no name is as ridiculous as Better Than Sex, though."

"I'll have one scoop of the super girly Pink Dream, then. On a sugar cone."

"Okay. I'll be right back." *Of course I'll be right back.* I shook my head. It wasn't like I was going to scoop his ice cream and flee with it. I was weird, but I wasn't an ice cream shoplifter. At least not yet, because I kind of did want to sprint out of here. I grabbed a sugar cone and put a heaping scoop of Pink Dream in it.

"Here you go." I handed it to him. I watched as he pulled a five dollar bill out of his wallet. "It's okay. It's on me. I owe you after yesterday."

"You don't really. I was just doing my job."

"I insist."

He smiled at me. "I'll have to save you more often then."

"Yes please." *What the hell? Yes please?*

He laughed. Again, I wasn't sure if he was laughing at me or with me. "Wow, this is really good. It's kind of awkward walking around with a big pink ice cream cone, though."

I laughed. "You actually look super macho." It was like I didn't know how to stop saying weird things. He didn't look macho, he looked like a Greek god. I found myself wishing there was an ice cream flavor of him.

"Super macho, huh? I feel like that's a compliment. Maybe this should be my new look then?"

If his new look meant visiting me after his lifeguard shift more often, then I was game. "Absolutely."

"Hey," my lifeguard said and waved to someone behind me.

I turned around. I hadn't even noticed my bosses walk in.

"Welcome back," Keira said. "Trying out the Pink Dream today?"

"Delicious as always. This really is the best ice cream I've ever had." He held up his cone like he was toasting them and then turned back to me. "I'll see you tomorrow at the beach, Jellyfish Girl." He put the five dollar bill he was going to use to pay for the ice cream into the tip jar and walked away.

I watched him disappear down the sidewalk. I had again failed to get his name or learn anything about him. I hadn't even caught his scent for Kristen. I turned my attention back to scrubbing the counter. It was probably for the best.

"He's cute, huh?" Keira said.

I was definitely not going to have this conversation with my boss. I could feel my face turning red. "He's okay."

She laughed. "Mhm."

"You'll have to excuse my wife," Rory said and put his arm around Keira. "For some reason she likes to think she's a great matchmaker even though she has zero experience."

"Well, I could be," she said. "That lifeguard was our first customer ever by the way. You'll probably be seeing him quite a bit here. But it sounds like the two of you already hang out on the beach." She raised both her eyebrows at me.

I wouldn't consider sitting near his lifeguard stand hanging out. Although, he had mentioned seeing me tomorrow twice now. Maybe everything was about to change. I shook the thought away. I didn't need anything to change. I was focusing on myself this summer. Keira was still staring at me expectantly, so I shrugged, hoping that was a good enough answer.

"I guess we'll just see where the summer goes. But is everything good here?" she asked before they headed back out.

"Great." I gave them two thumbs up and then realized I was being weird and picked my washcloth back up.

"Well, don't forget to grab your tips before you head out." She winked at me as they left. I guess she'd noticed the fact that my lifeguard had left me a big tip. It was only because I'd paid for his ice cream though. Right?

I watched Keira and Rory walk down the boardwalk hand in hand. They were newlyweds and pretty much the most adorable couple ever. But my life was far away from being anything like theirs. It's not like I really wanted to be in their shoes anyway. So why was I staring at them and daydreaming that it was me and my lifeguard holding hands and laughing on the boardwalk together? It was such a silly thought. I was happy to be focusing on myself this summer. So freaking happy. I realized I was holding the washcloth so tight that I had wrung out all the water. The soapy suds were dripping off the counter onto my Keds. *Ugh.*

CHAPTER 4
Thursday

I tied the string tight to my nicest bikini and looked in the mirror. This bathing suit always made me feel sexy. Probably because of the extra padding in the top. Luckily Kristen was at work, or else she'd be badgering me non-stop about wearing such a slinky bikini. She could read me like the back of her hand.

I stared at my reflection for a few more seconds. I was being ridiculous. Why was I trying to look good for a guy I didn't even really know? And had no desire to know. I turned away from the mirror and pulled on a tank top and jean shorts.

Stop lying to yourself, he's gorgeous and you want to get to know every inch of him. My mind came to a halt at my own thought. What the hell was that? Every inch of him? God, I had been reading too much romance.

But I was excited to see him. I had to find out his name. It was driving me crazy not knowing. Even though it was kind of fun referring to him as my lifeguard or Kristen's favorite…hot lifeguard. If I could just find out his name, I could be like, "Bye Blankity Blank. See you later. My heart has recently been stomped on and I'm not dating anyone…not that you asked to date me."

I grabbed my beach bag, locked the door behind me, and walked down the wooden steps outside. In just a few minutes I was on the boardwalk and then in the sand. I ran to my usual spot and sat down on my towel. I looked over at my lifeguard. He was preoccupied watching all the people in the water. I wasn't sure what I should do. I could go over and say hi. But I didn't want to bother him. And it wasn't like I knew how to be super casual. I'd probably end up face first in the sand and need mouth-to-mouth resuscitation. Not that the thought of that sounded so bad. It would definitely be embarrassing though.

I abandoned the thought of saying hello and decided to read instead. He continued to ignore me for hours. Or maybe he was just respecting the fact that I was reading. Or maybe he thought I was ignoring him. Before I knew it, I was halfway done my book. I knew it was supposed to be a romance, but I didn't realize how sexual it was going to be. I was a little hot and bothered.

"Hey, Stalker!"

I looked up from the pages at my lifeguard. He was gesturing me over. *Seriously? That's what he's going to call me now?* I put my book down and walked over to him. A few girls nearby stared at me as I approached him. They were probably jealous because they thought he was sexy too. Take that, beauty queens, I'm friends with the hottest man on the planet.

"You know, I like Jellyfish Girl better," I said.

"Okay, fine, Jellyfish Girl. Your stings look a lot better, by the way." The way he said stings made it seem like he had seen the one on my butt too. Which meant he had looked over at me when I had been reading on my stomach. I smiled to myself. I was very aware of his eyes on my legs. And I liked the attention.

"So much better. Thanks again for that."

He looked at the watch on his wrist. "It's getting pretty late, so if you're going to swim, do it now so you have time to dry off."

And he thought I was the stalker? He truly did know my schedule. "Time to dry off for what?" My only plans were to go back to my apartment to cook for Kristen. I usually dried off on the walk home. *Wait, did I just invite myself somewhere with him? What is wrong with me?* I was about to open my mouth to clarify when he started talking again.

"Lifeguards get free drinks on Thursdays at Grottos. You're coming with me."

Oh my God, he's asking me out. Or did I force him into asking me? God. "Umm..."

"Come on, Jellyfish Girl. It'll be more fun if you come."

"Okay." I didn't hesitate nearly as long as I thought I would. That I *should* have. I don't know if it was because of the erotic romance I was reading or because he was the most handsome guy I had ever talked to. Probably both. "I guess I'll go in the water now then." I quickly walked away before I had a chance to say anything weird.

"Be careful of jellyfish!" he yelled after me.

"Okay, smartass." *Oh shit, did I just curse at him?*

I heard him laughing as I made my way to the water. I shook my head. Every time we interacted I did the weirdest stuff. But he wanted to go out with me anyway. *There must be something seriously wrong with him.* I ran into the water and dove into a wave. I made my way past the breaking waves and treaded water. Part of me wished I'd get stung by another demon jellyfish so he'd have to touch me again.

I laughed at myself and looked back at him. He was so handsome. And maybe tonight I'd finally get to learn his name.

I didn't stay in the water nearly as long as I normally would. Knowing my lifeguard might be watching me made me nervous. All I could think about was the fact that he had asked me out. And how I hadn't even hesitated to say yes. What happened to my summer plans of no dating? I wrung my hair out and walked back toward my towel. I lay down on my stomach and pulled my book back out. *Stupid romance book, messing with my head.*

***

"So nothing stung you today?" I opened my eyes. My lifeguard was sitting on my towel beside me. I must have fallen asleep reading.

"Oh." I quickly sat up. "No, not today." I wiped the side of my face, grateful that there wasn't drool everywhere. I put my book in my bag before he got a chance to see what I was reading. *Why is he sitting next to me?* I thought him asking me out had been part of a bad dream. Well, actually a really great dream that involved some of that turkey business Kristen had mentioned. Of the non-anal variety. But I couldn't seriously go out with him. That wasn't part of my summer plans.

"Darn, I really wanted more free ice cream."

I laughed. "I can give you free ice cream whenever you want. I usually take some home with me after work."

"Your job definitely has better perks than mine. So are you ready to go?" He stood up and put his hand out for me.

I stared at his hand. A tiny voice in the back of my head warned me that this was a bad idea. Touching him should be a no-no. But my hand started moving on its own accord. "Yeah." I grabbed his hand and he pulled me to my feet. "One sec." I quickly pulled on my tank top and jean shorts. "Is this okay to wear?"

"Yeah, you look great. We all just wear our bathing suits." He was still wearing his lifeguard swim trunks but he had also put on a t-shirt.

"Are you sure it's okay that I come? You know...since I'm not a lifeguard?"

"It's fine. It just means I have to pay for your drinks." He smiled at me.

"You don't have to do that."

"I'm pretty sure I just scored free ice cream all summer. So yes, I do."

I smiled at him. It was hard not to smile when perfection in male form was staring back at you. "Okay." I shook out my towel and put it into my bag. We started walking toward the boardwalk. I kept stealing sideways glances at him. He was at least six inches taller than me. He was as tan as I expected a lifeguard to be. And he was lean yet muscular. He was starting to get a 5 o'clock shadow. For some reason I found myself wanting to reach out and touch it. I forced my hands to stay by my sides.

When we reached the boardwalk, he stopped and rinsed the sand off his feet at the little shower. "So all I really know about you is that you come to the beach every

Tuesday and Thursday around one o'clock. Jellyfish love you. And you work at an ice cream shop with really sexual flavor names. Maybe that means something. I don't know." He held the shower lever down for me so I could rinse the sand off my feet too.

I laughed. "No, it doesn't. I just needed a job to pay my rent. I'm renting this really cute, tiny apartment over this old lady's garage. I love it."

"Do you live there by yourself?"

"No." *Oh crap.* "Actually I have a roommate who I always have dinner with. I need to text her." Kristen would probably starve if I wasn't there to cook for her. I paused when I pulled out my phone. I knew nothing about my lifeguard. Maybe he was a murderer. He was probably going to get me drunk and kill me. Maybe he was a freaking cannibal. I could be seconds away from being in his tummy. "Umm…you said a bunch of people were going right? Do you care if she comes too? She'd kill me if she knew I was going to be hanging out with lifeguards all night and didn't invite her. She's violent like that." I stared at him, trying to see if he was sympatico with her murderous ways.

"Yeah, that's fine."

What a normal answer. I shot Kristen a quick text telling her to meet me there. She was going to lose her mind. It was good I'd invited her, because after her toast to hooking up with sexy lifeguards all summer, I'd be on her shit list for sure. This way I wouldn't wind up dead in a ditch and I'd make Kristen happy too. Plus it would make it less date like and more like a friend date. Which my mind could handle.

We started walking again.

"You are so lucky. I live in that big apartment building over there." He pointed to a building in the distance. "And I have three roommates. It's fun, but it's also kind of annoying."

He's not a murderer. He's a nice, apartment-living guy with living roommates.

"So, you just needed a job to pay rent, which means you're not saving up money for school?"

"No. I got a pretty decent scholarship. And my dad is paying for the rest of it. I haven't seen him that much since my parents got divorced when I was a kid. But he loves throwing money at me, not that I ever ask him to." I was rambling. I had a tendency to do that when I was nervous. I shrugged my shoulders to make it seem like what I had just said was normal.

"Sorry."

"It's fine. It's better that way." It wasn't. I was pretty sure he was paying for my college so I wouldn't bother him and his new family. Paid silence. "Honestly, he's kind of an asshole."

He laughed.

God he had a nice laugh.

"Okay. Tell me more."

"I mean, what do you want to know?" I wanted to ask him questions. I already knew everything about myself.

"Well, why are you here for the summer? Why didn't you stay in California?"

"I don't know." Lame answer. "It's complicated." Lamer answer.

"That means you do know, Jellyfish Girl." We stopped outside one of the Grottos pizza joints on the boardwalk. I knew of at least two more within walking distance. It was kind of ridiculous. But their pizza was amazing so I didn't mind. We walked past the hostess and went into the outdoor bar portion of the restaurant. Some of his lifeguard friends greeted him. I was waiting for someone to say his name, but none of them did. This was so frustrating.

He pulled a stool out for me at the bar. I sat down and he took the seat beside me. The bartender came over.

"What would you like?" my lifeguard asked me.

"Whatever you're having is fine."

He turned to the bartender and ordered two beers.

Before he could press me, I decided I should ask him a question. "So, are you in school?"

"No, I just graduated. I start my real job in the fall." The bartender came back with two beers. My lifeguard took a long sip.

"You wanted one last fun summer?"

"Something like that." He smiled at me. "So are you going to answer my question? Or do I have to get you drunk first?" It looked like he winked, but I couldn't be sure because he was still wearing his sunglasses.

How could I possibly word the answer to his question? That my boyfriend of two and a half years had cheated on me at the beginning of last semester with some girl with huge tits? I thought he was my forever. We had talked about our future all the time. I thought he was going to propose on the night I walked in on him in bed with someone else. He was the first person to befriend me on campus and all of his friends kind of just adopted me.

When we split up, those friends turned out to not actually be my friends either. The rest of spring semester had been lonely and unbearable. I hated SMU. And I hated California. I didn't want to go back. But I also didn't want to switch schools with only one year left. I needed to finish some degree. I was close enough on a few majors, I just needed to choose which one. Was that what he wanted to hear?

"You probably have to get me drunk first," I said instead of telling him the whole depressing story.

He laughed. "Okay. I'll see what I can do. Let's try a different question then. Do you have any siblings?"

"No, I'm an only child. Well, kind of. I have half-sisters. But they're a lot younger than me and I rarely ever see them." I looked down at my beer. "My dad's new family."

"Okay. Kind of an only child of divorced parents. Do they live around here?"

"My dad lives in Austin. But my mom lives about an hour from here. My original plan was to stay with her this summer. But she's dating this new guy and I felt like I'd be intruding." I tucked a loose strand of hair behind my ear. When I called her back the other day, she had been talking about some cruise she was going on later this summer. I decided it was better not to bother her with the fact that I was back in town since she was leaving soon anyway. I didn't want to make her feel bad.

We both finished our beers and he ordered us another round. "So, that leads me back to my original question. Why did you come back?"

I took another sip of my beer, wishing I could down the whole thing as unladylike as possible. "The simple answer is that I felt lost. I needed to come home. And when I couldn't go home, I thought that this was the next best place. I spent so much time here when I was younger that this seems like home to me."

"So what made you feel lost?"

My lifeguard was particularly nosey. But for some reason it didn't bother me. Or maybe the beer running through my veins made me forget about the fact that I shouldn't have even been out with him in the first place. "I think it was a lot of things all at once. I'm having trouble deciding what I want to do when I graduate for one. You're lucky that you have it all figured out."

"Yeah, lucky. I. Am. All. Set." He took a long sip of his beer.

The way he said it made it seem like he didn't really feel like he was all set or lucky. "You're not excited about it? What are you going to be doing?"

"Pushing papers in Corporate America. The dream job."

"If you don't want to work at the place that offered you a job, then why are you gonna do it?"

"I don't know. I had an internship there and they offered me a job. I accepted it. It pays well." He shrugged.

"Well maybe you should cancel."

"Being a lifeguard only in the summer doesn't exactly pay well."

"I don't know. I'm tempted to stay here. Maybe I'll drop out of school and be a beach bum."

He laughed. "I doubt you'd actually do that. But let me know if you do and I'll reconsider my position."

A girl walked over to us. "Hey, I need a teammate for pool. You in?" She touched his shoulder. It was the same lifeguard I had seen him with the other day. I disliked her even more.

"Do you need two more?" He looked over at me.

"Ben and Jillian are challenging *us*," the girl said in a rather rude tone. "Come on."

"Oh, it's okay," I said. "Go ahead. I'm horrible at pool, so it's better if I just watch. And my friend will be here any second." *Probably. Hopefully.*

"You sure?" my lifeguard asked me.

"Yeah."

"Okay. Come with me then." He grabbed my hand and pulled me to the back of the restaurant where there were some table games. It felt weird to have my hand held again after going so many months being alone. I looked down at his fingers intertwined with mine. I liked this. He stopped and I looked up at him. I wasn't sure when he had taken off his aviators, but they were now hooked on the front of his shirt. He was staring down at me with the most amazing deep blue eyes I had ever seen. He should not have been hiding those under sunglasses.

I wasn't sure if it was the booze, but I was speechless. *Screw this not being a date.* I could stare into his eyes for the rest of my life. It felt like I was swimming in them they were so blue.

He smiled at me and let go of my hand. "This won't take long. I'm pretty awesome at pool."

"This should be fun to watch then." There were a few seats next to an old jukebox in the corner. I sat down in the one closest to the pool table.

The girl clearly liked him. She was bending over rather seductively whenever she took a shot. And she kept lightly nudging his arm. She even asked him for advice on how to hold her cue stick so that he had to put his hands on her. But it didn't seem like they were dating. Whenever he made a shot he just high-fived her. Unlike the other couple they were playing. Ben and Jillian were clearly dating because they kept making out every few minutes. Almost a ridiculous amount. If they had been alone, they probably would have been banging on the pool table. I laughed silently to myself. The book I was reading was definitely messing with my head. Who had sex on pool tables?

Every now and then my lifeguard would look over at me. I kept giving him a thumbs up because I couldn't think of anything better to do.

I was halfway done my third beer by the time Kristen showed up.

She spotted me across the bar, waved like a maniac, and came running over.

"You could have told me which Grottos. I've been all over the freaking boardwalk searching for you."

"Ah, I'm sorry. I should have checked my phone."

"You think?" She adjusted her super short miniskirt and somehow made it even more inappropriate. "I'm not too late, am I? Which one is he?"

"Would you lower your voice?" I grabbed her arm and pulled her down onto the stool beside mine.

"I ran all over the boardwalk in *heels*, Mila. If you don't tell me who he is I'm going to kill you."

Apparently I *was* going to be murdered tonight. Just not by my lifeguard. "I didn't tell you to wear high heels. I just walked off the beach and came here. How was I supposed to know you were going to dress up?"

"Yeah…well…I wanted to look good. So which one is he?" She started moving her head around like a wild banshee.

"The one playing pool." I gestured to the pool table, hoping she'd stop being so obvious.

"Oh. I think he's seeing someone…"

I glanced back at the game. Ben and Jillian were making out again. "Not that guy. The other one."

"Well, now I get it. He's totally stalkable."

"I'm not stalking him." Why did everyone keep saying that?

"You kind of are. But he's super cute, I totally get it. So which other lifeguards are single?"

I shrugged. The only person I had talked to was my lifeguard. And the girl that was clearly desperate for his attention. *Not me.* The blonde lifeguard that was currently leaning so far over to make a shot that I could see her bathing suit bottom beneath her jean skirt. *Give me a break.*

"I thought you'd at least scope the place out for me. Just like I scoped out the place and I have bad news…you have competition." She nodded to my lifeguard's teammate.

"I think they're just friends," I said. "He did ask me here after all."

"So you're definitely on a date?"

Yes? No? "I don't know."

"People on dates don't usually ditch said date to hang out with another woman."

Fair point. But she didn't see how my lifeguard hesitated. And tried to include me. And how he held my hand. I watched his teammate laugh and flirtatiously touch his arm. He proceeded to laugh at whatever she whispered into his ear. Maybe Kristen was right. This certainly didn't feel like a date. Which was a good thing, because I didn't want to date anyone this summer. So why did my stomach suddenly hurt? And why did I suddenly want to bitch slap that bitch?

"Go be more assertive," Kristen said. "You can't let her walk all over you just because she's taller, blonder, and tanner than you."

I felt myself shrinking into my stool. Was that supposed to be an ego boost?

"Speaking of gorgeous people, I think I just found something I like." She was staring at some guy across the bar. "I'll catch up with you later." She squeezed my arm without really even looking at me and walked away.

Bye, Kristen? I watched her walk over to the guy and start talking to him. They immediately started laughing and he stepped closer to her. She made it look so easy. I had never been good at stuff like that. Aiden had been my only serious boyfriend ever, and my dating skills felt like they'd been stomped on and thrown to sea.

I heard someone cheering and looked back at the pool table. Apparently they'd won the game. My lifeguard high-fived the girl one last time and then walked back over to me.

"You two make a good team," I said. Better to push them together than pretend I ever had a chance. It was for the best anyway.

"Me and Abby? No." He laughed. "She kind of sucks at pool. I thought she was going to make me lose."

Maybe he didn't realize that she liked him. "I don't know. She definitely likes you."

He shrugged his shoulders. "We're just friends."

Huh. I hadn't expected that. My ego started to re-inflate.

"Did you want to play something?" he asked.

"Ping pong?" I had seen that there was a table on the other side of the bar. It was the only thing here that I was any good at. My ego would be huge again in no time once I whooped his ass.

"Sure."

We walked over to the table. There were two people already playing so we waited in line. I leaned against the wall and he stood in front of me. I looked up into his eyes. It was easy to get lost in them, even when I tried to tell myself I shouldn't.

"Why are you looking at me like that?" he finally asked.

"I'm not looking at you in any way." *Am I?*

"Yes, you are." He laughed.

"Has anyone ever told you that your eyes are the same color as the ocean?"

He smiled. "I can't say that anyone has."

"Oh. Well. It's true." I felt a little buzzed.

"Is your friend still coming?" he asked.

"Yeah…she's…" I looked around the bar but didn't see her. "She's somewhere. She got here while you were playing pool and wandered off."

He looked around too. For a second I thought maybe he didn't believe me. Like he thought I'd made up a friend and was a total loser.

"Her name's Kristen," I added quickly. God, it sounded like I was making her up by the second. "I swear she's here somewhere."

He nodded, although it was hard to tell if he believed me.

"Are you hungry?" he asked.

"Starving actually." And so grateful for the change of topic.

"Okay, how about the loser buys a pizza?"

"It is not your lucky day, because I'm like, really, really good at ping pong."

"Really, really good, huh? I guess I'm in trouble. I'm going to go place our order now so it's ready when we're done. What kind do you like?"

"Plain is good."

"My favorite. I'll be right back."

His favorite? Everyone always made fun of me for ordering plain pizza. I smiled to myself. I watched him go toward the front counter. Another girl stopped him along the way and hugged him. He seemed pretty popular with the ladies. Which made sense, because he was gorgeous. Really freaking gorgeous. I watched him lean against the counter and order the pizza. He laughed with the girl at the counter. It was the same way he had leaned against the counter at the ice cream shop yesterday.

I swallowed hard. *Is this not a date? Did he just invite me here as a friend?* I was having trouble focusing. I shouldn't have had so much to drink. I put my bottle down on an empty table. *Geez, this isn't a date.* He was just a nice guy, being nice to the weird girl who was always alone on the beach. Who made up fake friends. At least in his eyes. I felt so embarrassed. I looked down at my flip flops. Maybe I could just leave before he came back.

"Is it okay if we do doubles?"

I looked up. My lifeguard was standing in front of me with two guys.

"Um, yeah. That's fine." Now I was just reduced to one of the guys. I wanted to be okay with the turn of the evening. But for a while there, I'd given myself this small shred of hope that he liked me. My heart was still healing from the last blow and now it just felt like it exploded again. At least, whatever was left of it. I took a deep breath. *It's fine. It's for the best.*

"Stalkers aren't usually hot," one of them said. "Do you want to be my partner?"

I looked up at my lifeguard. He looked embarrassed. Why? Because he had told them that I was a stalker? Or because he hadn't realized that they'd talk about it in front of me? *Asshole.* This definitely wasn't a date. I was just the weird, loner stalker girl. "That depends," I said to the guy who had just talked to me. "Are you any good?"

"Yeah, we'll crush them."

"Perfect." The table had just freed up. I picked up a paddle. I wanted to win. I wanted to completely annihilate my lifeguard. He could have just told me he was inviting me as a friend. I felt like he had purposefully tried to embarrass me. And I was pissed. Or drunk. Drunk and pissed.

"You guys can serve first," my lifeguard said.

"You really shouldn't be cocky right now." I served the ball. It bounced low and went perfectly between them so that neither of them went for it.

"Shit, nice serve!" my partner said.

"Eh, it wasn't my best." I served again. This time my lifeguard made contact with the ball but missed the table by about a foot.

After my five serves, we were up five to zero. I grabbed the ball that my lifeguard's partner had just flubbed and tossed it hard at my lifeguard. He caught it.

They only had three points when I slammed the winning shot.

"Dude, that was awesome!" My partner high-fived me.

"Should we switch up the teams?" my lifeguard's partner asked. It looked like he wanted nothing to do with my lifeguard anymore either. "It's only fair that we each get a turn with the stalker."

Seriously? I felt a lump forming in my throat that I couldn't swallow down. "Actually, I have to get going. Thanks for letting me play with you guys. It was lots of fun." It felt good to win. But I was losing my composure. I put the paddle down and walked away from the table toward the front of the restaurant.

"Hey!" I heard my lifeguard yell after me.

I kept walking. I was supposed to stay single this summer. It was good that he had invited me here as a joke. I never thought I'd need a reminder that all men were assholes, but here it was. My eyes were starting to burn. I should have never come with him. I wasn't ready for anything like this. I just needed to be alone.

"Jellyfish Girl!"

I stopped in the middle of the boardwalk and turned around. "That's not my name. Or Stalker. Not that you care." People were staring at me. This was so mortifying.

"I'm sorry, I..."

"Please just leave me alone." I needed to get away from all the prying eyes. And most of all I needed to get away from him. I walked across the boardwalk and onto the beach. The sand was cold at night. I slid off my flip flops, picked them up, and ran as fast as I could down to the water.

CHAPTER 5
Friday

My alarm went off and I groaned. It couldn't possibly be time to wake up. I touched my forehead where I had a pounding headache. People who just got hit by a ton of bricks in the face shouldn't have to wake up in the morning. It was only fair. But the beeping was relentless despite how unfair it was.

I reached out to silence my phone. When the alarm stopped, I was about to let go of my phone when everything came back to me in a rush.

No. No, no, no. I pulled my phone close to my face and checked my most recent calls. *No!* There it was. At 10:30 last night I had made one outgoing call. To fucking Aiden.

My headache suddenly got worse. I remembered everything from last night. Drinking too much. My lifeguard making fun of me to his friends. Me stupidly thinking it was a date. Crying on the beach, the feelings mashing together with when Aiden broke up with me. And then…I called Aiden because drunk crying me apparently wanted my life to be worse at 10:30 last night.

I would have thrown my phone across the room, but my screen was already cracked. I was lucky it even worked. Instead, I slammed it against my pillow and tried not to start crying all over again. Why of all people did I call the devil himself? Being embarrassed and drunk shouldn't have made me need to hear his voice. But it was hard being so close to him for years and then getting cut out of his life. I was used to going to him when I was upset. It was a normal reaction, even if it was an accident. I never needed to hear his stupid voice again. Ever.

I closed my eyes and pulled the covers over my head. Luckily Aiden hadn't answered. But I remembered leaving a long, awkward message. I'd asked him why he called things off. I'd told him I was across the country and no matter how far away I was, it still hurt. I was pathetic. It would have been better if I'd stayed at the bar and gotten made fun of to my face for the rest of the evening. At least then I wouldn't have called my ex in a fit of despair.

My alarm started going off again. I'd hit the snooze button by mistake. Because there was no way in hell I was going to work today. Elephants were stampeding in my head and my soul hurt. I turned off the annoying beeping again.

"What are you doing?" Kristen asked with a yawn. "You're going to be late for work."

"I'm not going." At first I thought she didn't hear me because I was hiding underneath my blankets.

"You have to go to work."

"No." I felt the bed sag beside me.

"Did something happen last night?" she asked.

"No."

"Mila."

"Kristen."

She laughed and pulled my sheet down from my face. Her smile disappeared, probably because I looked like I'd been crying half the night and was about to burst into tears again.

"Jesus, what happened to you?"

If she kept looking at me with so much sympathy I really would cry. "Nothing."

"Clearly it's not nothing. What did the hot lifeguard do to you? Was it the anal thing we talked about? Because you're really supposed to work up to that slowly…"

I tried to pull the blankets back over my head but she grabbed them and held them down.

"So…not that. You have to tell me what happened. I know what he looks like now. Want me to go kill him?"

"No. He's just a stupid boy, if you kill him you might as well kill the rest of them too. And I don't want you to go to prison for killing half the population. I need you."

She smiled. "Will you at least tell me what happened?"

I sat up, wiping beneath my eyes. I was pretty sure I'd collapsed in bed right after sitting on the beach last night. My sheets felt sandy. And my hands were blackened by running mascara. "It was stupid. I thought that maybe it was a date, but I'm pretty sure he just brought me there to make fun of me with his friends. They called me Stalker Girl."

"Mila, I hate to break it to you, but you were stalking him."

"I was not stalking him!"

"You go to the beach the exact same time on Tuesdays and Thursdays specifically to watch him. That's what stalking is."

"Stalking is when you sit in a tree outside someone's window with binoculars and watch them change."

"No…that's a peeping Tom. Please tell me you don't do that too."

"Of course I don't! Because I'm not stalking him."

Kristen shrugged. "So the date was a bust. You gotta shake it off." She pushed my shoulder like she could shake it out of me. "There are plenty of lifeguards in the sea."

It wasn't really the date or lack thereof that I was upset about. It was the fact that I'd foolishly thought for a second that maybe I'd be able to put the pieces of my heart back together and then *bam*. I felt naïve and stupid. This summer was supposed to be about me figuring out what I wanted to do with my life. Not falling for the first guy who looked my way. Not that I was falling for my lifeguard. He was a dick. And on top of being beaten back down to my self-pitying ways? I made a horrible, awful mistake.

"It's not just the date I'm upset about," I mumbled. That would have been bad enough. But I had to go and put a cherry on top.

"Did he do something else?"

I shook my head and looked down at my phone. "I called Aiden."

"*The* Aiden? The one that never stopped saying he loved you, yet his dick was probably in some chick for months before you broke up?"

Vulgar. But I nodded my agreement.

"What did he say?"

"He didn't answer. He hasn't spoken to me since he kicked me out of his place. There's no reason for him to suddenly answer his phone now."

"Phew. Well, good. No harm no foul then." She patted my leg.

I wish. "I left a message."

"Oh, no." So much freaking sympathy on her face. "What did you say?"

"The usual…that I missed him, how could he do this to us, had I caused the breakup in some way. I just looked at my phone and I left him a five minute message. Five minutes! Who knows what other shit I said. So…I'm not going to work today." I lay back down, pulling the blankets up to my chin.

"None of that changes the fact that you have to go to work."

"I'm going to call in sick."

She looked at me. "Heartache isn't an illness."

"It is too."

"It's not." She pulled my blankets back down again. "And even if it was…I don't think you're actually upset about the stupid voicemail you left Aiden."

Of course I'm upset about that. I just glared at her.

"You put yourself out there and got hurt again. That really freaking sucks, Mila. And if I ever see that lifeguard's beautiful face again, I'll punch him for you. But two tools doesn't mean everything in the toolbox is rotten."

"That's a weird saying."

"But it's true. I met a great guy last night. And I'm sure he has cute friends. How about you do call in sick and we go down to the beach with two sexy, single guys and shove it in hot lifeguard's face?"

I stared at her. She was already wearing a bikini. I guess she had heard my alarm being ignored before she went on her beach date.

"I have a date with Ben and Jerry."

"Stop."

"And Tim Gunn and Swatch."

"Tim Gunn is gay and Swatch is a dog. Get out of bed."

"My heart hurts."

She pressed her lips together.

"I just need one day in bed. Tomorrow I'll be back to normal, you'll see."

"Are you sure? I feel like some fresh air would be really good for you."

I pictured myself sitting in the sand crying last night. I'd called Aiden for a reason. I felt completely and utterly alone. When would that feeling go away? Fresh tears were starting to form in the corners of my eyes. Besides, my lifeguard knew my work schedule. He might show up to apologize. *Fat chance.* I'd never seen him again. The thought of never seeing him again made the pain in my chest worse. "Just one day in bed," I said again.

"Okay. But don't you dare watch Project Runway without me. And I'll pick up some more Ben and Jerry's on the way home."

Thank you, bestie. I curled into a ball in my bed, holding my knees against my chest. She even closed the blinds for me before she left our apartment. As soon as she was gone, I closed my eyes again. I pictured the hue of my lifeguard's irises. Exactly the same color as the ocean. I thought I could get lost in them. Instead, I felt like I was drowning.

I was never going to let my guard down again. My heart couldn't take it anymore. I hugged my knees closer to my chest. When would it stop hurting?

CHAPTER 6
Friday

I had hibernated in my room for the past week pretending I was sick. Kristen kept threatening to pull me outside in my pajamas like some sort of monster, but then we'd end up binge watching TV instead. It turned out she wasn't a monster at all. Her threats were empty. If anything, she catered to my awful behavior by refilling the freezer with ice cream and helping me eat all the baked goods I started making. Depression now gave me a sweet tooth, whereas in Cali my depression had made it impossible to eat. And I couldn't eat everything alone. So in reality, Kristen was an angel.

If it was up to me, I'd still be hiding out. But my bosses apparently needed me. The girl who I usually worked with had taken the day off. Plus, if I took any more days off, I wouldn't be able to afford to eat. Which was a huge problem because cooking was one of the only things I still enjoyed doing. At this rate, instead of getting my act together this summer, I'd gain 100 pounds.

Fridays were my least favorite day to work because they were busier than Mondays and Wednesdays. But to-day it was good to have the distraction. I was training a new girl, which gave me even less time to think about my disastrous date. Or lack thereof. I hadn't had that much to drink in awhile. And I had never held my alcohol well, which I knew for a fact after margarita night when I'd first told Kristen about my crush in the first place. For the life of me, I wasn't sure why I'd allowed myself to have more than one drink with my lifeguard or Kristen. Alcohol led to bad decisions and bad behavior. *Shame on me.*

My thoughts wandered back to my date-pocalypse, which I was now calling it. I wasn't sure if it was meant to be a date or not, but it really didn't matter. Either way, I'd come to the conclusion that I'd acted insane. And he'd acted like a complete jerk. Hopefully avoiding him for the last week would have given him enough time to forget about me. Hell, he probably hadn't thought about me since. After all...he was labeled as a jerk in my mind for a reason.

I showed the new girl how to ring up a customer on the cash register. We didn't have a button for the different sizes, we just had to memorize all the prices. At night everyone had their own small credit card readers since there were so many people. I was supposed to teach her how to use that as well, but we were never overly busy during the day. I always just used the credit card reader on the cash register and had quickly forgotten how to use my small one. If Keira and Rory ever called me in for a night shift I wouldn't be much help.

The new girl, Becca, was still in high school. For some reason her optimism about this job was annoying me. Also the fact that Becca was short for Rebecca didn't help. It just reminded me that Aiden had left me for someone he deemed better. A Rebecca with bigger tits than me and new girl Becca combined.

All I wanted to do was go to the beach. I had worn my bathing suit underneath my clothes and was planning on a quick escape. I hadn't felt the sand beneath my feet since I ran away from my lifeguard. *My lifeguard.* I shook my head. I was so ridiculous. And technically I had felt the sand recently. It was still in my bed because I was a crazy nester who hadn't washed her sheets in weeks.

Becca needed to practice handling the customers, so I hung back and observed her. She was so bubbly. She was perfect for this job. Hopefully Keira and Rory hadn't hired her to replace me. I shook my head. I doubted that they'd fire me. My two bosses were amazing. Although, I wouldn't be surprised if they'd paired me with Becca to punish me for calling in sick for a week. But that was my own fault. Maybe I deserved to be punished for my pile of lies.

I looked down at my phone. I'd gotten in the habit of doing that ever since I'd called my ex last week. He hadn't called me back. I never expected him to. We hadn't talked since he broke up with me.

I had made so many ridiculous choices last Thursday night. Well, ever since Thursday. Being holed up in my apartment and ignoring Kristen's pleas for me to see the light of day again, hadn't exactly been healthy. At least when she left me to my own devices I read instead of watching Project Runway without her. I definitely never did that. Well, maybe one season. But I didn't mind watching it again. I'd be just as excited the second time around. I didn't care if Tim Gunn was gay or if Swatch was a dog. They were the only men for me.

Besides, after reading book after book after book, I'd run out of them. The only book I hadn't read was Twisted Love. I'd even removed the bookmark so I wouldn't be tempted to pick up where I'd last left off. I didn't want to read a romance anymore. It was good but I wasn't in the mood. It had made me realize that I still had dozens of books that I had left in my ex's apartment. I wanted them back. Getting a piece of my dignity back wouldn't hurt either. I'd made a fool out of myself by calling him last week. There'd be no more tomfoolery from me. Just poised confidence.

I took a deep breath and clicked on his name in my phone. It rang twice and then went to voicemail. I hadn't expected it to go to voicemail so fast. He must have seen me calling and rejected it. He was screening my calls. The answering machine beeped.

"Hey ba..." I coughed. *Did I seriously almost call him babe?* I coughed again. "Hey, Aiden. Sorry about the call the other night. Too much partying out here." I paused, knowing he'd probably just think I was trying to sound okay when I wasn't. *I'm not okay.* I hadn't been okay since I found him in bed with someone else. I cleared my throat. "I was just thinking about all those books I left at your place. Could you mail them to me? I can PayPal you the money for shipping if you want. Just let me know what it costs." I quickly gave him my new address and then repeated it. "And you know, if there's anything else that's mine. Actually, there was this sweater and a dress I really liked that I left...well, anything that's mine. Ship everything. I hope you're having a good summer." I felt my throat catch. "Thanks, Aiden." I quickly hung up. I shouldn't have called him again. I'd just buy new books and a new sweater and a new dress.

"How do you open the cash register?" Becca asked. She seemed distraught.

I laughed and walked over to her.

***

My shift was almost over. I was showing Becca how to make the cleaning solution for the counters when I saw my lifeguard coming off the beach and toward the ice cream shop. At least, it looked like he was coming this way. I wasn't about to stand here and find out.

"And that's it," I said as I poured in one more table-spoon of the awful lemon scented cleaning solution. I grabbed a washcloth and wrung it out. "I'll be in the back room for a sec cleaning up. Call me if you need help."

I dropped the washcloth on the table, sat down on one of the stools in the back room, and took a deep breath. Why was he coming here? I guess it was possible that I was wrong. He was probably just walking by after work to get to his apartment. That was it. I sighed with relief after a few minutes had gone by. There was no way he'd still be out there. I got up and wiped down the table.

"Are we allowed to do a bunch of little scoops of different flavors that in the end make up one normal sized scoop? And then just charge them for a single scoop?" Becca was standing by the doorway.

What the hell? "No."

"There's this guy that is insisting that he wants like a million different flavors. I don't know what to do."

"Sometimes customers are the worst. I'll try to talk to him." Our mantra was to always give the customers whatever they wanted. But some people were just horrible. I wish our mantra was, "Go away and just let me stand here doing nothing and make minimum wage." That would be amazing. The thought made me sigh. I still remembered how the ice cream counter girl stared at me after Aiden dumped me. She thought I was diseased or something. One of the reasons I took this job was so that I could make people's days better by having a smile on my face. I plastered one on, even though it felt super fake. Just because I was having a bad day, it didn't mean I needed to spread the frownies around.

I walked out of the back room. My lifeguard was standing by the counter. He smiled at me. Of course it was him being obnoxious. He had probably just been flirting with Becca. Ass. Face.

"No, you can't have a million different flavors and only pay for one scoop," I said. "That's ridiculous." I knew I was being rude, but I was pissed. He had no right to come here and antagonize me and my co-workers.

"I know it's ridiculous. I just needed to talk to you."

"I'm working. We're busy." He was the only customer waiting in line. At dinner time we were always dead, even on Fridays.

He looked behind him. "Okay. I'm just going to sit over there and we can talk when you get off at 5:30."

"How do you know that I get off at 5:30?"

"That girl that you usually work with told me. By the way, she really missed you. Apparently she doesn't have to do any work when you're around. You really shouldn't let people step all over you like that."

For some reason I wanted to slap him. "Are you seriously lecturing me on the fact that I'm a pushover? You have a lot of nerve."

"5:30. I'll be sitting right there." He pointed to a bench to the right.

"I can't stop you from sitting there."

"Alright then." He looked down at his watch. "See you in 20 minutes." He walked away. But he went past the bench and down the boardwalk.

Weird. Maybe he had changed his mind. I hope he'd changed his mind.

But he didn't. Fifteen minutes later he was back with a Grottos pizza box. He sat down on the bench and crossed his right ankle over his left knee. He took off his aviators, hooked them on the front of his shirt, and stared directly at me.

His eyes really were enchanting. I turned away from him. I needed to not look at his eyes. It was like they had a trance over me. When I turned around he was still staring at me. *Stop it!* I tried to pay attention to the new employee instead of my lifeguard.

"So how do you like your new job?" I asked Becca.

"It's lots of fun. I can't believe I was lucky enough to score a position at Sweet Cravings. We're both so lucky, don't you think?"

Of course that was her answer. "Definitely." I drummed my fingers against the counter. Our shift was over, and she was looking at me expectantly. But I didn't want to leave. Walking out of here meant walking toward my lifeguard. And I didn't want to walk anywhere near him. Even if he did have beautiful eyes and a pizza.

"Is it time to go?" Becca asked.

Classic Becca, not able to read my mind. In her defense, she didn't know me. And she certainly didn't know that I wanted to stay locked in here forever. Plus our replacements had already arrived. And it was in fact time to leave.

"Yeah," I said with a sigh. "Let's divvy up tips and we can get going." I dumped out the tip jar and counted it out. We each got fifteen dollars. The awesome tips were the only good thing about Fridays. "Well, hopefully we'll get to work together sometime again. It was nice meeting you."

"You too!"

I hung up my apron and grabbed my beach bag. Usually I had a purse, but since I had planned to go to the beach after work I had opted for my usual beach bag. I took a deep breath and went outside. My lifeguard stood up and walked over to me.

"I think I owe you a pizza." He smiled at me.

"No, it's fine. I'm actually not hungry." I was starving and the smell of the pizza had my mouth watering. But I wasn't hungry enough to eat with a dick.

"Oh, yeah, I heard you've been really sick." He said it normally, but I heard it in a sarcastic rude way. Because that's what I thought of him.

"I was sick." *I wasn't.*

"I'm not arguing with you." He shrugged his shoulders.

"I actually have plans right now," I said and started walking toward the beach.

He quickly caught up to me. "What are your plans?"

"I haven't been to the beach in a while."

"Okay, I'll come with you." He walked silently beside me across the boardwalk, through the sand, and close to where the water was breaking.

I glanced at him. I thought he'd have left by now. I didn't know what he wanted me to say. But the pizza did smell good. And I really was hungry. Choices, choices.

"Look, I do owe you a pizza," he said. "And you owe me an explanation. So let's eat and talk."

If anything he owed me an apology. But I wasn't about to play whatever game he was trying to play. "We don't owe each other anything."

"Actually we do. You won this pizza fair and square in a bet." He sat down in the sand. "And you walked out on me in the middle of our date with no explanation. I want to know why."

It was a date? I looked down at him. His blue eyes were so endearing. I grabbed my towel out of my bag and spread it on the ground. He brushed the sand off his swim trunks and sat down next to me on my towel. He opened up the box and raised his left eyebrow.

"What, is it drugged or something?"

He laughed. "No."

I took a slice. He grabbed one too and closed the lid to the box.

"I'm sorry about what my friends said. I told them about you being a stalker in a funny way. Like how I kid with you. I wasn't serious. I'm sorry if that's what upset you."

"It's fine. You don't have to apologize. I just drank too much." But even as the words left my mouth, I knew they weren't true. Because truly I had needed to hear that apology. It was nice to hear an "I'm sorry" after so much radio silence from Aiden. Maybe I'd misjudged this guy after all.

"Maybe you drank a little too much too," he said.

"Well even drunk me completely owned you in ping pong."

"That you did." He smiled at me.

I looked back out at the water instead of at him. "I convinced myself that you had been making fun of me behind my back. I thought maybe you were just being nice to the weird girl who always comes to the beach alone."

He laughed. "The sexy, weird girl. You're missing a very important adjective there."

I felt my face flush. "And I think watching you with Abby and all the other girls you talked to made me think I had misjudged everything."

"They're all just friends."

"You act very flirtatious with every girl you talk to."

"I didn't realize I was doing that."

"Well, you do. Which made me think I was just your friend too. I was embarrassed that I thought it was more. And that's when your friend came up and called me a stalker. I just snapped." *I'm on high alert for assholes because I dated one for almost three years and was blind to it the whole time.*

"Well, I thought it was date. It was with a bunch of my friends, but I was trying to get to know you. If you had stayed for pizza, we would have had more time to talk just the two of us." He pulled out another slice of pizza for me.

"Thanks," I said and grabbed it. I looked out toward the water. "But even if it was a date, it doesn't really matter. I shouldn't have said yes to going. I'm really not in any place to start a new relationship." *So you can leave now. But please leave the pizza. I appreciate your donation.*

"Is that one of the reasons why you came here? To get away from someone?"

Why was he so intrusive? Why was he still sitting here? I felt like I wanted to cry. It was so hard for me to talk about. Every time I thought about it, it was like it had just happened. But maybe it would help to talk about it out loud. And I needed another friend because Kristen was probably sick of me by now. Or literally sick from all the sugar we'd both consumed this week. Maybe my lifeguard was just what I needed. I kept my eyes on the water. "I went to SMU because I thought it would be this fun new adventure. But as soon as I moved into my dorm I realized just how far away I was from everyone I knew. I felt so alone. So when I met Aiden…" my voice trailed off. *I clung to him like a lifeline, without even really knowing him.* It was the first time I'd ever thought of it like that. But it was true. I just needed someone…and he fell into my lap. I shook my head. "We started dating right away and I pretty much devoted all my free time to him. I became friends with all his friends, but didn't take the time to make any friends of my own. I thought I was so in love with him. I thought he was all that mattered. I know, looking back at it now, how ridiculous that was. We were so young. I'm still young." I stopped talking for a few seconds, but my lifeguard stayed quiet. I could feel the tears welling in my eyes.

"Right before spring break I had this stupid idea in my head that he was going to propose. Instead, I walked in on him having sex with some slut with huge breasts. He broke up with me right there. With her watching from the bed. No explanation. Just...I was out of his life. I'm pretty sure they had been screwing around behind my back for months. And I didn't see it. He didn't even have enough respect for me to tell me the truth. It was so hard finding out and her watching me fall apart. And that was it. We were done in just a few minutes. The last two and a half years meant nothing.

"All of our mutual friends turned out to not really be my friends at all. I was so lonely. It was unbearable. And I was too upset to go out and make new friends. I just stayed in my room like a complete loser, thinking about everything that I had lost. I tried to think about what went wrong. I needed closure. I needed to know why. But he wouldn't talk to me. It was like I had never even existed in his life. So I walked around campus like a ghost."

I wiped away the tears from my cheeks. "I'm sorry, that was like the most dramatic..."

"Don't." He grabbed my hand so I couldn't wipe away my tears. "Don't act like it's nothing if it's not."

I looked up at him. "I want to feel whole again. That's why I came here. I need to figure out what I want by myself. I've spent too much time thinking about myself as half of a whole."

He squeezed my hand. "I get that. And I know what it feels like."

"For your boyfriend to break up with you?" I tried to lighten the mood.

"No." He laughed. "To feel broken. To be cheated on. All of it. I get why you ran out on me the other night. It takes time to trust people again after that."

I liked the feeling of his hand in mine. It was so nice having someone listen to me. But the fact that he understood made it even better. "Do you mind me asking what happened?"

He shrugged. "It was a long time ago. My high school girlfriend and I decided to stay together after graduation even though we were going to different schools. She cheated on me the first semester we were apart. I think you learn a lot from shitty stuff like that. I learned that long distance relationships don't work. I'll never try to do one again. And I guess from yours, you learned that you shouldn't date assholes." He smiled down at me.

"Yeah." I looked out back toward the water. He doesn't do long distance relationships. *So why did he ask me on a date in the first place? And why is he holding my hand right now?* I snuck a sideways glance at him. Maybe he was just being nice. It didn't matter either way though. I really wasn't ready to date again. But I could use a friend. "So now you know all about me, even down to my most humiliating moment." I pulled my hand away from him, ignoring the fact that my whole body suddenly felt cold. "What's your story?"

He shrugged. "I have a younger brother. My parents are still together. I'm boring. I've always done everything I was expected to do. And that's why I'm here this summer. I feel like this is the last time I'm going to know what it feels like to make my own choices."

"Your job can't be all that bad."

"I just have to sit there all day behind a computer screen. The whole day will be gone by the time I get home. I like to be outside. I don't want to forget what it feels like to have the sun on my skin. I'm dreading it. I feel like my life is ending." He laughed. "Now I'm the one being dramatic."

I smiled at him.

"Maybe I should think of this summer more like you do. I need to figure some things out too. And every day my mom keeps bugging me, reminding me that I need to get some work-appropriate clothes. I don't even know where to go for something like that."

"I can come with you if you want. There are some outlets really close. It'll be fun."

"Actually, that would be really great. What are you doing tomorrow?"

"I'm a weirdo with no friends. What do you think I'm doing? Just kidding, I do have friends. Well, one friend here. The girl I mentioned the other night does actually exist."

He laughed. "I never doubted that she did."

"Oh." Drunken me was great at jumping to conclusions. "Good."

His smile was contagious. "So, do you want to go tomorrow?"

"Sure. I need to buy a few books anyway, so it'll be good to go shopping."

"What was Twisted Love about?" He gave me a mischievous smile. He must have heard about it. Everyone had heard about it.

"It's a romance. It's just a really sweet story."

"Mhm."

"Clearly you already know what it's about. And I didn't finish it. I haven't exactly been in a romantic mood this past week."

"Well, maybe you can finish reading it now."

His sentence hung in the air. He had a new job starting in the fall. And I'd be flying back to California. But he was still flirting with me. Or maybe he was just being funny.

Regardless of his intentions, I found myself wanting to be flirtatious back. He had called me a sexy weird girl earlier. Compliments were nice, even if they were only half nice. And his words had given me a surge of confidence. It felt like ages since someone looked at me the way he was looking at me. I stood up and pulled off my tank top.

"What are you doing?" he asked.

"I haven't been in the ocean in a week. I need to be wet."

He started laughing really hard.

Why did I choose that phrase? A normal person would have said they wanted to go in the water. I decided silence was the best response. If I explained myself it would just end up getting worse. I was the queen of word vomit when I was around him.

Finally he spoke again. "But it's getting dark. Aren't sharks out at night?"

"I don't know, you're the lifeguard."

"I'm pretty sure they feed at night. And I'm worried that they might be as attracted to you as jellyfish are."

"So you can watch out for me. Isn't that kind of your job?" I started to unbutton my jean shorts.

"During the day..."

"Oh my God, are you scared of sharks?"

"Who *isn't* scared of sharks?"

"But you're a lifeguard."

"I'm still a person."

I laughed. "You don't have to come with me." I pulled off my shorts and tossed them onto my towel.

He stared at my legs and then quickly stood up. "Well I kind of have to. I need to protect you from everything that wants to bite or sting you." He pulled his shirt off, revealing his perfectly sculpted torso.

That was the sweetest thing anyone had said to me in a long time. I smiled at him. "I'll race you."

He didn't say anything. Instead he started running.

"Hey!" I ran as fast as I could after him and into the water. "Oh my God, it's so much colder at night!" I said after I came up from a wave. I grabbed his arm as another wave came crashing down. He pulled me against his chest so I wouldn't get crushed. His hand was pressed firmly against the small of my back.

"Shit it's cold," he said.

"It is." But I wasn't cold. His hands on me felt warm. I felt myself pulling even closer to him. And even though the water had settled, he kept his hand on the small of my back.

"Okay, you made me come in, so it's kind of your job to keep me warm." He grabbed my thigh and brought it up to his waist.

I lifted my other thigh and crossed my legs behind him.

Both his hands drifted to right under my ass.

No, I was definitely not cold. My body felt like it was on fire. "Better?" I asked. My voice came out weird, and I hoped he couldn't tell how much I loved being in his arms.

"Much better." He looked down at me. His Adam's apple rose and then fell.

Oh, he can tell. Despite everything we had just talked about, I wanted him to kiss me. And it seemed like he wanted to kiss me too. But he just stared at me with his perfect blue eyes.

I wasn't sure what felt better, his eyes on me or his hands holding me against him. Who was I kidding, it was the hands. They were so close to...my mind suddenly took a weird turn. Was he a butt guy? Was he going to want to Thanksgiving turkey me? *Stop ruining the moment!* Now that my mind was racing it was hard to stop, though. He didn't look like he'd be into anal. But what do guys who are into anal look like anyway? For some reason I was thinking bald. Probably everywhere. Luckily he broke my dirty train of though.

"Are you wet enough now?" He raised his left eyebrow.

I was. In more ways than one. "Are you?" Again with the weird voice. I cleared my throat, trying to rid it from neediness.

He laughed. "Yeah, and I'm frozen. I can't feel my legs." But he didn't move to get out.

It was like we were locked in a trance. And if either of us broke it, we could never go back. He didn't do long distance. I didn't have time to focus on a relationship, I needed to focus on myself for once. And yet...I didn't move to get out either. I could have stayed like that forever. I liked the feeling of his hands on me. And I liked being so close to him. "Then let's get out." For a second, I didn't realize who said it. But from the disappointment on his face, I knew it was me. My brain was sensible, even though my body was absolutely not. I reluctantly unclasped my hands from around his neck.

He looked down at me as he let go of my thighs. "Yeah, let's get the hell out of here before we get eaten by sharks." He grabbed my hand and we ran together out of the water.

Even though it wasn't cold outside, we were drenched in the icy water and there was a constant breeze coming off the ocean. My lifeguard picked up the towel before I could reach it and wrapped it around himself.

How rude. "Stop hogging the towel." My teeth were chattering.

He spread out his arms. "We can share, I guess."

I laughed as he wrapped it around the two of us together. The side of my face was pressed against his chest. He smelled like sunscreen, sweat, and saltwater. He smelled just like summer. Kristen was going to be so proud of me for finally figuring out what he smelled like.

I wrapped my arms around his torso. His back was so muscular. I kept my hands completely still and tried to absorb this moment. Maybe I wrong about what I needed. Maybe I was ready for another relationship. He was so nice and handsome. And he actually listened to me. I liked him. I liked him a lot.

"It's getting late," he said.

He didn't feel the same. I quickly unwound myself from him and the towel. I must have imagined the disappointed look on his face earlier. But it didn't feel like I could just be imagining the chemistry between us.

"Yeah." I looked around for my clothes that he'd dumped into the sand. "I should get going." I grabbed my shirt off the ground.

"I'll walk you home."

I was about to protest, but then I realized I didn't want to. I wanted to spend more time with him. "That would be really nice."

He pulled his shirt back on and I quickly pulled on my shorts. I could feel his eyes on me as I zipped my jean shorts back up. I looked up at him but he quickly looked away. He ran his hand through his wet hair. Everything he did was so sexy.

I grabbed my bag and he draped my towel over his shoulder. We made our way back up to the boardwalk. We were both silent. I began to wonder if he was thinking about me the same way I was thinking about him. It was complicated. Maybe it was too complicated. We turned off the boards onto a quiet sidewalk. My place was only a block away and before I knew it, we were there.

"That's me." I stopped and pointed down a driveway.

"It's so close to the beach. You're really lucky."

Unlucky circumstances had brought me here. But I felt so lucky tonight. I smiled at him.

"What time do you want to go shopping tomorrow?" he asked.

"Do you want to go after lunch? Maybe around one?"

"Sure, I'll pick you up then." He stood there for a second, looking at me. He put his hands in his pockets. "Okay then. Goodnight, Jellyfish Girl."

"Wait." I reached out and grabbed his arm.

He stepped back toward me. It looked like he wanted to kiss me. Maybe he wanted me to make the first move. We had both basically agreed that we couldn't date. He was being respectful, but I wished he'd cut it out.

It took all my willpower to not stand on my tiptoes and run my hands through his wet, shaggy hair. I realized I was awkwardly staring at him. "What's your name? I'm tired of referring to you as my lifeguard." *Shit!* "I mean the lifeguard. The. Not mine. You're not mine. I know that people say that in an endearing way sometimes, but that is not at all what I meant. Because I didn't mean to say it at all. Besides...I mean...you can't own people. I definitely just refer to you as the lifeguard. Like the lifeguard for all the people at the beach. And sometimes hot lifeguard when I'm talking about you with Kristen." *Why am I still talking?* "Not that I talk about you a lot. Or at all." *Shut your face, Mila!*

He smiled down at me. "So you think I'm your lifeguard, huh?"

"No. It was just a classic case of the word farts." *Word farts? What the fuck am I saying?* I bit my lip.

"I kind of like that you refer to me as your lifeguard." He shrugged his shoulders. "You can just keep calling me that."

"But..."

He took my towel off his shoulder and draped it behind my neck. My heartbeat quickened. I thought he was going to pull me in for a kiss. But instead, he dropped the ends of the towel.

"I'll see you tomorrow, Jellyfish Girl," he said and walked away.

I'm in so much trouble.

CHAPTER 7
Friday

There were butterflies in my stomach as I unlocked my door. I knew I shouldn't have them, but I couldn't help it. And even though we were supposed to just be friends, I didn't even want them to disappear. I wasn't even sure I could get rid of them if I wanted to.

He liked when I called him my lifeguard. It felt like that meant he liked all my idiosyncrasies. That he liked me just the way I was. The butterflies started flapping around even more. I smiled to myself as I pushed the door open. Tonight was just what I needed.

The door slammed into something hard on the other side.

"Ow! Son of a bitch!" Kristen fell with a thud and sprawled out on the floor, blocking my way in. "Why did you hit me?"

"Were you spying on me?"

"Don't flip this around. I think you broke my whole body."

I tried not to laugh as I helped her to her feet. "That's what you get for spying."

"I wasn't spying."

I just stared at her.

"It just so happened that I was looking through the peephole at the exact same time you and douche bag dick wad were standing there."

"And who's the stalker now?"

She rolled her eyes. "Sue me. And speaking of su-ing...you'll be hearing from my lawyer about all the broken bones in my body. I'm basically a professional athlete! My bones are precious."

"Did I actually hurt you?" I wasn't at all afraid that she'd sue me, but I didn't want her to be in pain. And I definitely didn't want it to my fault that she didn't make the cut for the U.S. volleyball team.

"Yes." She waved her hand in front of her face, torso, arms, and legs. "Everywhere."

Dramatic much? "I'm sorry."

"You don't sound sorry. But I guess I won't sue you if you tell me what the hell you two were doing together? I couldn't hear properly through the door. I could have sworn you said word farts."

If only that hadn't happened. I was in too good of a mood to care though. I laughed and walked past her and into our apartment. "He came to the ice cream shop to talk to me. He even brought a pizza since I missed out last week. We ate on the beach and…"

"I know. I had to order in because you abandoned me without any warning." She stuck out her bottom lip and motioned to the Chinese takeout boxes on the coffee ta-ble. "But if the next thing out of your mouth is that you two made out under the stars, all is forgiven."

I wish. I think I wish? God, I don't know. I shook my head. "No, we didn't kiss. We talked and went for a swim. He apologized about the other night. It was just really, really nice."

"Nice? You have to give me a better adjective than that. And more details. Did you hold hands? Did you skip first base and go straight to second?"

I thought about his hands precariously close to my ass. There was no way I was going to have this conversation with her. I had a bad feeling it would just go straight into talking about anal. And I was done thinking about that. Besides, tonight felt…personal. I didn't want to spill all the details. I wanted to bottle them up and keep them forever. What could I say to distract her from prying questions? "Well, I know what he smells like now."

"Oh…you were close enough to get a good whiff of him? Does he smell as amazing as we thought he would?"

Even better. "He smells just like summer."

"So…like…sweaty?" She made a face that squished all her features together.

I laughed. "No. Well, kind of, but in a good way. It was a mix of sunscreen, sweat, and saltwater. It was intoxicating. We hung out after he had worked all day, so it was ocean goodness."

"Now we have to find out what he smells like when he cleans himself up properly."

"Okay?" What was with her and male aromas? I liked how he smelled after work. I really really liked it. Probably too much for my own good.

"I guess this means you don't want me to kill him anymore?"

I shook my head. "Definitely not."

"So you're going to date?"

"No. I think we're going to try to be friends, I guess."

"That was a weird sentence."

I shrugged. "What? Why?"

"I think. I guess. Try. You're going to land straight in his bed for sure."

"Not going to happen. He doesn't do long distance."

"And summer doesn't end for two months. Right now you're super close distance. Why not take advantage of that for as long as possible? A sexy summer fling never hurt anyone."

I laughed. "I'm focusing on myself, remember?"

"And just imagine how good you'd feel with his dick in you."

So freaking amazing. I should have been reprimanding her, not daydreaming about the possibility of what she'd proposed. "You know what I mean, Kristen. I need to figure out my major. And figure out how to run for more than ten minutes at a time without feeling like I'm dying."

"All of which you could do together. Besides, I'm sure he's great at running. Doesn't he have to run in slow motion every day as a lifeguard? He could teach you how to do that."

I laughed.

"And I wasn't watching you guys for very long, but girl, it looked like he was going to go in for the kiss for a second there. I'm not sure the two of you are on the same page."

"Of course we are."

"Mhm. So when he said he was going to see you tomorrow…that's not another date?"

"We haven't been on and are not going to go on any dates. We're just friends." But he had actually admitted going to Grottos was a date. And tonight certainly felt like a date. I glanced toward my closet.

"Are you thinking about what you're going to wear tomorrow?"

"Maybe…"

"Then it's a date!" She squealed. "Want me to help you pick something out? Oh, I have an idea! Tell me where you're going and I'll try to get a good view of wherever you are and I'll text you great advice the whole time."

"It's not a date. So I don't need advice. And please, don't ever ever do that."

"You're no fun at all. At least let me help you find an outfit then. What are you two friends doing on your non-date? I feel like you'll need assless chaps."

I stifled a laugh. "Promise you won't show up?"

"Sure." She didn't sound sincere at all. But I was also pretty sure she worked tomorrow. So even if she wanted to be creepy, she wouldn't have the chance to.

"We're going shopping. He starts his fancy new corporate job this fall and doesn't have anything to wear. And I need some new books."

"What you need is to kiss hot lifeguard."

"Yeah, well, maybe in my next lifetime."

"Or this one." She pulled out a skimpy, sparkly red dress from her closet. "You'll definitely get him to kiss you if you wear this."

"We're going at one in the afternoon. I'm not wearing a party dress in the middle of the day. Besides, we're meeting up after lunch. We won't even be sitting down at a restaurant. I was thinking jean shorts, a tank top, and Keds."

"Huh. Maybe you are just friends. Because you literally wear that every day. You're not even trying."

"Sometimes I wear pajamas all day instead."

Kristen laughed. "True. At least you're out of your depressing phase. But can we still watch Project Runway tonight?"

"Yes. The answer to that is always yes."

"The next challenge looks so freaking good. Who knew bathing suits were so hard to make?"

"Right?" I started to walk over to the couch.

"Wait, we still have to pick your outfit. Work first, play second."

"I already told you what I was going to wear."

"And unless you want me to murder you in your sleep, you're going to pick out a better outfit than that."

"You're scary sometimes."

"Only because I love you. Now try this one." She tossed a much more suitable sundress at me. But it was still a dress, and it seemed way too fancy for an afternoon of shopping. "Can't we stick to my closet?"

"Are you saying you don't like the way I dress?"

Only she could turn my question into an insult on her. "That's not…"

"Good." She pulled out several more outfits. "Time for a runway show. Strut your stuff and I'll judge you like Nina Garcia."

I was currently wearing something I'd be very comfortable in tomorrow. Minus the bathing suit of course. I started walking in my best runway model strut. "How about this?" I reached her and put my hand on my hip.

"You look like you woke up in a sewer," she said with a surprisingly spot-on Colombian accent for Nina Garcia. "What is it that you're wearing, exactly? Trash? Only a sewer rat would be caught dead in that ensemble."

"Why are you so good at that? And stop saying that my outfit is from the sewer."

"And the styling...what happened with the styling?" she continued with the accent.

I laughed. "Stop, you're freaking me out."

"What? Did you run out of time?" She was still perfectly in character. "You should have used the Lord & Taylor wall more thoughtfully. I can't look at this girl any longer."

I picked a pillow up off the couch and threw it at her.

She caught it with a laugh. "Sorry, I'll stop. I was weirdly good at that though, right?"

"Creepily so."

"Maybe I should get a job in fashion." She pulled the pillow to her chest as she collapsed backward onto the couch. "Try on at least a few outfits I picked out. Please? And then I'll be able to peacefully focus on Swatch and Tim Gunn." She cleared her throat. "This is a make it work moment, Mila," she said in a pretty awful Tim Gunn voice this time. At least she wasn't good at both voices. That would have just been weird.

I laughed and looked at all the ridiculous garments she had pulled. I wanted my lifeguard to like me for me. And nothing on the couch screamed "me." But if it appeased

Kristen, I'd try on a few. Besides, she wouldn't be here when I left tomorrow. She'd never know what I wore.

"Fine," I said. "But we get to eat lots of ice cream during the show after this torture." I may have been finished moping around, but I was pretty sure I was now addicted to binge eating ice cream every night.

"Deal. But, Mila, you need to hurry," she said in her bad Tim Gunn voice again. "We're going to the runway *now!*"

CHAPTER 8
Saturday

I changed my shirt for the fifth time. Kristen had gotten into my head about my outfit and I'd spent all morning obsessing until the point where I decided I hated everything in my closet. But what I wore didn't matter at all. I was thinking too much. My lifeguard and I were just friends. That was it.

I stared at my reflection in the mirror. A tank top was a tank top. Which was kind of Kristen's point. It was tempting to go to my closet and pull out a few dresses, but I knew that I was being ridiculous. I blamed the butterflies in my stomach. They were betraying my mind. *We're just friends, butterflies. Fly away. Or stay. Oy vey.* I laughed out loud at the weird rhyming in my head. *Oh God, I'm losing my mind.* Maybe the butterflies had scattered and some had gotten stuck to my brain. I shook my head, like that would fix the problem.

A knock sounded on my door. My heartbeat kicked up a notch. *Calm down.* I leaned closer to the mirror to check my makeup one last time. I added a bit more mascara, grabbed my purse as I rushed through the apartment, and opened the door.

My lifeguard was leaning against my doorframe with his arms crossed. He looked like sex on a stick. I had only ever seen him in his lifeguard swim trunks. He had ditched the sunglass and was wearing khaki shorts and a tight V-neck shirt. His eyes matched his shirt and I had the strangest sensation that I wanted to maul him.

"Hey," I tried to say casually, but it came out breathless after my rush over to the door. I needed to start exercising, I was truly out of shape. Or maybe I was breathless because of him.

He smiled and looked over my shoulder. "Nice place."

"Oh, thanks." I stepped to the side to block his view of the clothes strewn all over the studio apartment. If he was waiting for an invitation in, that was 100 percent not going to happen. I wasn't sure if I knew how to keep my hands to myself, so being alone with him was out of the question. You weren't supposed to touch friends inappropriately. Even sexy ones.

"You ready?" he asked.

"Mhm." I stepped outside and closed the door behind me. Luckily he didn't reach for my hand or anything. If he had, I probably would have melted into a puddle at his feet. Instead of turning into liquid, I walked down the wooden steps after him.

There was a motorcycle parked in the driveway and I almost felt compelled to roll my eyes. *Of course he rides a motorcycle.* Because his current hotness level wasn't already off the charts.

He grabbed a helmet off the seat. "Have you ever been on one?" he asked and handed it to me.

"No, I haven't. But I've always wanted to." My mother had warned me at a young age that only bad boys rode motorcycles. Boys that I shouldn't get tied up with. Not that her love life could be trusted. She'd probably dated more men than she could ever remember. Including said motorcycle guy where her advice had originated. And honestly, being a good girl hadn't exactly landed me in a good place. My life was in shambles.

All my own issues rolling around in my head came to a stop when I thought back to my mother's warning. What the heck did she even mean by boys I shouldn't get tied up with? What kind of kinky stuff was my mom into? *God, why am I thinking about this?*

"It's your lucky day then." He picked up another helmet and put it on.

It did feel like my lucky day, and I was glad he was here to distract me from my overactive imagination. Besides, how much of a bad boy could he be? He was wearing a helmet, so he was at least practical. I pulled my helmet on and fumbled with the straps.

"Here, let me." He clipped the straps together and then looked into my eyes as he tightened the cords.

I gulped. The way he was looking at me made my whole body feel warm. I was glad I remembered deodorant or I'd be a few seconds away from embarrassing pit stains.

He let go of the straps and got onto the motorcycle. "Hop on," he said.

I climbed on behind him and held my breath. Was I supposed to grab onto him? Would I fall off if I didn't? *Just grab him. Get it over with.* I lifted one arm and right before I touched him, I pulled back. Maybe you only had to hold on to the person in front of you in movies. Like a romantic thing. And this was a friend date. It wasn't like I'd go flying off the back of it. I could just lean forward a little without actually touching him.

He laughed and turned his head. "You have to hold on to me."

Well, since he was offering...I wrapped my arms around him right away. I could feel his abs through his shirt. *This really is the best day ever.*

He started the engine and the motorcycle roared to life. "Hold on tight!" he said as he pulled out of the driveway. As soon as the front wheel hit the pavement he really hit the gas.

I screamed and gripped him tighter.

He responded by accelerating even more.

If I hadn't been holding on to him, I would have flown off the back of the motorcycle and onto the car behind us. The way they showed it in movies was exactly right. I needed to hold on for dear life. And the fact that his ab muscles seemed to tense beneath my fingertips was a very nice added bonus.

I pressed the side of my head against his back and watched as the houses flew by. I felt alive when I was with him. It was the same feeling I had when I was in the water with him the other night. That I wanted to cling to him and never let go. I had wasted so much time believing that life had taken a crap on me and feeling sorry for myself about it. But maybe I was exactly where I was supposed to be. Right here on the back of a motorcycle about to be tied up with a bad boy. As friends.

The ride ended far too soon. He pulled smoothly into a parking spot and pulled off his helmet. I was still holding on to him.

"So how was your first time?" he asked and looked over his shoulder at me. He put his hand on top of mine.

"So much fun. Why does anyone ever drive a car?"

"Probably so that they can go shopping and have a place to put stuff." He got off the motorcycle. "Did I mention that I'm just going to abandon you here after we're done?"

I laughed. "That would be very ungentlemanly of you."

He unstrapped my helmet for me, taking his time. He'd practically held my hand a few seconds ago. And now he was staring at me in that way again. It felt too intimate. Or maybe perfectly intimate. Which was why it had to stop.

I cleared my throat. "Stranding your friend at the outlets would also so be a very rude thing to do. Especially a new friend." I pulled the helmet off and handed it to him. As he put it down, I quickly ran my fingers through my hair to make sure it didn't look crazy. "And it would also be an awful way to repay me for helping you."

"We'll see how the day goes I guess."

"Don't you dare leave me here," I said and lightly nudged his arm.

"I would never leave you." He rubbed the back of his neck and looked over at one of the signs.

I would never leave you. The words repeated in my head like they were lyrics in a super lazy and repetitive chorus. Why was he making it so hard to just be his friend? *I would never leave you.* My heart couldn't even handle the sweetness after the months it spent turning sour and bitter. I knew he just meant it in a today way. Like he wasn't going to abandon me in the middle of a parking lot just because he needed space for his purchases. But it still felt nice to hear.

Especially after how Aiden treated me. And my dad too. *I would never leave you.* My throat suddenly felt like it was constricting, like I was holding back tears. *Do not cry on this friend date, Mila. Do not make this weird.*

"So, where to?" he asked.

"Um..." *Thank you for another perfect distraction.* I swallowed down the lump in my throat and willed it to stay away. I hadn't really thought today through. I had never gone clothes shopping with a guy before. The only store I knew on the sign that had men's clothing was Express. "This way," I said.

We walked together into the store and into the men's section. "What size pants do you wear?" I asked.

"Medium."

"No, I mean like the number size."

He shrugged his shoulders.

I laughed. "This is going to be a long afternoon."

We walked around and grabbed some work-appropriate things. I stood outside the dressing room and waited for him. *He said he would never leave me. Why had he said that? Of course he would leave me. All we had was this one summer together.* I was beginning to think that every relationship was limited. Nothing was forever. Relationships were as fleeting as the summer sun.

When he came out, I couldn't help but laugh. The dress pants were too short, but the collared shirt fit really well.

"You're pretty terrible at this," he said with a smile.

"Actually, you look very trendy. Besides, you have other pants back there that are longer. I was trying to figure out your size. Come here."

He walked over to me. I rolled up the sleeves on his dress shirt so that his muscular forearms showed. He had looked good before, but now? He was going to go off to his fancy new job and get a new girlfriend in a snap. The thought turned my stomach.

"This shirt looks really good on you," I said. "Don't I get any credit for that?"

"It's uncomfortable."

"What do you mean it's uncomfortable?" I had just touched it and the fabric felt fine to me. "It's just a normal shirt." I reached behind his neck and looked at the collar. "It's 100% cotton."

"I'd rather wear a t-shirt."

I laughed. "You're acting like I'm forcing you to buy clothes like this. I'm just here to help."

He smiled at me.

"Go try again."

He pretended to sulk back into the dressing room. He was so cute. When he came back out the next time, he had completely abandoned the idea of a shirt. He just had on the same pants and a tie.

I laughed. "What are you doing?"

"What, is this not work appropriate?" He turned around in a circle. "I think I look pretty great."

"I didn't say you didn't look good. But it's not suitable office attire." His muscles were distracting. And he actually looked amazing. Business casual should be replaced with the outfit he was rocking.

"This is ridiculous. I don't know what I'm doing," he said. "Just come in here with me."

"It's the men's changing room," I said in a hushed voice.

He looked both ways. "Yeah, well, no one's looking." He grabbed my hand and pulled me into the dressing room. He closed the door to his stall and locked it.

"We're going to get in so much trouble." My heart was beating so fast that it was all I could hear. But I wasn't really worried about the store's security. I was more nervous about being in a confined space with him. Where he'd be stripping. I closed my eyes for a second. *Stripping? Really?* I was making this weird and it didn't have to be. I opened my eyes again. *Nope.* I was going to get in trouble. But not with the store's security. I was in so much trouble with him.

"It's not like we're going to bang in here," he said. "You're just helping me pick out some clothes. The worst that could happen is they'll ask us to leave. You need to learn to live a little."

I crossed my arms. "I rode a motorcycle today and I'm in a men's changing room. I think I'm doing fine."

"Yeah, but you only did those things because of me."

"So?"

He shrugged. "I think you need me. That's all. Now close your eyes again so I can change."

I sat down on the bench in the changing room and closed my eyes. I heard his pants unzip. And then the awkward sound of me swallowing wrong. A strange squeaky noise that I barely recognized came from me. *Jesus, Mila, it's not the first time you've heard a man unzip his pants before. You've seen a penis. Why did my mind automatically go to his dick?* But now that I was thinking about it, it was so very hard to stop. It was so tempting to take a peek, but some- how I mastered the art of restraint and kept my eyes closed.

"Okay," he said.

I opened my eyes. He was just wearing his boxer briefs. One of his legs was up on the bench I was sitting on. He was posing in the most ridiculous way, with his hands behind his head.

"Oh my God." I picked up a shirt and tossed it at him. I couldn't help but notice the bulge in his boxers since I had been obsessing over it a few seconds ago.

He laughed and caught the shirt. "Now that you've seen me almost naked, you don't have to bother closing your eyes."

"I think that since I've seen you in just your underwear I deserve to know your name." I was glad I said that in- stead of what I really wanted to. Which was more on the lines of, "Now that I've seen you in just boxers you might as well just show me the package." At least I had a filter even though my mind was being attacked by butterflies.

"Yeah, probably." He looked uncomfortable now, when a moment ago when he was posed in his underwear he looked as confident as could be.

"So...are you going to tell me what it is?"

"Nah."

"Oh come on."

He looked at me as he pulled on his shirt. "Well, even if I knew your name, I'd still call you Jellyfish Girl, so I'm not sure what the point is."

"You really don't want to know what my name is?"

He buttoned up his shirt. This time he rolled up the sleeves himself. "If I'm being completely honest, I already know your name."

"What? How?"

"The girl from Sweet Cravings told me when I was trying to find you." He stopped getting dressed and looked down at me. He was wearing just the shirt. It didn't matter what he wore, he was sexy as hell.

"And?"

"And I'd rather call you Jellyfish Girl than Mila. It seems a little more personal. Don't get me wrong, Mila is a very nice name. It suits you almost as well as Jellyfish Girl."

"Okay." I could feel my cheeks turning pink. There was definitely something personal about a nickname. But that didn't take away from the fact that I wanted to know his real name too. "It's only fair that I know your name if you know mine."

"What's to know? I'm your lifeguard."

"I didn't mean it like that."

"Yeah...you did." He pulled on a pair of pants. They were the right length, but the waist was too big.

"Come on. You have to tell me."

"How do I look?" he asked, ignoring the question.

"They're too big."

He turned around and looked in the mirror. "Yeah, you're right." He started to unbutton them.

While he was distracted, I grabbed his shorts and pulled out his wallet. I opened it up.

"Wait." He turned around and tried to grab his wallet back. "Mila, come on." He grabbed my arm, but I turned around.

I quickly pulled out his driver's license and read the name. He gripped my other arm too so that his arms were around me, trying to prevent me from looking at the driver's license. But it was too late. I'd seen it. I was about to tell him, when I felt his pants fall, the fabric dropping between us. And then I felt him. The package that I wanted to take a peek at earlier was now pressed against my ass. I didn't need to see it to know it was big. I was torn between being aroused and being mortified. I was being hugged by a pants-less man I barely knew in a men's changing room. A man who had quite a silly name. I turned my head to see him and started laughing because I didn't know what else to do.

"Shit." He snatched his license out of my hand and let go of my arms.

"Your name is Jaime Jamison?" I tried to keep a straight face.

"My name is J. J." He grabbed his wallet back as he kicked off the pants.

"I'm sorry." I bit my lip. It was such a ridiculous name. It was hard not to laugh.

"Yeah, my parents are the worst." He put his wallet back in the pocket of his shorts. "They're pretty much the only ones that know my real name."

"Your secret is safe with me."

"Yeah, I'm not sure about that."

"It is. You can trust me."

He looked at me for a second. "I do trust you."

"And I like the name J. J." I smiled at him. "It suits you."

He rubbed the back of his neck. He looked embarrassed.

"You know, you could name your kid Jaime Jamison Junior."

"Yeah, but I'm not an asshole."

I laughed. "And I wasn't just laughing at your name. I was laughing because you were kind of holding me and your pants fell…"

He picked up a new pair of pants and pulled them on. He looked in the mirror as he tucked in his shirt. They fit perfectly. They were snug but not too tight. His ass looked amazing.

"So?" he asked and turned toward me as he tightened his tie.

"You look great. Very grown up. All you need is a belt."

He lifted the tie and pretended to choke himself.

"Oh, come on. You look really handsome."

He dropped the tie. "I do, huh?"

"You do."

"You know what? This shirt is actually a lot more comfortable than the other one. I think I'll just buy this outfit in a few different colors."

"Guys are so much easier to shop with than girls."

He laughed. "Okay, now get out of here while I change, you pervert. You're going to get us in trouble."

I laughed and exited his stall. I looked both ways before running out of the men's changing room. Maybe he was right about me. Maybe I was a pervert. It was pretty easy for him to convince me to go in the changing room in the first place. And then I'd basically just thought of his dick the whole time. It was like my body had a mind of its own. It was screaming at me to forget about being single. To forget about the promises I'd made to myself this summer. And the scary part was that I wanted to listen. Because J.J. was incredibly sweet and charming and so freaking gorgeous. Jaime Jamison was a pretty silly name, but J.J.? J.J. was exactly the kind of name I pictured him having.

I made my way over to the women's section as I waited for him. A blue dress caught my eye on one of the racks. It was the same blue as his eyes. I picked it up. The fabric was so light and soft. There was a peephole in the front that probably showed off way too much cleavage. It crisscrossed at the neckline and the fabric crossed again in the back, leaving most of the back exposed. It was really sexy. I flipped over the sales tag. *And way out of my price range.* I went to put it down.

"Try it on."

I looked up at J.J. "Oh, no. I was just looking."

"Seriously, try it on. It would look great on you."

I laughed and hung it back up. "I'd have nothing to wear it to."

He looked at the dress. "If you say so. Are you ready to go? I'm starving."

***

I took a bite of my hamburger. "This is amazing," I said.

"I told you. I can't believe you've never been to Red Robin before."

"They didn't have any near SMU." Thinking about SMU almost made me lose my appetite. But the burger was so good that it was impossible to put down.

"Right." He looked down at his plate for a second. "Have you ever thought of transferring back east?"

That's what was going on. He thought there was a chance I was coming back since I told him how much I hated it. *Is there a chance?* "I don't know. It's probably easier if I just finished at the same school. Transferring credits is a nightmare. Isn't it?" I had heard that it was, but I wasn't actually sure.

"I wouldn't know." He took another bite of his burger. "But how bad could it be?"

I shrugged. He wanted me to stay. I smiled to myself. If I was being honest, I wanted to stay too. It wasn't just as easy as changing schools and transferring credits, though. I had a scholarship at SMU that would go to waste. And I wasn't sure what the deadlines were to apply for other schools. But I could look into it. The thought of going back to Cali was certainly less appealing than staying here with J.J. Not that it would be here. I doubted his job was anywhere near the beach. "Where is the job you took located?"

He finished chewing his last bite. It felt like it took forever for him to answer. "It's in New York City."

"Oh. New York." I didn't have to say NYC wasn't my favorite, it was probably pretty clear from my voice. New York City was not on my list of places I ever wanted to live. I'd been there once in the summer and it was hot and sticky. And once in the winter and it had been snowy and smelly. In the city's defense, I think their trashmen had been on a strike or something. But it still left a bad taste in my mouth. Literally. I thought about my mom's house nearby. She was about three hours from NYC. This had to be at least half an hour more than that. "That's pretty far from here."

"Yeah." He sighed in this adorable disgruntled way. "It'll definitely take some getting used to. Especially after being here for the summer." He pulled out his wallet.

I grabbed my purse to get my share of the bill.

He put down some money on the table. "I got it, Jelly-fish Girl."

"But..."

"I have a really good job lined up for the fall. I got this."

"Have you ever thought of not doing it? The job, I mean." I locked my eyes with his. He'd asked me if I'd ever consider moving back here. And even though I didn't specifically word it that way, I was trying to see if he'd ever consider changing his plans. If he'd ever think about moving to Cali. It was ridiculous, I knew that. If I came back to this area, I'd be moving home. If he came to California, he'd be moving there for me. And we barely knew each other.

"I think about it all the time. I know I'll end up doing it though."

"Why?"

"I need to eventually grow up."

The thought of growing up wasn't at all appealing to me. "Maybe. But why work in an overpopulated city when

I'm sure you could get a decent job doing the same thing right here?"

He smiled at me. The sound of thunder made me turn away from his intoxicating stare. A light rain pattered against the window.

"Crap, we have to go." He grabbed his bag of clothes and I grabbed my purse as we slid out of the booth. He took my hand in his and we sprinted through the parking lot, trying to ignore the drizzle. There was a small bag on the back of his motorcycle. He shoved his clothes into it and slammed it shut. He quickly strapped my helmet on and we both climbed onto the motorcycle.

I wrapped my arms tightly around his abs again. His shirt was damp and it made it even easier to feel his six pack. He sped away from the outlets and onto the road. Even though it was only drizzling, the raindrops hurt a little as they hit my bare skin. I held on to him even tighter. I didn't want to ever have to let go. My thoughts were swirling with credit transfers and NYC. It was possible. I wanted it to be possible. Because as I held on to him speeding through the streets, I knew it wasn't possible to just be his friend anymore. That wasn't what I wanted at all.

I held on to him a little tighter, not wanting my day with him to end. But we were back at my place way too soon. He pulled into my driveway, cutting the engine. It was raining a little harder now and we were both completely drenched. He unclipped my helmet and grabbed my hand. We ran up the steps to my apartment door.

"Thank you!" I almost had to yell over the raindrops. I held my breath as he stared at me. Steam was coming off the driveway below. It made it look like we were standing in clouds. "This was the most fun I've had in a really long time."

We both just stood there, staring at each other. It was like he was waiting for me to do something.

But I didn't know what to say. I could tell him that I didn't know how to just be his friend. That I wished our paths in the fall aligned better. The rain started to fall faster. And all the words stayed lodged in my throat. All that escaped was, "J.J.," when he took a step closer.

He grabbed both sides of my face and kissed me hard.

Holy shit.

He moved into me, pressing my back against the door. His hands slid to my waist.

I grabbed the back of his neck and deepened the kiss. It was everything I wanted and more. I moved my hands to the scruff on his cheeks. The tiny prickles of his facial hair on my palms made my skin tingle.

I felt his thumb dip beneath my tank top and trace the waistline of my jeans. His touch made my whole body feel alive. His other hand slid to my ass.

"Fuck." He pulled away from me and ran his hand through his hair.

I didn't want his hands to leave me. I didn't want him to stop kissing me. "J.J."

"I...I'm sorry, Mila." He turned and ran down the stairs.

"J.J.!"

He hopped on his motorcycle and sped off into the rain, leaving me a wet mess on the porch.

CHAPTER 9
Sunday

I traced my lips with the tips of my fingers as I stared at a list of universities in the northeast. It would be crazy to transfer schools for someone I just met. I knew that. But there were a lot of other reasons to transfer too. I was miserable at SMU. I was miserable in California in general. Even if I'd never met J.J., I would have at least looked at this possibility.

I stopped touching my lips. That wasn't true. I'd waited until the day after J.J. kissed me to look up new universities. Which meant I was doing it for him. I bit the inside of my lip as I looked at tuition prices for some of the colleges I recognized in New York. It didn't hurt to do a little research. And regardless of J.J., I was committing myself to a year of depression if I went back to Cali.

My eyes almost bugged out of my head when I started reading the tuition prices. One of them was almost $60,000 a year. Were they fucking kidding me? Not to mention the cost of living in NYC would be astronomical.

I sighed and leaned back on my pillow. It was stupid to look. I had a great scholarship to SMU. Aiden would be gone in the fall, so it wasn't like I was going to run into him. And all his friends had just graduated too. I'd be able to start over. I'd meet new people and make new friends. I thought of J.J. and Kristen. They were both more fun than anyone I'd met at SMU. *Ugh*.

I glared at the ridiculous tuition costs. Even with a decent scholarship, which was unlikely since I would be applying so late, any school in New York would be more expensive than SMU even before you factored in the cost of living. Which meant I couldn't do it. I wasn't going to call my dad and ask him for more money. And I wasn't exactly making lifechanging money at Sweet Cravings three days a week. I glanced over at Kristen who was still sleeping soundly.

Just because a school in New York wasn't an option, it didn't mean I still couldn't transfer. After all, J.J. was absolutely not a factor in this decision. Definitely not. Kristen went to a college nearby. I typed the University of New Castle into google. A state school even without a scholarship might be cheaper than SMU was. Which meant I wouldn't have to bother my dad and I wouldn't have to be in hell for one more year. And I wouldn't have to say goodbye to Kristen at the end of the summer.

I clicked on the University of New Castle's undergraduate admissions page. My eyes scanned the information about transfers. Right above the application button there was a note that space was limited for fall admissions based on major. I still didn't even know what I wanted my degree to be in. I'd bounced around so much at SMU that I was close to having enough credits for three different majors. I clicked on the link anyway just to see if they listed the majors where there was still room. No luck. And the page said that the normal deadline for fall applications was May 1st. So whatever spaces they had left were probably very limited. If I was going to do it, I needed to do it soon.

I glanced over at my phone. If I'd had J.J.'s number, I would have called him to talk about it. Yesterday at dinner he acted like he wanted me to transfer. He kissed me. It was possible that we were exactly on the same page. But...I didn't have his number.

My fingers went back to my lips. No one had ever kissed me the way he had. It didn't matter that he apologized and ran off. He did that because of what I'd told him about focusing on myself this summer. The next time I saw him, I was going to tell him I'd changed my mind. This summer didn't have to be all about me. It could be about us. And a few states between us in the fall was a lot better than a whole country between us. If he was willing to try long distance, we could make it work. We had all summer to figure out logistics.

I stared back at my screen. It was only $75 to apply. I'd eat ramen noodles for a few days and I'd never miss the money. I clicked on the big blue button labeled AP-PLY NOW.

***

My application was completed, minus the essay portion. The question I had to answer was, "Why do you want to transfer to the University of New Castle?" And it needed to be 500 words or less. I had somehow written a 3,000 word essay about Aiden cheating on me, how I was a total loser, how the beach didn't smell the same on the west coast, and how I was kinda sorta falling for a lifeguard.

None of it was acceptable for an admissions essay. It was more of a rant. I backspaced for what felt like the millionth time. *Why do I want to transfer to the University of New Castle?* I let the question roll around in my head. Delaware was home to me. And for the first time in a long time, I didn't feel alone. That was the honest truth. I deleted everything I had written and started typing again.

***

"I have to kill him, don't I?" Kristen asked.

I wiped the tears from beneath my eyes. I hadn't realized that Kristen had woken up. "What? No."

"But he made you cry." She sat down on the edge of my bed. "What the heck happened on your date that made you wake up like this?" She waved her hand not just at my face but in front of my whole body.

I glanced down at my pajamas. There was absolutely nothing wrong with them. She was starting to think she was a fashionista after watching so much Project Runway.

"I'm not crying because of yesterday." I wiped away my remaining tears. I had pretended to be asleep when she came home last night. For just a few hours, I wanted to keep what happened between J.J. and I to myself. But if she had seen me when I got home, she'd know my tears weren't over him. And she certainly wouldn't be threatening to kill him. "I actually had a really great time."

"So what is this?" She did the thing with her hands again.

"I'm going to pretend you're just asking why I'm crying, and not insinuating that I'm a hot mess." I turned my laptop toward her. "Can you read this and tell me if it's okay?"

Her eyes started scanning my essay. "You're applying to the University of New Castle?" She looked up way before she could have possibly finished the essay. "You're applying to the University of New Castle!" She leaned forward and threw her arms around me. "Mila, we're going to have so much fun there together."

I laughed and hugged her back. "I don't even know if I'll get in. Applications are past due, but they have a few spots open on a case by case basis." I released her from my hug. "So I need this essay to be perfect."

"Right." Kristen looked back down at my computer screen. A few minutes later she lifted her head. "Is this really how you felt? I mean…I know you said it, but…now I *feel* it. I'm so sorry, Mila."

"It felt like I couldn't breathe. I'd never felt so alone in my entire life." I shook my head. I didn't want Kristen's pity. "But life is pretty good right now. After all, I have a new best friend." I kicked her shin with my foot.

A smile spread over Kristen's face. "Best friend, huh?"

I had called her my bestie in my head a few times but never out loud.

"I like the sound of that," she said before I had a chance to overthink it. "And you'll definitely get in with that essay. Goodbyes suck, and I was already dreading ours. Now I won't have to. What major are you declaring?"

"I chose marketing just because I was close to finishing that degree at SMU already. And also undeclared as my second choice. I'm hoping that if they don't have any room left in marketing they might still take me. Honestly I still have no idea what I want to do after I graduate, so maybe I haven't tried the right courses yet."

Kristen clapped. "You're definitely going to get in. Do you think you'll live in the dorms? Or an apartment?"

"I think I'll hold off on planning all that until I hear back." I turned my screen back to me. "Any changes you'd make?"

"Zero. It's perfection in written form. Hit submit!"

I held my breath as I pushed the button. That was that. I quickly filled out the billing information for the application fee and shut down my computer.

"So…" Kristen said.

I looked up at her. "So?"

"Your date must have been good if you're moving all the way back to little old Delaware to be closer to him."

"His new job is in New York, not Delaware. Me wanting to transfer has nothing to do with J.J." *Well, maybe a little. Or a lot.*

"Oh you learned his name! What else did you learn about him?"

That he rides a motorcycle and his kisses make my knees feel weak. "Well, the whole he's moving to NYC at the end of summer thing, which is a bummer."

Kristen shrugged. "That's not very far away from the University of New Castle. What else did you learn?"

"That he looks amazing even when he's wearing a shirt." *And not wearing pants.* "He loves a good burger. He rides a motorcycle…"

"God, of course he does. Did he wear a leather jacket? Did he make you wear a leather jacket?"

I laughed. "No, and no."

"All he's missing is the jacket and tattoos. Everywhere."

Tattoos and a leather jacket would definitely scream bad boy a little louder. But I liked that J.J. was a good bad boy. I smiled to myself.

"Anything else?" Kristen asked. "Anything in particular to get you to look into transferring schools in the fall? Because I could have sworn we talked about that a few weeks ago and our conversation certainly didn't spur you into action."

"Well, he maybe mentioned transferring credits and the possibility of moving back to the east coast."

Kristen squealed. "He didn't even hint at it? He just flat out asked?"

I couldn't conceal my smile any longer. "Yeah. And we also kissed." I decided that leaving off the fact that he apologized afterward and drove off on his motorcycle was for the best. He was definitely just worried about how I'd react to the kiss. He was worried that he crossed the line. And I couldn't wait to see him again so I could tell him there was no line anyway.

Kristen picked up one of the pillows off my bed and threw it at me. "And who said it was a date date? Not just a friend date?"

"You," I said as I hugged the pillow to my chest. "I just...I never expected him to actually like me as more than a friend. I mean, I've opened up to him about Aiden. He knows I was a loner out in Cali. And he doesn't do long distance relationships." That was the only troubling thing about our kiss. I hoped it was the fact that I told him

IVY SMOAK

I wanted to be single this summer that made him stop kissing me, and not the fact that he was worried about me being unfaithful to him if we were ever apart. I wasn't the kind of girl that cheated. Apparently I was just the kind of girl that got cheated on. *Ugh.* I hugged the pillow a little tighter.

"Well, it looks like he's singing a new tune about long distance relationships. So when is your next date?"

"Um...I don't know. I figured we'd just see each other on Tuesday when I usually go to the beach."

"Oh. Huh."

"What, is that bad?" I couldn't exactly extract plans from him when he was running away from me.

"No, it's..." her voice trailed off. "Didn't you say he has the weekends off too? I figured you'd have plans again today. But he's probably just doing that whole guy thing." She rolled her eyes. "I hate when guys act like there's a two-day rule. When two people like each other that only have one summer...they should be hanging out at every opportunity."

She was right. June would be over before I even knew it. We only had two months in the same state.

"Screw the two-day rule. Text him something sexy and go out to dinner. I can manage on my own for a couple of nights in a row."

"I don't have his number."

"Oh. Huh."

"Would you stop saying that?" I laughed and threw the pillow back at her. "I only just learned his name, and I had to force it out of him." Actually I had to steal his wallet and get him practically naked, but Kristen didn't need to know the specifics. "I'll definitely get his number on Tuesday."

"Well, in the meantime..." she turned my laptop back toward her. "We should stalk him on Facebook."

"How about *you* stalk him and *I* make pancakes?"

"Even better." She started typing as I climbed out of bed.

When I was little, my dad used to make pancakes every Sunday morning. It was one of the only good memories I had of him. I pulled out the flour. I wondered if he was making pancakes for his new family now. The thought made my stomach twist into knots. I needed to call him if I was transferring schools. Before he got a chance to send a check to the wrong place.

I cracked an egg in the mixing bowl. My dad probably wouldn't even ask why I was transferring. He'd just try to get off the phone as quickly as possible. I started to beat the batter a little harder than I should have been. I hoped to God that J.J. was nothing like my father. Or Aiden. Or anyone who found joy in making my heart hurt.

CHAPTER 10
Tuesday

My lifeguard was looking at the ocean and I was staring at him. It was almost time for his shift to end. I needed to talk to him. If I had his number, I absolutely would have called him before today. The more time that passed, the more I was worried about why he had kissed me and run off. I had hoped he'd show up for ice cream on Monday, but he didn't even walk by the shop. And now he was ignoring me. Or maybe he was just focusing on doing his job. I was probably just reading into everything too much. After all, there was a two-day rule for a reason.

If Kristen hadn't been able to find him on Facebook, I probably would have felt calmer. But she had found him. And his page was just like he was in person...surrounded by tons of random girls. It seemed like every picture of him had another beautiful girl with her arms wrapped around him. It made me wonder who he was spending time with on Sunday. And Monday. And this morning.

He stood up and blew his whistle, signaling for everyone to come in from the water. Instead of walking over to me, he pushed his lookout post to dryer sand.

So that was it? It felt like he had sucker punched me in the gut. Was he really just going to ignore me now? I looked out at the water. I had told him about how much it had hurt me that Aiden had done that to me. One kiss was different than two and a half years. But it stung. It was like he was ghosting me because he knew how much it would bother me. I wrapped my arms around my legs and put my chin on my knee. *Why does it hurt this much?*

"I've been thinking."

I looked up and saw my lifeguard standing next to my towel. *Oh, thank God.* I was just overthinking everything. He wasn't ignoring me at all. He was just working. I smiled up at him. "I was beginning to think that you were never going to speak to me again."

He didn't laugh. He didn't even give me one of his signature smiles. "Can I sit down?" he asked.

I nodded. He sat down on my towel beside me. The relief I felt a moment ago was gone. J.J. seemed...off. The distance between us on the towel was even more than between friends. The pain in my stomach came back in a rush.

"I'm sorry about the other night."

"I'm not." I wanted to reach out and grab his hand. Instead I balled mine into a fist.

He sighed. "We can't do this."

"This?" I swallowed hard.

"Us."

I had thought about nothing but us for the last two days. And I had come to the complete opposite conclusion. "I think that you're exactly what I need right now." He made me feel alive again. I didn't want to give him up. We were both here for two more months. Why was he doing this?

"I'm not what you need. You told me you wanted this summer to find yourself. So that's what you need to do."

He scratched the back of his neck. "I think we should probably just be friends, Mila."

He didn't call me Jellyfish Girl. His flirtations were gone. It felt like he had slapped me.

"Okay." I kept my arms wrapped around my legs. It felt like I was sinking into the sand.

"Things are just too complicated right now. Maybe after you're done school..." his voice trailed off. He pushed his heels into the sand.

"J.J.! Come on!" shouted a girl across the beach.

I turned my head and looked at her. It wasn't his friend Abby. It was some other girl with bigger breasts. It felt like Aiden was breaking up with me all over again.

"Right. Of course," I said. "You don't have to say anything else. I totally get it. I'll see you later then." I tried to make my voice cheery. It sounded weird. And definitely fake. Probably because I wanted to punch him, not be his stupid friend.

"Mila." He put his hand on my knee.

Don't touch me. I glared at him.

"I'm sorry. I shouldn't have kissed you. I just..."

"It's fine. Really. I completely understand." I didn't. We had so much fun on Saturday. Why was he doing this? "It wasn't even a good kiss." It was kind of true. Because in reality it was a great kiss. Describing it as good didn't do it justice.

His hand fell from my knee. "Did you want to come to dinner with us?"

I looked over at the girl with big breasts and the rest of his friends. "I'm actually in the middle of a really good chapter." I picked up my book off the towel. It was the romance I had started and stopped. We didn't have a chance to go to a bookstore the other day because of the rain. And I had no desire to pick this book up where I left off. Especially now. "But I'll catch you later, okay?" I opened up the book to a random spot and started reading. My eyes stung from my imminent tears. I tried to blink them away.

He sat there for a minute in silence. I wasn't sure if he wanted me to say something else. I kept my eyes locked on my book. *Please go away.* I wiped under my eyes as discreetly as possible. Was he trying to torture me? Humiliate me? Make me feel like shit? He'd accomplished all three in record time. He deserved an asshole medal.

"Okay," he finally said. He stood up. I heard him walk away but I didn't look up. I waited for as long as I could before dropping my book and putting my forehead down on my knees. I cried for a long time. Rejection had never felt worse. I was prepared to tell him that I didn't care if our relationship was short. I just wanted to see where the summer took us. I had let myself get excited about the idea of starting something new. Being home wasn't supposed to hurt like this. I was just starting to feel whole again.

***

I plopped the box of wine onto the kitchen counter. I had stood in the aisle at the liquor store for half an hour trying to figure out how many bottles it would take to get really freaking drunk. I'd decided it was more bottles than I could afford. Hence the box. I opened it up and filled my glass all the way to the top. And it didn't take me long at all to get all the way to the bottom of the glass. I topped it off again.

I needed pizza. And not Grottos pizza, because that would remind me of J.J. and I didn't want to be reminded of J.J. I started pulling ingredients out of the pantry. Also, I couldn't really leave my apartment because I was two huge glasses in and there was no going back.

"Woah," Kristen said from behind me. "Do you want to talk about whatever happened today?"

I slammed my fist back into the dough instead of kneading it the way I was supposed to. "There's nothing to talk about."

"Then why are you assaulting the dough?"

I laughed. And then I couldn't stop laughing. "Assaulting the dough? You can't assault an inanimate object." *Weirdo.*

"I don't know if that's true…"

I picked up another wine glass, not caring that my hands were covered in flour, and filled it up all the way to the tippy top like mine.

Kristen accepted it without complaint. But she did grab the dish towel and wipe off my flour fingerprints. "So back to my earlier question…do you want to talk about it?"

"There's nothing to talk about." If she could repeat herself, so could I. At least…I thought I was repeating myself. What had we been talking about again? I took another huge sip of wine as I started rummaging through the drawers in the kitchen. "Do we really not have a rolling pin? What kind of rental doesn't have a rolling pin?"

have imagined his voice, but he was definitely there. It was so good to see him. *I mean bad.* It was bad to see him.

"I'm not crying." I was happy my voice sounded sassy instead of sad. Apparently my new diet gave me quite the attitude. At least on the outside, because on the inside I was dying.

"I meant at the beach yesterday."

Oh. My sudden weird confidence was pulverized. "You saw that?" I had tried so hard to hide it.

"Yeah. And I'm sorry that I did that to you."

"I wasn't crying because of you, J.J. It had nothing to do with our conversation. I had just gotten some bad news earlier is all." I looked away from him.

He didn't say anything. But his silence made it seem like he didn't believe me. What did it matter if he knew I was crying over him. He already thought I was a mess. He didn't want to date me. He didn't want to be my friend. Why was I always so worried about what people thought of me?

"It's okay," I said quietly. "Don't worry about it. Really." It wasn't like he was the first person to give me the boot.

"It's not okay. I acted like a complete dick."

What an appropriate word choice.

"I approached that whole conversation wrong. What I should have said is that I like you. I've missed you the past few days. When I wake up, you're the person I want to hang out with. If I'm being honest, I used to look forward to seeing you on the beach on Tuesdays and Thursdays even before we met. I don't care if that makes me a stalker." He flashed me a smile.

I laughed. I couldn't help it. "I looked forward to see-ing you too."

"But you're going back to California at the end of the summer. You're only going to be here for two more months."

There was no point in telling him about my applica-tion to the University of New Castle. It didn't matter either way. "I know."

"And I know you aren't looking to date anyone. I'm not in any place to date someone either. I get that it's complicated. It's messy." He sighed. "I don't want to hurt you. That's why I said we should just be friends."

"I know." I didn't actually know that. And it was really nice to hear it. I exhaled, not even realizing I had been holding my breath while he spoke. He still liked me. I stared at him. Did I still like him? My eyes traveled to his lips. *Affirmative.* But I really wished I didn't. Especially since he was only offering me friendship.

He tapped the counter. "Are you hungry?"

It would be easy to turn him down. I could tell him I was working a double shift. But I didn't want to push him away. I just wanted him to want me, even though it was pathetic. And he was standing here telling me he was sorry. That he still wanted me in his life. Us being friends didn't exactly break my new diet. I looked at the clock behind me. I still had a few minutes left of my shift, but my re-placement was already here. "Is it okay if I get going early?" I asked her.

"Absolutely." She looked at my lifeguard and then winked at me.

I laughed and pulled off my apron. Before I walked out of the shop, I turned to J.J. "Would you rather go get dinner or just have ice cream?"

"Bring me my ice cream, woman!" He slapped his palm on the counter.

I laughed, grabbed two bowls, and put a few scoops of Pink Dream ice cream in each one.

"I'm glad we made up," he said and stole one of the bowls out of my hand as soon as I came out of Sweet Cravings. "I missed this ice cream."

"I thought you missed hanging out with me." *Stop being desperate.*

"Eh...not as much as the ice cream." He smiled at me and took another bite. We started walking down the boardwalk.

When I was younger, I had always wished I was one of those girls walking down the boardwalk with a boyfriend. I glanced at my lifeguard. I completely understood everything he had said. But it didn't change how I felt. I wasn't sure if I could just be friends with him. Whenever I saw him, I got butterflies in my stomach. And his smile made my knees feel like jelly. And I started to sweat more than usual.

My head was completely logical. Friends only. My mind was one hundred percent into that idea. But my body? It was trying to betray me. I inched closer to him while we were walking and silently cursed myself. My body could be really stupid sometimes.

At the end of the boardwalk we turned down a side street and walked past some more shops. Normally I'd find silence unnerving, but it wasn't awkward with him. Somehow I was comfortable yet nervous at the same time. I tried to squash those nerves. There was no reason to be nervous around a friend. And J.J. and I were doomed to be only that.

"So I was thinking we should have a rematch," he said and stopped on the sidewalk.

"A rematch? You mean in ping pong?"

"Yeah."

"Do you really think that's a good idea? I completely smoked you."

He laughed. "You're so cocky."

I shrugged my shoulders. "Well, if you really want to get beat again, I'm game. We passed the Grottos already. Is there one closer or should we head back?"

My lifeguard scratched the back of his neck. "I actually have a table in my apartment if you want to just play there. It's probably closer."

He's inviting me back to his place? Even though we had just had a conversation about being friends, it felt like he was giving me mixed signals. Was he as conflicted as me? Or was he trying to torture me? I bit the inside of my lip. Going to his place didn't mean like a hookup or anything. Friends hung out alone all the time. And I did want to see his place...

"Or we can head back to the Grottos if you'd rather."

"No. I'd like to see your apartment." I smiled at him. He had pointed it out before. It was just farther down the street we had already turned on. I thought we were just randomly walking, but maybe he was trying to get me to come see his place the whole time. The thought made me smile. And then frown. But then I smiled again because it was a lot easier to silence my brain than my body.

"Great. It's actually just a couple more blocks." We started walking again.

"So...I have a question for you," I said.

"Shoot."

"If you have a ping pong table in your apartment, why are you so incredibly bad at it?"

J.J. laughed. "I'm not *that* bad. You just took me by surprise, that's all."

"Mhm. Sure."

"Geez, you really are cocky, Jellyfish Girl."

He called me Jellyfish Girl again. Maybe we were right back where we were before the kiss. Before he royally screwed up and I gave up men. Before it felt like he stabbed my heart with a knife.

Whatever it was that we had now, I liked it. He and I were natural together. There was no awkwardness. It seemed like maybe we could actually be friends, as long as I could keep my hands to myself. If it meant keeping him in my life, I had to try.

When we got to his apartment building, he opened the door for me. I couldn't help but think how much of a gentleman he was. Aiden had never opened doors for me. I silently cursed myself for even thinking about Aiden. There was no comparison between him and J.J. They were on totally different levels. J.J. had apologized to me the day after he stomped on my heart. Aiden on the other hand...I was still waiting. And I wasn't holding my breath.

"So, are your roommates home?" I asked as we stepped on the elevator.

"I'm not sure. Why, are you scared to be alone with me?" He smiled.

He was being flirtatious again. The butterflies started flapping around in my stomach on command. *He's like this with all girls. It means nothing.* I just needed to get used to it. He wasn't coming on to me. I glanced at him out of the corner of my eye. *Or is he?*

"Not at all," I said. "Anyone who's that bad at ping pong isn't very scary."

"You're relentless. I really want to beat you now."

"Well, good luck." He'd need it. The elevator doors opened and we stepped out into a hallway.

"This way," he said and put his hand on the small of my back for a second.

My whole body felt alive even with a slight touch from him. *Calm down. We're buddies.*

He took his key out of his pocket and unlocked the door. It was dark inside. "I guess we're alone," he said and switched on the light.

My heart began to race. He invited me back to his apartment and we were all alone. He was definitely coming on to me. Maybe he realized whatever it was between us wasn't worth fighting. I couldn't be the only one who felt this amazing spark between us. I followed him into the main living area. There was a couch, a TV, a pool table, and a ping pong table. The ping pong table had several red cups on it, the remnants of a game of beer pong. The room was open to a small kitchen that was only big enough for one person to cook in. I wondered if his place came with a rolling pin. The only decorations in the living room were a few posters of scantily clad women. *Gross.*

I turned to him. "I like your decorations."

"Why thank you."

I rolled my eyes at him.

"I actually didn't pick those posters."

"Mhm."

He laughed. "I didn't."

I looked around the room again. There was a bath-room next to the kitchen and two closed doors on either side of the living room. "So, where's your bedroom?"

He leaned against the kitchen counter. "That's rather forward of you, Jellyfish Girl."

"What? Oh, no." I laughed awkwardly. "I didn't mean I wanted to hop into bed with you. Obviously. You know what? You don't even need to show me. I was just curious what it looked like because you mentioned these decora-tions weren't yours. So I was wondering what kind of decorations you chose. But I'm good. Curiosity killed the cat, you know. I'm too young to die." *What the hell am I saying?*

"Geez, I wish I hadn't left my whistle in the lifeguard shed. It could have doubled as a rape whistle. I feel like I'm going to need it tonight." He smiled at me.

"You won't need your whistle. I'm not rapey. I'm a sophisticated lady." *Yeah, right.* "Besides, I heard your friend-speech loud and clear. You're completely off limits." I put my hands up.

"If you say so."

If I say so? I don't want him to be off limits. I thought that's what he wanted. What the hell is going on here?

"My bedroom is over here." He pointed to the closed door on the left of the living room. And then he started walking toward it.

I guessed that was an invitation. I followed him into the small room. There were two beds. My lifeguard's eyes were on me as I leaned down and looked at some photos on his dresser.

"Is this you?" I asked. I picked up the picture frame. There were two young boys in it. They both had the same captivating blue eyes.

"Yeah, that's me and my brother."

I smiled at him. "You were really cute." I set the photo down and leaned against his bed as I looked around the room. There were more posters of half-naked women in the room but they weren't on his side. Clothes were strewn along the floor, but it was pretty clean. For some reason I had pictured four guys living together being a mess. But I guess I was wrong. I looked back at my lifeguard.

His eyebrows lowered slightly.

I gulped. *Why is he looking at me like that?* I could feel my face flushing. God, I wanted him. I wanted him to push me against his bed and kiss me again. I wanted his hands on me. I wanted to taste him again.

He pulled off his shirt as he looked at me.

Holy fuck. Is this really happening? Everything below my waistline clenched. His abs looked amazing. I wanted to run my hands down his six pack, tracking every contour of his muscles. I remembered how they felt when I was holding on to him on his motorcycle. But touching them now? I felt like I was going to combust.

He tossed his shirt on the floor. "I'm going to change out of my swimsuit real quick."

I continued to stare at him. He smiled at me. *Oh, shit. He's trying to dismiss me, not Thanksgiving turkey me.* I stepped backward and stumbled over something, falling to the floor.

My lifeguard started laughing. "Shit," he said. "Sorry, are you okay?" He laughed again.

"I'm fine." *Mortified, but fine.* "Sorry," I mumbled.

His knelt down next to me. "You are unbelievably cute."

Cute. I didn't want him to think I was cute. I wanted him to think I was sexy. He grabbed my hands and helped me stand up.

I stood there for a second. "Right. You need to change. So, I'll be out there." I pointed to the living room. "Do you have a rolling pin? My place didn't come with one, which I thought was strange. I'm just going to go look." I quickly walked out of his room.

I heard him laughing as he closed the door. *What is wrong with me?* I needed to calm down. We had just talked about how we were going to be friends. I was being crazy. But he had looked at me like he wanted me too. He liked that I had leaned against his bed. Maybe he was having the same dirty thoughts that I was. And if I was flirtatious enough, maybe he would forget about his decision to just be friends with me. I plopped down on the couch.

A minute later he came out of his room. He was wearing basketball shorts and a t-shirt. *Holy fucking hotness.* I crossed my legs, trying to ignore the fact that my body reacted to him in ways it never reacted to anyone before.

"Did you find a rolling pin?" he asked.

I had forgotten to look. But Kristen had said she doubted any beach rentals came with them. So I was going to trust her on that. "Nope. You don't have one either. So freaking weird. Right?"

He pressed his lips together instead of responding.

"All the locals must be anti-baking. Not that I was using it for that. I was trying to make a pizza. Usually I'm great at making pizza, but it's harder when you've consumed a large amount of wine."

He laughed. "Is that your way of asking for a drink? Do you want a beer?" He made his way over to the fridge. "We don't have any wine."

Could I have a drink and not be weird? Probably if I only had one. I was only bad on margarita night. Or when I had like three beers. Or when I drank half a box of wine. "Sure," I said and walked over to him.

He took two beers out of the fridge and popped off the caps before handing one to me. I took a long sip. Hopefully this would help me calm down a little. I was so turned on I was having trouble thinking straight.

"I liked your room," I said.

"For a second I thought I was going to need that rape whistle."

I laughed. "Oh, come on. Just because I'm attracted to you doesn't mean I have no self-control." *Shit did I just say that out loud?*

His lips pressed together.

"Where are the paddles?" I almost screamed. I looked away from him. *Shit, shit, shit.*

"Here," he said and handed me a paddle. He looked pleased with himself. "So what are the stakes this time?" He walked over to the table and tossed me the ball.

Was he trying to see if I was attracted to him? Was that what this was about? I had just admitted it to him, so whatever game he was playing should be over. My lifeguard was the most confusing boy I had ever met. I shook my head, trying to clear away my thoughts. "Hmm," I said as we hit the ball back and forth.

The door to his apartment opened and my ping pong partner from Grottos came in with his arm wrapped around the girl I had seen at the beach with the huge breasts. They were laughing loudly and almost stumbled into the room. They were clearly drunk.

"Stalker Girl!" my partner yelled and lifted up his hand.

"Hey, you." I said and high fived him. I had never learned his name.

"Oh my God, are we playing ping pong again? Game on!" he said and pointed at my lifeguard.

"Oh, I want to play!" the girl with huge tits said and jumped up and down.

I tried not to sigh. "Umm..." I looked up at my lifeguard. It felt like that night at Grottos all over again. Except this time I knew he just wanted to be friends. *Maybe.* I didn't know that for sure. Because he said that's what he wanted. But he never looked at me like just a friend.

He shrugged apologetically.

"Okay," my partner said and grabbed a paddle. "Me and Stalker Girl against you two."

I laughed. This was going to be interesting.

"Clint!" the girl yelled from across the table. "Let's play strip ping pong."

Hell no. I looked up at my lifeguard and his eyes locked with mine.

"I think that's a great idea," he said. A smile cut across his face.

Holy shit, he wants to see me naked.

CHAPTER 12
Wednesday

I was about to protest, but I stopped. No one had ever looked at me the way that my lifeguard was looking at me right now. He wanted to see me naked. And I definitely wanted to see him naked, even though I was trying really hard to not want that. Friends were supposed to hang out in clothes. But I never had a friend who looked like J.J. How much could it hurt to see him completely naked just once? Probably not much. Honestly, I was more concerned about the fact that he'd see me naked. Bathing suits were revealing but…not as revealing as no clothing.

I bit my lip and glanced at Clint. He and his girlfriend were probably too drunk to ever remember this. Besides, I was really good at ping pong. There was no way I'd actually have to get naked. J.J. would be the one stripping. So in my case…no harm no foul.

"What are the rules?" I asked. *I can't believe I'm even asking this.* Yesterday I had sworn off all men and now I was standing here with a ping pong paddle weighing the odds of how likely I was to see two dicks. So much for my diet.

"How about every time a team scores five points, each person on the opposite side has to lose one article of clothing?" My lifeguard smiled at me. "And once one person on a team gets fully naked, the other team wins."

I didn't know why he was smiling. He was about to lose horribly. Like the worst loss in the history of losses. I was about to put him to shame. I gripped my paddle a little tighter and picked up the ball. "Game on," I said. I tossed the ball toward them and we began to volley for the serve. Clint and I won easily. This was going to be fantastic.

I served first. It hit the table and sailed between the two of them. My second serve was just as good but my lifeguard effortlessly returned it and Clint missed. I looked up at my lifeguard and he shrugged.

"I told you not to be so cocky, Jellyfish Girl."

I laughed. It was one lucky shot. He was the cocky one. "But..."

"Oh, did I forget to tell you that I'm actually really good at ping pong?"

Seriously? Oh fudgesicles! I shook my head and tried to ignore him. He was just trying to get in my head. He sucked at ping pong, I knew it for a fact. I took a deep breath and served again. Clint flubbed the shot. "Clint, what the hell?"

He laughed. "I don't have any body issues. Besides, everyone here has already seen me naked."

"Well I haven't."

"Maybe it's your lucky day then."

Fuck. I picked the ball up off the ground. "Just because you like running around naked doesn't mean we have to lose. Don't you like winning?"

Clint shrugged. "After this game I'm getting naked either way." He winked at his girlfriend.

Good God. I was going to have to steal all the balls that came his way. He was completely off his rocker. And I couldn't send it over to J.J. anymore. The whole left side of the table was off limits now. I served it at Clint's girlfriend. She wasn't as bad as I was hoping. Clint lost us the next two points as well.

I picked up the ball and threw it at my lifeguard. They had gotten their first five points.

"Take it off!" he yelled and high fived Clint's girlfriend.

Clint pulled off his shirt. Of course he didn't have any body issues. He was a lifeguard. He was fit and tan and almost had as nice of a six pack as my lifeguard. *Stop staring at him, you're being so awkward.*

"Hey, Stalker Girl," Clint whispered to me. "We got this. They're both going to be incredibly distracted now. It's all part of the plan."

"Well, we could just beat them." *Ass hat.*

"But where's the fun in that?" He winked at me and turned back to the table.

I grabbed the hem of my shirt and slowly lifted it over my head. My lifeguard had seen me in a bikini. This wasn't any worse. And I always wore nice pushup bras to work because it usually got me better tips. Since Clint had zero desire to help me win this game, maybe taking his advice wasn't such a bad idea. J.J. was in dire need of a distraction. I tossed my shirt as seductively as possible to the side, leaned down, and picked up the ball off the floor.

J.J.'s eyes were locked on my breasts. And Clint's girlfriend was certainly staring at him. Maybe Clint was right. I took a deep breath. This was going to be more fun than I realized. Now that we had the upper hand, I'd be winning in no time. I was already prepping my victory lap...which included me putting my shirt on first. Maybe after I shoved it in J.J.'s face.

It was his turn to serve. He served it toward me. It was a good serve, but not too good that I couldn't return it. *Because I'm awesome like that!* We got the next four points so that we were tied five to five.

"Your turn," I said and folded my arms across my chest. *Take that.*

My lifeguard shrugged. He grabbed his shirt by the collar and pulled it off. I should have been desensitized to his sculpted torso from seeing him at the beach all the time, but I wasn't. I was practically salivating. And he aced his next serve.

"You okay there, Jellyfish Girl?" He flashed me his smile that made my knees weak.

"Yes, I'm fine." I wasn't. I was clearly way more distracted by him than he was by me. *Stupid perfect lifeguard body.* It was Clint's serve and he was clearly distracted by his girlfriend too. We lost the next four points in record time.

I tried to think of what underwear I was wearing. I was pretty sure it was a thong. Not just pretty sure, positive. I had to wear a thong with these shorts or else I'd have a visible underwear line. *Fuck my life.* Clint dropped his shorts. I looked down at the floor. I didn't want to see him in his boxers. *This isn't a big deal. We've all seen people naked of the opposite sex. This is normal. How is this normal again?* I unbuttoned my shorts while my brain started having a panic attack of its own.

Because I was wrong. This was mortifying. And humiliating. And awkward as all get out. Why couldn't I have worn a normal pair of underwear? *Stupid underwear lines.* Underwear lines deserved a slow and painful death. I slowly lowered my shorts to the floor. I couldn't make eye contact with my lifeguard. Or anyone for that matter.

Clint picked up the ball. "Your face is bright red, Stalker Girl," he whispered. "Chill, you have a great ass."

Holy fucking shit. My face probably turned five shades redder. My lifeguard cleared his throat. I finally looked up. He was smiling at me.

That smile did something to my heart, because it was beating so fast I felt faint. I couldn't lose any more clothes or I might have a heart attack. We needed to score the next five points to tie it up. I tried hard to focus on the ball. We won the last serve Clint made. Luckily his girlfriend was bad at serving and we won four out of the five points that she served.

My lifeguard quickly took off his shorts and kicked them to the side. He wasn't embarrassed at all. Granted, I had already seen him in just his boxers. He'd flaunted himself around that changing room like it was no big deal. So why did all of this feel like a big deal to me?

He didn't glance at all at Clint's girlfriend. His eyes stayed locked on me. I wasn't sure if he actually liked what he saw, or if he was just trying to embarrass me. My eyes drifted down his torso. There was definitely a big bulge in his boxers. If we got five points I'd get to see him naked. And if they got four more, he'd see me topless. That couldn't happen. It was not a possibility. I needed to step up my game or live the rest of my life under an actual rock.

I grabbed the ball. I did one of my best serves and my lifeguard returned it. The volleys were long. Just like his penis probably was. *Shit, focus!* My lifeguard and I had taken over so that we were hitting the majority of the balls while Clint and his girlfriend barely got to hit any. Even though Clint wasn't screwing me up, I was still distracted and we lost three out of five of my serves. *No, no, no.* This wasn't happening.

"We just need one more point and then we win," my lifeguard said. It was really more of a taunt.

"Stop gloating. You haven't won yet," I snapped. *This can't be real.* Maybe I was having a really awkward vivid dream. I pinched myself. *Nope, I'm living this nightmare.*

I tried to reach over to return a shot, but Clint hit it instead. The ball missed my lifeguard's side of the table by a fraction of an inch.

"You've got to be kidding me!" I threw my paddle down on the table.

"Sorry, Stalker Girl," Clint said. He grabbed the waistline of his boxers and pulled them down. I quickly looked away. "Your turn," I heard him say.

Why didn't I wear more layers today? Fuck. I can't believe I'm doing this. I reached behind my back and unhinged my bra. I turned around and let my bra straps slide down my arms. Before I turned back around I strategically folded my arms across my chest. At least my nipples were covered. My very hard nipples, thanks to my stupid lifeguard.

"Now, if you'll excuse me," Clint said and walked over to his girlfriend.

"Clint!" she screamed as he lifted her over his shoulder. The two of them laughed as they disappeared into J.J.'s bedroom, which I was hoping was their shared bedroom. Or else that was super weird.

"Well that was fun," my lifeguard said.

"Okay, can I put my clothes back on now?" I kept my arms folded across my chest.

"Hmmm." My lifeguard walked over to me.

"I can't believe you lied to me about being good at ping pong."

"I didn't lie. The first time we played I was too distracted to play well."

"By what?"

"You."

I swallowed hard. He put his hand down on the table and leaned toward me. His face was only a few inches away from mine.

"Close your eyes," he said.

I immediately shut my eyes. Partially out of embarrassment, and partially because I was hoping something was about to happen. *God, he's going to kiss me.* I'd wanted another kiss ever since our first one. A second later he slapped my ass.

"What the hell?" I opened my eyes. My lifeguard was holding *all* my clothes. "Oh my God, give those back!"

"Clint was right, you know."

"About what?"

"You have a great ass."

"Damn it, give me back my clothes, J.J."

"I kind of prefer you without clothes."

"J.J.!"

"I'll give you back your clothes if you put your hands down."

"I'm not doing that."

"But I won the game."

"I don't care if you won," I said.

"You agreed to play."

"I did play. And I took off everything but my thong, just like I had to. Now give me back my clothes." I kept one arm across my chest and reached toward my clothes.

He took a step back. "I feel like I should be allowed to see."

I laughed, but it wasn't an "I'm having a great time," laugh. It was more of a "tortured soul" kind of laugh. "Why?"

He continued to back away from me around the table. "You've seen me topless a bunch of times."

"That's different!" I started to chase him around the table. The victory lap I had pictured in my head was not anything like this humiliating moment.

He stopped when we were back where we started and held up my clothes out of reach. "It's not that different. You're acting like no one has ever seen you naked before."

"I am not. I'm just acting like *you've* never seen me naked before. Which you haven't."

"Well how many guys have seen you naked?"

"J.J., I'd rather not play 20 questions right now."

"I think it's the perfect time to play 20 questions."

"J.J."

"Mila." He raised his eyebrow at me.

"Oh, come on! How would you feel if I pantsed you right now and saw *you* completely naked?"

"I'd feel like it would be hard to control myself."

I gulped. I stopped trying to reach for my clothes. Whatever friendship he'd proposed had just been thrown out the window. He couldn't control himself around me.

And I didn't want him to try. I was just about to tell him to stop trying to control himself when the front door to his apartment creaked. *Shit.* I quickly kneeled down so that the ping pong table would hide me. He put his hand on the top of my head.

"J.J.!" Someone yelled when they walked in. "Whoa, sorry, man."

"Oh." J.J. cleared his throat. "We're not..."

"Dude, I didn't mean to cock block you."

Shit. Does J.J.'s roommate seriously think I'm giving him head in the middle of their living room? I scrunched up my face. That was worse than the real story. I stood up, keeping my arms across my chest. "We were just playing strip ping pong." I recognized the guy as J.J.'s ping pong partner from Grottos the other night.

The boy's eyes drifted down my body. I had never felt so exposed in my life. I looked over at J.J.

He stepped in front of me to block the guy's view of me. "Get the fuck out of here, Logan."

"Right, sorry." Logan disappeared into the room I hadn't been in.

J.J. started laughing as he turned around to face me. "I'm so, so sorry," he said between bouts of laughter.

"J.J. give me my clothes before someone else walks in."

"Okay, okay. Here, catch." He tossed my clothes at me.

I instinctively moved my arms away from my breasts so I could catch the clothes. *Shit. Balls! I'm a nudist!* I pulled the clothes against my naked torso. I looked up at J.J. He looked so satisfied with himself.

"You're such a smug ass," I said and turned away from him. I quickly put my clothes back on. When I turned back around he was still staring at me. But I wasn't really focused on his eyes. I swore the bulge in his boxers had grown significantly. *Stop staring at his dick, you gave those up!* My eyes gravitated back to his face.

I thought about what he had said a second before Logan had walked in. He was having a hard time controlling himself around me. I didn't want him to control himself. Maybe I should have played his game a little longer. My eyes wandered down his body again. The bulge in his boxers definitely looked even bigger than it had been before. There was no denying it. *I should have pantsed him! If I had played that differently, he might be kissing me right now.*

He cleared his throat, drawing my attention away from his boxers.

"Are you happy with yourself?" I asked, putting my hands on my hips. God, it was nice to be wearing clothes again.

"I'm very happy with myself." He sat down on the arm of the couch. "Did you want to watch a movie or something?"

My first instinct was to ask what time it was. But even if it was 3 a.m. I'd still rather stay. And even though he'd just seen me almost completely naked, it didn't feel awkward between us. It felt like we'd known each other forever. *Like we're besties? No, definitely more than besties.* "Sure."

"Awesome." He walked over to his clothes and pulled his shorts back on. His shirt remained on the ground as he grabbed our beers off the counter.

I looked away and sat down on the couch to one side. I silently cursed myself. *I should have sat in the middle so he'd have to sit directly next to me.* When he walked back over, he handed me my beer and sat down in the middle of the couch. For some reason I held my breath. I didn't care what we had talked about. Clearly neither of us wanted to be just friends. He turned on the TV and put his arm behind me on the couch without touching me.

"Oh, I love this movie," he said. "Have you ever seen it?"

"The Internship? Yeah, I love Vince Vaughn and Owen Wilson." I smiled at him.

"Yeah, they're freaking hilarious together. This movie was so underrated. I can't believe people didn't find it funny."

"I know!"

He put his feet up on the coffee table in front of the couch. It was hard to focus on the TV when all I wanted to do was look at him. I wished that Logan hadn't interrupted us. I began to wonder what would have happened. It had been so tempting to pants him. And if I was being honest with myself...do way more after said pants were gone. Way, way more. My diet was over. I was craving his dick more than I'd crave ice cream if I ever gave it up. Well, maybe. Either way, it was a lot of craving and a lot of diet cheating going on in my head.

I yawned and leaned back so that my head was resting on his arm. He didn't flinch at all. Maybe he was hoping I'd do that. His intoxicating smell of saltwater and sweat made me want to kiss him even more. I closed my eyes and pretended that Logan had never shown up.

CHAPTER 13
Thursday

I couldn't remember the last time I had slept so well. I slowly opened my eyes and then snapped them shut. *Oh my God.* I was still at my lifeguard's apartment. I was resting my head on his lap. His cock was directly underneath my right cheek. It felt slightly erect. And it definitely felt big. *Oh. So. Big.* I knew I should move. That was the logical thing to do. But since when was I logical?

Instead, I stayed completely still. I had almost seen him naked last night. I wondered if that opportunity would ever present itself again. This might be the closest I ever got to him.

My lifeguard's hand must have dipped below my shirt while we were sleeping and I could feel his palm pressed against the skin right below my bra. His hands were rough and I liked how his skin felt against mine. I didn't want to move at all. I wanted to stay in this moment forever. As soon as one of us moved, the perfection would be over. I slowly opened my eyes and strained to see his shorts right by my head. This was no normal snuggling session. It was a very inappropriately sexualized snuggle fest. This was 100 percent not the way it would feel like to snuggle with Swatch from Project Runway. I had it all wrong at the beginning of summer. *No offense, Swatch.*

Every time he breathed, my head moved slightly up and down. I stared at his legs and feet. How was even this part of him so sexy? I bit my lip. It was hard not to reach out and touch him. Since when had touching leg hair climbed so high on my bucket list? *Stay still.*

My lifeguard groaned and I quickly closed my eyes again. His breathing no longer sounded shallow. I felt him shift below me. He was definitely awake. His hand slowly moved down my torso and his fingers traced right above the waistline of my shorts. *He thinks I'm still asleep.* His hand slid to the small of my back and his fingers traced up my spine. The way he was touching me made my whole body tingle. With his other hand, he ran his fingers through my hair.

He was staring at me the way I'd just been staring at him. There was something vindicating about that. It also made me feel less weird for pretending to be asleep. Our friendship was completely whack.

I heard a door open and close.

"Hey," someone whispered. It sounded like Logan. "Our shift starts in 20."

No!

"Okay," my lifeguard whispered back. He ran his fingers through my hair once more and pulled my shirt back down my torso. "Hey, Mila?" He put his hand on my shoulder, all innocently, like his hand hadn't just been up my shirt.

I rolled onto my back and looked up at him. "You're handsome in the morning." I put my arm over my face. *Why did I just say that?* Our skin touching had forced the butterflies back into my brain.

My lifeguard laughed. "I have to be at the beach soon and I need to take a shower. Do you want to wait and I'll walk you home on my way to work?"

I took one last moment to savor having my head on his lap and slowly sat up. "No, that's okay. I'll see you at the beach later?"

"I'll be there." He smiled at me and got up off the couch.

I stood up too. I suddenly felt extremely awkward. It seemed like I should at least hug him goodbye. That would be a very normal thing to do. So of course, I took a step back instead. *Smooth.*

He rubbed the back of his neck with his hand.

"Okay, see you later," I said and started toward the door. Before I walked out, I turned around. His hands were in his pockets and he was staring at me. Did he feel it too? It felt like my heart was beating in my throat. I quickly left his apartment.

***

I was sitting on my bed cross-legged holding my phone. Aiden had just texted me. This was the first time I had heard from him since he broke up with me. I don't know how many times I had called him and texted him last semester. He always ignored me. Every single time. Like I was a ghost. Like I never meant anything to him.

I looked down at his text. He said he hoped I was having a good summer. The only reason it was good was because he wasn't in it. If he had never broken up with me, I may have stayed with him for the rest of my life. The thought was chilling. I would have never come here for the summer and never met my lifeguard. That was the hardest part to swallow. This was the best summer of my life. I had thought my world ended when I walked in on Aiden and that slut. But I truly felt like I was exactly where I needed to be. Having felt what it was like to lose love had somehow made me open to finding a better love.

I didn't need the summer to find myself. I felt more like myself here than I ever had in California. And my lifeguard was who had fixed me. He held the cure to whatever problem I had. I knew he was keeping his distance because he respected me and I was going back to California at the end of summer. But I wanted it to be more. I didn't want to miss out on my chance with him.

I looked back down at Aiden's text. A few weeks ago I would have been ecstatic that I had finally heard from him. But he was probably only texting me because he needed something. I no longer cared about his needs. I wanted nothing to do with him. For some reason this was the closure that I had been longing for. I was done thinking about him. *Fuck him.* I couldn't believe I had wasted so many months wallowing. Losing him wasn't a loss at all. He was an asshole. How could I have not seen it before? I kept thinking I had done something wrong. I kept blaming myself. But it wasn't my fault. He was just a shitty human being. A complete and utter goober butt. I rolled my eyes at myself, wishing my name calling was more on point.

The apartment door opened and Kristen walked in wearing spandex shorts and a sports bra. "Hey, where were you last night?" She wiped the sweat off her forehead with the back of her hand.

I couldn't help the smile that spread across my face. "I'll give you two guesses."

"I only need one." She pulled a water bottle out of the fridge. "You broke your dick diet and went to town on J.J.'s dick."

"No. Well...no. It's a no. I was with J.J., yes, but we were just hanging out as friends. But...I think I'm ready for more than that. I'm pretty sure he is too. And I think I'm ready to tell him exactly what I want. Which is him, in case that wasn't obvious."

Kristen laughed. "Yeah, I got that. But why the sudden change of heart? Less than 24 hours ago you were still cursing his name and giving up men."

"He apologized." I said the word apologized really slowly because I was still super surprised it had happened. I laughed and lifted up my phone. "Plus, Aiden texted me and I felt *nothing*. Well, that's not entirely true. I felt something even better...closure. I am so over him." I tossed my phone onto my bed. I didn't need to hold it and stare at it every few minutes anymore. I was free.

"It's about time." She downed the rest of her water bottle. "So you spent the night at his place as friends? What did that involve exactly?"

Strip poker and waking up with my head on his dick. "Just, you know...friend stuff. We fell asleep watching a movie. It was all very PG-13."

"What movie?" She raised both her eyebrows at me.

Did she think I was going to say porn or something? "We watched The Internship. It has..."

"Vince Vaughn and Owen Wilson? Yeah, I know. One of the most underrated movies of all time. Or at least since I've been born."

I laughed. If J.J. wasn't my soulmate, maybe Kristen was. "Agreed. I love me some Owen Wilson."

"I love me some Vince Vaughn. I'm glad we don't even have to fight over celebrity crushes. And speaking of fighting…next time text me if you're going to spend all night out. I was worried you were dead in a ditch."

"Sorry. But I'm alive and better than ever so you can't be mad." I gave her my most innocent smile.

"I'm not mad at you. I was just worried. Are you heading out to stalk him already?"

"It's not stalking him anymore. He even knows I'm coming."

"Ha! I just got to admit you were stalking him in the first place."

"Touché. See…I can use that word when I'm sober." I grabbed my beach bag and headed toward the door.

"Cell phone. We literally just talked about this." Kristen picked it up off my bed and tossed it to me.

Luckily I caught it because if the screen cracked anymore it would be totally unreadable.

"Nice catch. Text me later if you're not coming back for dinner."

I nodded. "Are you sure you don't want to come with me? You never come down to the beach."

"I go down to the beach all the time." She gestured to her running shoes. "I just exercise instead of lying there reading. *You* should join *me* sometime. I'm running more than ever since you feed me such delicious, addictive food. I don't want those calories to catch up to my ass."

"You're right. Let's do that tomorrow morning." I was giving up my dick diet. But I still wanted to better myself this summer. And exercising was at the top of my list.

Kristen put her hand on her hip. "Am I hallucinating or did you just agree to go on a five mile run with me tomorrow?"

"Five miles!" *Who the hell said anything about five miles?* Her level of training was clearly too intense for a normal human. "You know what...we can discuss that tomorrow morning. Bright and early."

"Deal." She waved me goodbye.

I made a point not to say deal. I was pretty sure I'd die if I ran five miles right now. But I made a deal with myself that I could do it by the end of the summer.

CHAPTER 14
Thursday

The sun felt good on my skin as I walked to the beach. Walking was so underrated. Kristen didn't realize that a long walk on the beach was better in every way than a run. But despite the fact that I just agreed to be tortured tomorrow, it felt like a huge weight had been lifted off my shoulders. I was over Aiden. So over Aiden that even thinking about his name didn't make me feel sick to my stomach anymore. I smiled to myself. I was free from that feeling that I'd failed and had no idea how I'd failed. Aiden was basic AF and it only took me one awesome date with someone else to realize it.

Now I just needed to let my lifeguard know that I wanted to be more than his friend. A lot more. It seemed like he felt the same way. We never acted like friends. I had the biggest crush on him. He definitely knew it. And he seemed to like me back. I thought about his fingers running through my hair this morning and my smile grew even bigger. He was probably crushing as hard as I was.

I looked up at him as I made my way to my usual spot in the sand. When I reached it, I stood there for a second. There was room for my towel right next to his lifeguard stand. I didn't want to keep my distance anymore. *Be bold, Mila.* I walked over to the empty spot.

"Hey!" I said and tapped the side of the lifeguard stand. I immediately pulled my hand back to my side. There was no need to knock on wood.

He looked down at me. "You're late," he said.

I was pretty sure my smile couldn't get any bigger. "Yeah, well, I slept over at some random guy's apartment last night and it threw my whole schedule off."

"Some random guy, huh? Sounds like a sexy evening."

"It was almost really sexy. But his roommate walked in on us." I couldn't believe that actually came out of my mouth. One pep-talk on being bold and I'd jumped right into the deep end. I mentally high-fived myself.

My lifeguard laughed. "Almost really sexy? I'm not sure I even know what you mean by that." He glanced at the ocean and then back at me. "You'll have to show me what really sexy is sometime, because now I'm just curious."

He wants to have sex with me. I gulped. That wasn't exactly what he said. Really sexy could mean anything. To me it meant *all* the sex. In every position. Including the gross Thanksgiving turkey one. "I think I'd like that." I wished he wasn't wearing his sunglasses. I wanted to see his reaction to what I said, but it was impossible to tell. *Stupid sunglasses.* His silence was unnerving. It felt like a few minutes ticked by with me just awkwardly standing there. He was staring out at the ocean again. But I wanted his attention, even if it was for just another second. I craved him more than Pink Dream ice cream. So I was basically addicted. "One," I almost shouted.

"One?" He smiled at me. "One what?"

God, why was that the thing I said into the awkward silence? I leaned in closer to him so that the people around us couldn't hear me. Why I chose a super public place to answer his question from last night at the top of my lungs, I had no idea. "Only one guy has seen me naked."

"The asshole?"

"Yeah."

"Well, I hate to break it to you, but I've kind of seen you naked too. So have Clint and Elle. You're racking up the points here."

"Not naked, naked. I was wearing underwear.

"Which revealed a whole lot of your ass."

I could feel my face turning red. He was right. My ass had been on full display. I swallowed hard when he didn't look away. It was like he was picturing me in nothing but my thong again. "How many girls have seen you naked?"

"Ummm." He looked back out at the water. "Hmmm." He didn't answer for an agonizing minute. "More than one."

"What does that even mean? You can't remember? Or it's like…a lot more than one?" *Please don't be a lot more than a few.* I didn't know where we were going, but I hoped I'd be going wherever it was with him. And the thought of him ogling tons of naked women really bothered me. Even if it was in his past.

"It means I've gone streaking and I have no idea how many girls saw me."

I laughed. That was not a serious answer. Besides, I'd asked the wrong question in the first place. All I really wanted to know was how many girls he had slept with. That was something someone who was more than a friend would want to know. But he wasn't giving up the information easily. "What if you don't count the streaking incident?"

"Completely naked? Or like, wearing boxers?"

I smiled. I'd seen him in his boxers twice and I wouldn't be forgetting either occasion anytime soon. "Completely naked."

"Probably four."

"Probably?"

"Yep, probably."

"Your answers are extremely vague."

"I'm trying to work, Jellyfish Girl. It's hard to focus on more than one thing at a time." He smiled at me.

Fair point. Hopefully there weren't a bunch of children drowning because of me. "I'll leave you alone then." I laid my towel on top of the sand and sat down on it. I had decided to finish Twisted Love after all, so I pulled it out of my bag. A steamy hot summer beach read fit my mood perfectly. And it was easy to imagine that it was about J.J. and me.

I lay down and hoped that he really did like my ass. Because even though I was wearing a bikini bottom, it was basically on full display. Every now and then as I read, I'd glance up at my lifeguard. I caught him staring at me once. For some reason my response had been to wink. I wasn't used to being so bold, but I was finding it fun. The wink had gotten me a smile and a wave of confidence.

After a few hours of reading, my lifeguard cleared his throat. I looked up at him.

"I think some of the lifeguards are playing touch football after our shifts are over. Do you want to play?"

Anything that involved touching him was a go for me. "Yeah, that sounds fun."

"Do you know how to play?"

Well, now he was just being insulting. "Of course I know how to play. I love football. I used to throw the ball around with my dad on Sundays before Eagles games." *Before he left.* I tried to squash that annoying voice in the back of my head. But I was already picturing him teaching my half-sisters. All three of them laughing together. The perfect family. Why did this still hurt so much? I was fine without him. I had been for years. If he didn't need me or my mom, I didn't need him either. That was what I always told my heart, but sometimes it was too stupid to listen. Or too naïve to care. Or too hopeful that things could one day change.

"Really?"

I looked back up at him. "I'm sorry, what did you say?" I'd gotten lost in my annoying daydream of what would never be me and my dad.

"You really know how to play?"

"Why are you so surprised? Does it not seem like I'd be good at it? My dad didn't have a son so he taught me everything instead." *Before he realized I'd never be good enough. Before he realized he could start over with a new, younger family.* These thoughts were coming out of left field. I was finally in a good place after the Aiden fiasco. The last thing I needed was to revert back to my broken-hearted tween years when my dad walked out. I shook my head, hoping the annoying thoughts and butterflies would fly away. "I'm a freaking beast."

My lifeguard laughed. "So you're super cocky about your football skills too?"

"No, not as cocky. I'm just super competitive."

"I've noticed."

I got up and put my book in my bag. I wanted him to keep noticing me. And I wanted it to be unrelated to my football skills...which really were pretty amazing. "I'm going to go cool off. Blow the whistle if a shark comes. Since we both know you won't come in and save me."

"Of course I'd come in."

"I thought you were scared of sharks?"

He shrugged. He didn't say it, but I'm pretty sure that shrug meant he'd fight a shark for me. Which was probably the nicest thing a guy ever didn't say to me. I pulled my hair out of my elastic band and walked down to the water. When I looked over my shoulder I could tell he was watching me. Sunglasses be damned, he had eyes only for me.

I dove under the water before a wave caught me. And again I was reminded of my dad. All the vacations with him I'd taken for granted. Now I just saw images flash through my head of him with his new family on their summer trips. He'd never once invited me.

I broke the surface of the water and took a deep breath. I was worried I was thinking about all the times my dad hurt me for a reason. Aiden wasn't the only dick out there. There were a bunch of them. I looked back at my lifeguard.

He waved and broke down my walls a little. J.J. wasn't like Aiden. And he certainly wasn't like my dad. I just had this gut feeling that he'd never hurt me. I hoped I was right. Because I was really tired of temporary.

Then I realized why I was really thinking about my dad. I needed to call him. I needed to tell him to hold off sending tuition to SMU. I was coming back home.

CHAPTER 15
Thursday

The whistles blew and I looked up from my book. My lifeguard hopped off the stand and quickly pushed it up away from the water. A second later he collapsed beside me on my towel. He was so close I could smell the intoxicating mixture of sunscreen and sweat on his skin. I felt myself leaning a little closer. Kristen was right. There was just something special about a guy's scent.

"We're going to play in like ten minutes." He put his hands behind his head and lay down on his back.

"Okay." I sat up so I could look down at him. But then I wished I had stayed lying down too. Because now all I wanted to do was lean over him and kiss him. It had been far too long since our first kiss and my lips were craving him.

"So why are you suddenly so interested in that number?" he asked.

I shrugged. If the number of girls that had seen him naked wasn't important to me, I probably wouldn't have even realized what he was talking about. But it was important and I was interested in the fact that his number was four. "You asked me last night. And then I was wondering about you. So...you've had four girlfriends?"

"No. I've had two girlfriends."

"Oh. So what were the other two girls?"

He sat up. "Girls that I wasn't serious about."

"Hmm." His response was a warning sign. I thought about the fact that he drove a motorcycle and my mother's warning. He was a very bad boy.

"Don't look at me like that, Jellyfish Girl."

"Like what?"

"Like you think I'm a bad person."

"I don't think you're a bad person." It was true, I had been thinking he was a bad boy. But a bad person? I tucked a loose strand of hair behind my ear. J.J. definitely wasn't a bad person. "When did you break up with your last girlfriend?"

"It's been a while. A few years maybe. Yeah, over two years."

I already knew that his first girlfriend cheated on him when they went to different colleges. So that left the mystery of the other people who had seen him naked. "And where do the other girls fit in?"

"My last year of college."

"Were they like…one-night things?" It felt like I was pulling the information out of him in an extremely awkward friendship way.

"You're suddenly awfully curious about my sexual history. What about you? You've only had sex with Aiden?"

I scrunched up my face. "Yeah."

My lifeguard laughed. "It seems like you want to change that."

"Maybe I do." I dug my heels into the sand. *With you.* Why couldn't I just tell him that I liked him? Every time I came close, my lips seemed to press together, keeping my secret locked away. "So…about those other girls…"

He laughed. "You're very nosy today."

"And you're avoiding the question."

He turned away from me and looked up at the sky. "I told you that I'm not thrilled about my job this fall. I was kind of a mess my last year of college. I know that's not really an excuse."

"And I told you that I don't think you're a bad person."

"So you still like me?" He flashed me a smile.

"I really like you." I coughed. "As a friend. Of course as a friend. You're my buddy."

"Right." His smile faded.

Fuck. What is wrong with me? That had been my best opportunity yet. *Just tell him how you feel!*

"You guys ready?!" Clint yelled over to us.

I was happy that I was being offered an avoidance tactic instead of just creating them in my head. I quickly stood up. I was still a little wet from my dip in the ocean. Hopefully that would prevent me from getting too sweaty. Whenever I worked out, I always seemed to get way sweatier than anyone else. And being nervous around my lifeguard wasn't going to help the situation. I was lucky that he wasn't coming on my supposed five mile run tomorrow. He'd probably just keep on running away from me if he saw how sweaty and red I got.

My lifeguard slowly sat up, took off his sunglasses, and tossed them onto my towel. He looked up at me with his blue eyes.

I didn't want to play football. I wanted to fall asleep with his arms wrapped around me again. I wanted more than whatever it was we were. Somehow I needed to make him realize that. And since the words escaped me, maybe I could show him in a different way. By body tackling him into the sand during touch football, even if that was technically against the rules. It was the only logical option. I put my hand out for him. He grabbed it and I pulled him to his feet.

"Can I be on your team?" I asked. I didn't let go of his hand. *Or would it be better to not be on his team? How could I flirt more?* Tackling meant being on the opposite team. Unless I was going to throw in the towel and be really bad and tackle my own teammate. Which would be really hard for me to do because I loved winning. Maybe that's why my being bad at love was so hard for me to accept.

"I'm not sure it's up to me, *buddy*." He squeezed my hand and then let it go.

"Oh, come on. You knew what I meant."

"Actually, I didn't. Maybe you could describe it in more detail." He smiled at me.

I knew he was messing with me, but it seemed like another perfect opportunity to tell him the truth. *Why is this so awkward?* I swallowed hard. His eyes were so distracting.

"Yo, guys! Come on!" Clint yelled again.

I smiled at my lifeguard and started walking toward the group of lifeguards that had formed away from the water. It was impossible to talk to him, so being more flirtatious was definitely the only thing I could do. I walked over to Clint. "Hey, your girlfriend seemed nice. Is she going to come play?"

"Who? Elle?" Clint laughed. "I don't have a girlfriend, Stalker Girl."

"Oh." *Awkward.*

"Okay, Reggie and I are the captains," Clint said. "I'll take J.J."

My lifeguard walked over and stood next to Clint. He whispered something in Clint's ear. My heart started beating fast. It felt like I was in high school all over again. I didn't want to be picked last. It was always so mortifying just standing, waiting. And I wanted to be on my lifeguard's team. I hoped he'd just told Clint to choose me next. I wouldn't let them down. After all, I was a beast.

I started to pull my hair up into a ponytail. It was time to get serious.

"Hey, are you any good?"

I turned my head toward Reggie. He was looking right at me. I turned around to see if there was some big strong man behind me who Reggie was actually staring at. *Nope.* I looked back at him.

"Who, me?" I asked.

"Yeah, you." He smiled at me.

"I'm...okay." I was standing next to two tall, muscular lifeguards. He couldn't seriously be about to pick me. It didn't make any sense. From a competitive standpoint, I should be one of the last picks just because I was so much shorter than everyone else. Smaller legs meant slower.

"Come be on my team," Reggie said.

I definitely didn't expect to be picked first for someone's team. I looked over my shoulder at my lifeguard as I walked toward Reggie. He looked kind of pissed. Maybe this was just what I needed. If I could make him jealous, then maybe he'd admit that he wanted to be more than friends too. Besides, now the tackling strategy was a go. We were about to take a sexy roll in the sand.

Reggie leaned down and whispered in my ear. "I haven't seen you around. What's your name?"

"Mila." I put my hand out for him.

He shook it. "It's nice to meet you, Mila. Are you just here for the summer?" He was completely ignoring the fact that it was his turn to pick someone again.

"Um, I think it's your turn to choose someone."

"Right. Alex!" he said and turned back to me. "Are you going to the 4th of July beach party?"

"I actually didn't know about it. Is it just on the beach somewhere near here?" Rehoboth beach wasn't that big, but if it was on the other end of it, I might miss it. How had I not even heard of it?

"Yeah, and it's going to be a lot of fun. They set off fireworks and there's tons of food and drinks. You should definitely come." He called out another name.

"That sounds great. I'll think about it." I looked over at my lifeguard. His hands were in his pockets and he was scowling slightly. *This is working.*

"I'll give you my number after we're done so that I can tell you where it is," Reggie said.

I wanted to say, "Can't you just tell me now?" But I knew he was probably just flirting with me. It made me realize that I didn't even have my lifeguard's number yet. Why didn't I? Wasn't exchanging numbers one of the first things that people who liked each other did? *This is so frustrating.*

After both teams were selected, my team got in a circle and listened to Reggie. Apparently they did this all the time. And they had terminology that I had never heard of before. All I understood was that Reggie was the quarterback. Embarrassing J.J. wasn't what I wanted to accomplish today...but it was looking like that was what was about to happen. I shouldn't have told him I knew how to play. Tossing a football around with my dad didn't exactly make me an all-star.

"Sorry, what do you want me to do?" I asked.

"Just try to get open," he said.

"Okay." I stood next to Reggie when we got into formation. We were running something called a slant route. Fortunately it had nothing to do with me.

My lifeguard positioned himself directly across from me.

"You're going down," he said.

"In your dreams."

"I have dreamt of you going down on me."

What? "Shit," I mumbled. The play had started and I was still standing there staring at him. "Stop distracting me," I hissed and tried to run past him. My heart was racing from his comment. Was he serious? Had he really dreamt of that? *Focus on the game!*

He kept moving in front of me so that I couldn't get past him. I put my hands on his abs and tried to push him out of the way. He just laughed and kept blocking me. Someone else caught the ball and was stopped a quarter of the way toward the line in the sand that signaled the end zone.

"Shouldn't you be paired up with someone your own size?" I asked and playfully shoved J.J.'s arm.

"I'll go easy on you the next play. Show me what you got."

I got back in position. This time my lifeguard let me run past him, but Reggie threw the ball to someone else. When I walked back over to Reggie, he high-fived me.

"Great job getting open. The next one is coming to you," Reggie said.

I smiled to myself. I so badly wanted to score against my lifeguard. Then I could do a touchdown dance and rub it in his dirty mouth. Thinking about his mouth was distracting again.

"And, hut!" Reggie yelled.

I ran past my lifeguard again and turned around. The ball flew toward me. I reached up and caught it perfectly. But before I could turn back around to start running, my lifeguard wrapped his arms around me.

"J.J.!" I screamed as we both fell into the sand.

He laughed as he rolled on top of me.

"Isn't this supposed to be two hand touch?" I couldn't help giggling. This was so much fun. He had done to me exactly what I was hoping to do to him. Tackling was so much better than limiting it to two hands. I liked my whole body pressed against his.

"I did touch you with two hands. And then I tackled you. I can touch you again if you need me to, though." He raised his eyebrow.

My body felt like it was about to combust.

"Hey, lovebirds!" Clint yelled. "Let's keep it going."

My lifeguard pushed himself up, put his hand out for me, and helped me up. "Oh, sorry," he said and pulled me in close. "I got sand all over you." He wiped his free hand across my ass and down the back of my thigh."

Holy shit. "J.J." I pushed my hand against his chest. "Stop trying to distract me."

"That's not exactly what I was doing, but that's an added bonus."

He released me and walked back over to his team. If he wasn't trying to distract me, what was he doing? I walked back over to my team as I brushed the rest of the sand off my ass. This time Reggie completely ignored me. *Oh. Was my lifeguard really just trying to make Reggie back off?* The thought made me smile. J.J. was jealous. I wasn't just smiling, I was beaming. He was basically laying claim to me. Which was old-fashioned and should have infuriated me...but I wasn't really a feminist. *He likes me back!*

On the next play, someone from my lifeguard's team intercepted the ball. They were stopped close to the end zone. Now I needed to try to stop my lifeguard from scoring. It was time to stop flirting and focus. He was going down. My lifeguard ran towards me and easily sidestepped me. Clint tossed him the ball and they scored.

Shit.

The game went on for a long time. After an hour or so, I was completely exhausted from trying to chase my lifeguard everywhere. He was too freaking good at football. Actually, they all were. I was definitely the weak link on my team. We were down by one touchdown and we were really close to the end zone. I ran past my lifeguard and turned around just in time to see the football sailing toward me. It was only the fourth one that had been thrown my way all day. I caught it. *Because I'm a baller.*

I started running. *I'm going to score!* I was a few feet away from the end zone when my lifeguard picked me up and hoisted me over his shoulder.

"J.J.!" I screamed.

He started running in the opposite direction toward his own end zone. His hand slipped to my ass. I wasn't sure if it was to steady me or because he just wanted to touch me. But I loved the feeling of his hands on me.

"J.J.!" I yelled again as he crossed the line.

He started to do a victory dance while still holding me.

I leaned down and slapped his ass. "Put me down. Obviously that doesn't count, cheater."

He slowly lowered me, keeping me against his torso. "I think it does count. You're such a sore loser."

"No, it doesn't count! You can't pick up players."

"Well, it might not count as a touchdown, but that was your last down. Which means you lose." He let go of my waist and grabbed the football out of my hands. He ran over to his team and high-fived all of them.

I walked over to my team. "Sorry, guys."

"Don't worry about it," Reggie said. "We'll get them next time." He leaned in closer to me. "Hey, I'm sorry about earlier, I didn't realize that you were dating J.J."

I looked over at J.J. He was giving some super tan girl with long blonde hair a hug. It felt like his hands lingered a beat too long. And the way he smiled at her when he pulled back from the hug was the exact same way he smiled at me. My stomach rolled over. I thought I had made him jealous, but maybe I was wrong. Maybe he was just trying to distract me during the game. "I'm not dating

J.J.," I said. Just because I wanted to be, it didn't make it true.

Reggie smiled. "In that case, I think I promised you my number."

I watched J.J. talking to the girl. It was like he had eyes only for her. Maybe I hadn't successfully made him jealous, but he had sure made me jealous. "Right. For directions to the party?"

"Yeah. Do you have a pen?"

"Um. In my bag." I pointed to my towel in the distance and we both started walking toward it. "I'm really sorry about blowing the game. I've really only ever tossed the ball around in my backyard before." He didn't need to know that it was years ago. Or that my dad had probably gone easy on me.

Reggie laughed. "It wasn't your fault. Like I said, we'll get them next time."

I tried to brush some of the sand off myself as we approached my towel. When I got to my bag, I looked back at my lifeguard. He was still talking to the same girl. The rest of his team had started to disperse, but J.J. and that girl were practically glued together. I grabbed the pen out of my bag and handed it to Reggie.

"Do you have any paper?"

"I'm sure I do somewhere." I leaned over to rummage through my bag again, but he grabbed my hand.

"Here," he said. He held my hand as wrote his number on the back of it. He rubbed his thumb against the ink and it smeared slightly. I wasn't sure if it was because I was sweaty or because I was wearing sunscreen. Just the thought of sunscreen was a lie. It was definitely the sweat. I was a mess.

Reggie brought my hand up to his mouth and blew on it. I swallowed hard and looked up at him. He was handsome. He had sandy blonde hair and his skin wasn't nearly as tan as the other lifeguards. There was something about him that just seemed normal and somehow familiar and comforting. He was more like a person than a model. But he was still ripped and his smile was bright. I quickly looked away when he dropped my hand.

"Thanks. I'll text you later."

"Okay, great. I'll see you next week if I don't see you sooner. It's going to be lots of fun."

"Sounds good."

"It was nice meeting you, Mila." He went to hug me at the same time I put my hand out for him to shake, so I ended up rubbing my palm against his chest.

"Oh, sorry," I laughed.

"Geez, you're already trying to feel me up? I'm going to have to keep my eye on you. See you later." He smiled at me and walked away.

I sighed and went down to the water. The breeze coming off the ocean felt refreshing. I didn't want Reggie to like me. I wanted J.J. to like me. I folded my arms across my chest. Liking J.J. was like being on a rollercoaster ride. I just wanted us to both be on a carousel or something instead. I was done with the ups and downs.

"Hey," J.J. said. He had run over to me. "It's Grottos night. You in?"

I looked behind me. The girl with blonde hair was staring at us. "I'm all sandy. I think I just want to go take a shower. I'll come next time." I smiled at him.

"You sure? You can just rinse off on the boardwalk. It's not a big deal. I'm sandy too."

"That's because you kept cheating and tackling me."

"Tackle football is more fun. Come on, let's go."

"I just feel all gross. I'll catch you later. Besides, tons of other people are going with you. You don't need me." *What am I doing? Am I just giving up? I'm such a coward.* I looked out at the water. I didn't want to compete for his attention. This was exhausting. I wanted to curl up in my bed and go to sleep. Where had my boldness from earlier gone?

"Are you okay?"

"I just feel really tired. All I want to do is shower and sleep."

"Okay. Do you want me to walk you home?" He rubbed the back of his neck with his hand.

It was pretty clear that he didn't want to. All his friends were already leaving. "No." I laughed. "I'm not sick. Just tired. Go. Have fun."

"Okay, Jellyfish Girl. I'll see you tomorrow." He put his hand on my shoulder for a second and then walked away.

I watched him go up to the girl he had been talking to. She bumped her shoulder against his and they started laughing as they walked toward the boardwalk together.

Maybe I was wrong about being ready to date. When Aiden had dumped me I felt so pathetic and worthless. I felt worthless again right now. I wasn't as pretty as the girl

J.J. was talking to. I couldn't compete with her. Besides, if J.J. really did like me, he'd probably already be with me.

And what was with that crap about seeing me tomorrow? He didn't have my number. He'd never asked for it. All he meant was that he was going to stop by Sweet Cravings to get a free scoop. I was just the schmuck that had offered him a summer of free ice cream.

I could feel the tears running down my cheeks. I didn't want to feel like this again. I grabbed my stuff and stormed back to my apartment, trying to hide my tears the whole way.

CHAPTER 16
Sunday

I sat down in the back room of the ice cream shop and pulled out my phone. It was hard to get out of bed in the morning. It felt like I was back at school, moping around. But I knew I had to fight the feeling. I couldn't get sucked back into that hole again. And if I thought once more about that blonde slut falling asleep in J.J.'s arms, I'd lose it.

To J.J.'s credit, he did stop by the ice cream shop on Friday. And he hadn't asked for free ice cream or anything. He just asked if I wanted to hang out. I'd told him I had plans with Kristen. Which was true...dinner with Kristen was one of my favorite things.

Regardless, I was pretty sure he was growing very suspicious that Kristen didn't exist. But I didn't care. I wasn't sure if I knew how to be just his friend, so I had to keep turning him down. It was the only thing I could do to keep my heart intact. How was I supposed to hang out with him for hours as friends when all I wanted to do was reenact our kiss? Or the way he touched me in the sand? It wasn't possible. There was no way to go back to being platonic.

I looked down at my hand. Reggie's number had vanished a few showers ago. But I found myself constantly staring at my hand like maybe it had all the answers anyway. I wanted to go to the party tomorrow. I'd taken today's shift partly because I didn't want to work on the crazy busy 4th of July and partially because I didn't want to miss the party. And maybe I didn't want J.J. to know my schedule anymore. To get tomorrow off I'd also had to grab a Tuesday shift. Maybe I'd just change all my days to avoid him.

I sighed. That was ridiculous. I couldn't avoid him forever. I couldn't stay fixated on J.J. for the rest of my life. I needed to get out there and make more friends and meet more people. And maybe if I let a few more people in, I wouldn't be so obsessed with him.

Reggie had invited me to the 4th of July party. I owed it to him to give at least a friendship between us a chance. It wasn't like J.J. had asked me to the party. We were just friends right now because I was too much of a coward to tell him how I felt. If he was even going, he was probably taking the blonde girl. Maybe she was offering him something I couldn't...a move to New York. And I definitely couldn't offer him that. The closest I could get was Newark. Even that was a stretch. I hadn't heard back from the admissions office yet.

I took a deep breath and typed out a text to Reggie. "Hey! It's Mila. So, where exactly on the beach is that party?" I pressed send.

A few minutes later I got his response. "Hey, Mila! I forget what street it's near. How about I just come to your place and we can find it together?"

I smiled to myself. He was cute. And he probably didn't flirt with every girl he talked to like J.J. did. I gave him my address and pressed send. Then I pulled up the text from Aiden. I was suddenly feeling bold again. And that shithead hadn't mailed me my books yet.

"I'm having a fantastic summer. Although I haven't gotten my books yet. Did you mail them?" I pressed send.

My phone buzzed a minute later. I swiped my finger across the screen, expecting a text from Reggie. But it was Aiden. "Mila, I need to talk to you. Can I call you?"

I put my phone down on the table. *Now* he finally wants to talk to me? His text from last week was the first time I heard from him since we broke up. I didn't want to talk to him now. I never wanted to talk to him again.

I walked out of the back room.

"Hey, do you mind if I get going a little early? I'm not feeling well," I said to Becca, who I was being teamed up with more and more. Probably because she was always so cheery and I was so…not. The thought of hearing Aiden's voice made me want to throw up. Besides, J.J. might be showing up any minute to ask if I want to hang out. He probably knew I was randomly working here today. Because clearly he was the stalker, not me. And I didn't know what to say to him. I mean…what was there to say? He knew I liked him. Of course he knew that. I didn't need to say it out loud for him to see it. And being around him was just too hard.

"Sure. Feel better, Mila. Oh, are you going to the 4th of July party tomorrow? I heard it's going to be awesome!"

"Yeah, I'm thinking about going."

"I hope I see you there," Becca said. "Feel better!"

"Thanks!" I quickly took off my apron and went out the door. A second later my phone started buzzing. I looked down and Aiden was calling me. *What the hell?* I felt like I was going to throw up. What could he possibly want to talk about now? I ignored my phone and it eventually stopped buzzing. But then it started buzzing again. I looked down. Aiden was calling me again. *Fuck.*

I stopped at a bench on the boardwalk and sat down. For a few weeks I thought I was fine. But apparently I wasn't. I was still a fucking mess. Pining over a guy I could never have was probably just a coping mechanism. Maybe it was one of the stages of grief or something. Anger was definitely one of the stages, and I had plenty of that.

How many times had I called Aiden and he hadn't answered? *Too many to count.* Could I really give him the satisfaction of calling twice and me answering? *No.* A few seconds later the phone stopped buzzing again.

I sighed and leaned back against the bench. Maybe he was calling to apologize. What else could he possibly be calling for? And a late apology was better than no apology. Wasn't it? If I was ever going to be able to let it go, maybe I needed to hear what he had to say. My phone started buzzing again. *I can do this.*

But then I looked back down at the cracked screen and remembered how it broke in the first place. There was nothing left to say to Aiden. There was no point in taking the call. My phone eventually stopped buzzing and I sighed. *Leave me alone.*

My silent prayer was not answered. The buzzing started again. *You know what? Fuck it. And fuck him.* I wanted the apology. He owed me at least that. Maybe it would help me finally move on.

I picked up my phone and answered the call. "Hey," I said much quieter than I meant to. My body was coursing with anger but my voice was barely audible.

The line was silent. Maybe he hadn't heard me.

"Aiden?"

"Hi, Mila." There was an awkward pause. "It's so good to hear your voice."

What the hell? The feeling wasn't mutual. Hearing his voice made me feel like I was going to throw up again. "Why are you calling me, Aiden?"

He laughed. "It's weird hearing you call me Aiden. You never really called me that."

He was right. After we had started dating, I always called him babe. My stomach felt like it was twisting in knots. "Yeah." My voice sounded weird.

"I'm sorry that I haven't mailed you your stuff yet. It's just...I feel like you'll really be gone as soon as your stuff is gone."

Why do I want to cry? I swallowed hard. I needed this phone call three months ago. Not now. "I was gone as soon as I walked in on you sleeping with..."

"I know," he said, cutting me off. "Mila." His breathing sounded heavy. "I'm such an idiot. I'm so sorry."

"You're right. You are an idiot."

He laughed. "I know." He was silent for a long time. "I made a mistake. I'm so, so sorry."

That's what I had wanted to hear. But for some reason it wasn't enough. "We both know it wasn't just one mistake, Aiden. You don't have any reason to lie to me now. How long did it go on?" I didn't need to know the answer.

I shouldn't have even asked the question. Nothing he said could fix the hurt.

"I know. I know. Fuck, Mila. I don't know what's wrong with me." He sighed. "I'm sorry."

He didn't answer the question. I should have ignored it and ended the call. Instead, I heard myself asking it again. *For the love of God, why am I torturing myself?*

"I don't know. Six months maybe. But I'm sorry. I screwed up and I'm really fucking sorry."

"Okay." Nothing he just said was okay, so I wasn't sure why that was my response. Six months? Was he serious?

"I'm sorry," he said again. "I know I'm an asshole."

I wasn't sure if he was looking for me to say I forgave him. But I didn't. My heart wasn't big enough to forgive and forget. I hated him. I hated the way he had made me feel. And I felt that way again right now. I put my face in my hand. Six months. He'd slept around behind my back for six months.

"I miss you."

I didn't say anything. Did I miss him? I felt angry and sad. But I wasn't sure I missed him anymore. I closed my eyes. No, I didn't miss him. I hadn't missed him for a while now. Ever since I met J.J.

"When are you coming back?" he asked. "I need to see you."

"At the end of summer." *Maybe. Hopefully not.* "Aiden, why didn't you ever call me back? I needed you." *Shit.* I could feel my tears welling in my eyes. "I needed you last semester. I needed to know why."

"I'm sorry."

His sorry felt empty. It didn't mean anything to me now. "Why did you do it?"

"I don't know. But I can't stop thinking about you. I miss you so much."

"Was it something I did?" That's what had bothered me the most. It felt like it was my fault somehow. Tears started running down my cheeks.

"No. No. I just made a mistake."

Why did he keep saying that? He had made the same mistake over and over and over again. I had walked in on him making one of the hundreds of mistakes. "I'm going to go."

"Mila. Please, you have..."

"I don't want you to call me again."

"I want you back." His words hung there.

He wanted me back? After cheating on me? Humiliating me? Abandoning me? *Fuck him.* "It's too late." I hung up the phone.

CHAPTER 17
Monday

"You're getting really good at this," Kristen said from beside me.

"Thanks." I picked up my pace even more. I'd decided that a broken heart could go one of two ways. You could eat your feelings and get a permanent food baby. Or you could get buns of steel by working out non-stop with the queen of fitness herself. This time I was going with the latter and I truly felt amazing. Physically at least. Mentally, I was a freaking mess.

But I actually liked running, which was the strangest combination of words ever. Ever since the game of touch football, I'd been running with Kristen every morning bright and early. I was like a machine.

"So...have you talked to J.J. yet?"

That was the only bad thing about running with Kristen. She loved talking the whole time. I don't know how she managed breathing through the workout and speaking at the same time. Maybe she was a genie. "No, not really. He stopped by the shop a few days ago but I was busy."

"Right...binge watching Project Runway. You need to talk to him."

"And say what exactly? That I'm madly in love with him?"

"Are you madly in love with him?"

My sneakers made a squishing sound in the wet sand. It was like the beach was trying to make me admit the truth. "I don't know. Maybe. But it doesn't really matter."

"Of course it matters."

"I'm not going to set myself up to be hurt again." I tried to focus on my stride.

"That's kind of what taking a chance at love is. Putting yourself out there even though it might end up with you getting hurt."

I sighed and my pace seemed to slow. "And that's why I'm just going to avoid love completely." If I couldn't have J.J., there wasn't anyone else I wanted anyway. There was an impenetrable iron wall around my heart now. Period.

"And what about your date tonight?"

"It's not a date." At least, it wasn't to me. Maybe it was to Reggie. I never should have agreed to go with him. What had I been thinking?

"Are you sure about that? It kinda seemed like he asked you out."

"I'm sure." I wasn't, but I had just gotten an amazing idea. A wonderful, terrible, perfect idea. "And you should come. It'll be more fun if you're there."

"I was going to call in for another shift…"

"Come on. It'll be fun."

"Being a third wheel is never fun. But…I do kind of want to go. I just didn't have anyone to go with."

I suddenly felt really guilty. I should have turned Reggie down days ago and just asked Kristen to go with me. What had I been thinking? I wasn't the only one in a love pickle. The lifeguard she had been dating turned out to be an asshole too. With a girlfriend no less. And here I was, trying to throw a pity party for one when it could easily be two. "Then come with us! Pretty please?"

She laughed. "You're sure it's okay? Reggie won't be weirded out?"

"Of course! I mean, of course he won't be weirded out and of course it's okay." It would at least help me avoid an awkward conversation with Reggie. I couldn't go on a real date with him. All I did was think about J.J. It wouldn't be fair. Besides, it would be more fun if Kristen came. Maybe she and Reggie would hit it off. In a strange way, I was actually doing them both a favor. I had sworn off love, but Kristen hadn't. This was going to be perfect.

"Is J.J. going to be there?"

My pace was starting to slow as a cramp spread along my left abdomen. I wasn't sure if it was caused by running or thinking about my lifeguard. I missed him. And I hated how much I missed him. But I had no way of talking to him. I couldn't just show up at his apartment. I didn't want to walk in on him with the blonde girl. Or some other girl. I couldn't take that again.

"Earth to Mila."

"What? Oh...I'm not sure. We never talked about it."

"Well, fingers crossed he is. Although I love this new energetic version of you, the last time I saw you really smile was after one of your many hang out sessions with him."

"That's not true. See?" I plastered a huge smile on my face.

She laughed. "Stop. That's a terrible grimace."

"It is not." I took a huge gulp of air. "Fine, it is, but it's only because I have a cramp the size of Mount Helena."

"Fine, let's head back. We need the rest of the day to get ready." She started running backward, which she swore worked out different muscles.

I didn't need to work out different muscles. The ones I was focusing on were sore enough. "It's 8 a.m. at the latest right now. And the party doesn't start until five."

"Exactly, we gotta hurry. Race you!" She turned around and started sprinting.

"But it's a beach party! We're supposed to dress casually!"

She started running faster.

Kill me now. Who knew volleyball players were like machines? "Wait up!"

***

I knew it was getting close to when Reggie was supposed to pick me up, but I still wasn't dressed. Mostly I had been procrastinating by brooding over whether or not to tell him that Kristen would be coming too. But there were only a few minutes left before he'd arrive. It was too late. I'd just spring it on him. It would be fine.

I pulled on the lacy red tank top that Kristen had helped me pick out earlier. Now that it was time to actually leave the apartment, I wasn't sure how I felt about how low-cut it was and how it showed off my stomach. It was a little...over the top in a bad, slutty way. And this date was supposed to be anything but sexy.

But…maybe J.J. would be there. And maybe, just maybe, this shirt would be his wake-up call. I quickly pulled on a pair of low-rise jean shorts over my bikini bottoms and slid into a pair of flip flops.

My makeup had been done over an hour ago, thanks to Kristen. Which was good because she had been hogging the bathroom ever since.

The knock on the door made my stomach drop. I really should have told him about Kristen in advance. "He's here!" I called toward the closed bathroom door.

"I'll be out in one sec!" she called back.

I walked over to the door and opened it very slowly. Like horror movie slowly because I was hoping Kristen would pop out and face the awkwardness with me. No such luck. "Hey," I said when the door was finally open.

"Hey, Mila." Reggie smiled at me. "You look amazing."

I could feel my face flushing because I had a feeling he was just saying that because my tits were everywhere. "Thanks. You clean up well yourself." And he did. He was wearing khaki shorts and a blue polo. His face was freshly shaved. He looked really handsome. If I wasn't hung up on the unattainable J.J., today would have been so much fun. As soon as I thought it, I realized how unfair that was. Today could still be really great. Maybe Reggie was secretly the man of my dreams. Or at the very least, the man of Kristen's dreams. She had dated the wrong lifeguard before…Reggie could be the right one.

"You ready to go?" he asked.

"Mhm. But Kristen will just be another minute. She's almost ready though." *Smooth. Don't introduce her at all, just pretend she was always part of the plan.*

"Kristen?"

"Yeah, my roommate. I thought we could all head down together."

"Oh, okay. That makes sense."

Does it? Great!

"Hey, sorry it took me so long!" Kristen practically ran out of the bathroom. I had at least attempted to hide my bikini under clothes. Kristen, on the other hand, was embracing the fact that she had great boobs. She was wearing a push-up bikini and a teensy tiny sarong coverup around her waist. I felt immediately inadequate. But also great, because my outfit that I thought was slutty was apparently not.

"Hi, I'm Kristen," she put her hand out for Reggie.

He smiled and shook it. "Reggie."

"Nice to meet you. Thanks for letting me join you guys tonight. I know it was super last minute."

Reggie glanced at me and then back at her. "Oh um…yeah, no problem. You ladies ready to head out?"

"Yup." Kristen walked past both of us and outside. I closed the door and locked it.

Reggie cleared his throat. "So…is it just the two of you that live there?"

"Yes, we got so lucky. Well, I got lucky. Mila was in need of a roomie and I was in need of a place. It was a match made in heaven."

"That is lucky," he said. "I live in that big apartment down the boardwalk and I have three other roommates. It's always hectic."

"Oh...do you live close to J.J.?" I asked.

His eyebrows lowered slightly when he turned to me. "He lives down the hall from me. A bunch of the life-guards live in that building actually."

"I didn't know you were a lifeguard," Kristen said.

"Yeah, Mila didn't tell you?"

"She mentioned that you played football with her. And that you were really bad, but that's about it."

He laughed.

"I did not say that." If Reggie wasn't standing between us, I would have hit her. "I just told her we lost."

Kristen shrugged. "Logical conclusion then."

He turned back to me and smiled.

I noticed how he seemed more intent on looking at me than Kristen. I never knew with my lifeguard, but it was very clear with Reggie that this was supposed to be a date. It was refreshing. I thought I no longer knew the difference. But at the same time, it also made me feel hor-rible. He seemed really nice and he was definitely cute. But I had a thing for tall, dark, and handsome idiots.

"I don't know if Kristen plays any football, but she plays volleyball and she's a seriously amazing runner," I said. "She runs like five miles every morning."

"Oh really?" He turned back to her. "I run every morning too."

"On the beach or the boardwalk?" she asked.

"The beach of course. Running in the sand is an even better workout."

"I know! I can't believe how many people I see running on the boardwalk. Amateurs."

They were definitely hitting it off. I was starting to like running, but they were on a whole different level. I mean...what was wrong with running on the boardwalk? At least you wouldn't get sand in your shoes.

"Well that was easy to find, I probably didn't really need an escort," I said as we stepped onto the boardwalk. The music could be heard as soon as I had exited my apartment. It would have been impossible to miss it. A huge stage had been erected on the beach and there was a live band playing music. At 8 a.m. none of this had been here. It was impressive how fast they'd put it together.

"Yeah, well, I wanted to make sure I got to see you again." Reggie smiled at me.

Stop it. "Psh. But I sucked at football. Like...hard."

"You don't suck at football. It was ridiculously unfair that they put J.J. on you. He's one of the best players."

I sighed at the mention of J.J.'s name. And over the fact that Reggie was staring at me instead of Kristen again. "So where do you two want to sit?" I asked.

"Oh." Reggie glanced at Kristen and then back at me. "The three of us? Well..." He looked around the crowd as we walked toward the stage.

I had technically told him Kristen would just be walking down to the party with us. I could tell he was confused, but couldn't he see that he had more in common with Kristen?

There were at least a couple hundred people already there, sitting on blankets and beach chairs, and dancing near the stage. One extra person on our kind of date seemed perfectly normal in the chaos. Plus, I was going to flip it so that I was the third wheel.

"Sorry, I should have thought to bring a blanket," Reggie said.

"That's okay. We don't mind sitting in the sand." I immediately sat down. *See, I'm a weirdo who sits in the sand. Like my friend instead of me!*

"Do you want something to drink?" he asked. "I mean…either of you?" He glanced at Kristen.

I knew he was searching for clarity in this awkwardness, but I didn't know what to do. "I'll just have one of whatever you're having," I said.

"Same," Kristen said. "Here I have some cash…" she started rummaging around in her purse.

"I got it. I'll be right back." He disappeared into the crowd.

Kristen sat down next to me. "Yeah…this is a date. And I'm totally in the way."

"It's not and you're not. Actually…I think the two of you could make a cute couple."

"First you make me awkwardly crash your date and now you want me to steal your date? Have you lost your mind? I'm leaving." She started to stand up.

I grabbed her arm and pulled her back into the sand. "Please don't leave."

"I'm third-wheeling so hard right now and I hate it."

"God, I swear it's not a date," I said. "I barely know him."

"That's what dates are for, Mila. It's a chance to get to know each other."

"So…he'll get to know you instead."

"You are the worst," Kristen said.

I laughed.

She shook her head and started laughing too. "I hate you."

"You love me."

"No, I hate you," she said.

"Please don't leave."

"You're forcing me to be the opposite of a wingman. I should have taken that shift." She started laughing again. "You're insane, you do know that, right?"

I stuck my bottom lip out at her.

"Put that away." She pressed her hand against my face, making us both laugh again. "So what exactly was your plan here?"

I shrugged. "I don't know...I thought maybe it would be good for me to go on a date with someone new. J.J. clearly isn't into me like that. But now that I'm here? I just miss him."

She sighed. "Fine, I'll stay and be a total cockblocker. You're lucky that Reggie is really cute. But here's the new plan...we need to find J.J. If you're going to spend all night being awkward anyway, you might as well be making J.J. jealous."

"I don't know..."

"Give that dirtbag a taste of his own medicine."

"He's not a dirtbag."

"Actually, he kinda is. He's the reason my girl is always sad. So tonight we're going to flip the script on him. Do you see him anywhere?" She started scanning the crowd. "I'm going to go look. I'll be right back." She disappeared into the crowd.

Instead of looking for J.J., I stared down at the sand. This was a bad idea. A really bad idea. I already felt guilty for trying to force Reggie and Kristen together. But using Reggie to make J.J. jealous? This was a mess. And even if I did do it...J.J. wasn't going to change his mind about me. We were destined to be friend-zoned forever.

"Mila!" someone shouted.

Speak of the devil. I looked up at my lifeguard. He was holding two shot glasses and smiling as he wove through the crowd. He sat down next to me in the sand.

"I was hoping you'd show up. Here," he said as he handed me one of the shots and tapped his cup against mine. He downed his shot.

He hoped I'd show up? If he hoped I'd come, why hadn't he asked me himself? "Hi, J.J." I tried not to wince at the burn in my throat as I drank my shot.

"I came by the ice cream shop yesterday but your friend said you had left early because you weren't feeling well. I guess you're doing better now?"

"Oh, yeah. I'm feeling better now. Are you here with someone?" Pushing him away always felt like the easiest solution.

"All my friends are over there. Come hang out with us."

I didn't want to hang out with him and all his friends. That always just ended up with him flirting with some other girl. Kristen's voice was in the back of my head, urging me to go forward with the plan. And then I saw her in this distance walking back toward us. She had both her thumbs up, thinking I was already partaking in it. I took a deep breath. What was the worst that could happen? "I'll ask Reggie what he wants to do when he gets back."

"Reggie?"

"Your friend from touch football. He'll be back in a second, he was getting us drinks."

"Wait, are you here *with* Reggie?"

"Yeah, I wouldn't have known about the party if he hadn't told me about it. That would have sucked to miss out on all this fun." This was literally torture.

"I was going to invite you, but you were avoiding me again. Every time I stopped by Sweet Cravings you either sent me away or were missing."

"I wasn't avoiding you. Besides, I didn't want to interfere with any of your plans with that blonde girl you've been hanging out with. Actually, she's looking for you right now." I gestured to her. She was staring at us.

He looked over at her. "We're just friends."

"Oh…like us?"

"No, not like…what, are you here with Reggie because you're mad at me?" He started laughing. "Come on, let's go dance. Stop being weird."

"Hey, J.J." Reggie was holding three cups and looking down at us. He looked kind of pissed.

How much of that conversation did he hear?

"Hey, man." J.J. stood up. "The rest of us are over there." He pointed to a group of people nearby. "Come on."

I looked up at Reggie. "I don't mind staying here, if you want."

"Nah, let's go over." He handed me one of the cups and put his hand out for me. After he helped me to my feet, he kept his fingers intertwined with mine.

Now J.J. was the one who looked pissed. We followed him over to the other lifeguards.

"Hey, Mila?" Reggie stopped me a few feet away from everyone.

"Yeah?"

"Does J.J. know that you guys aren't dating? He looks like he wants to kill me."

I took a sip of my drink. It was strong. "Honestly, I told him I liked him a little while ago and he said he just wanted to be friends." I shrugged.

"Do you still like him?"

"It doesn't really matter. Nothing's going to happen between us."

"Gotcha." He took a long sip from his cup as he stared at me. "And your friend Kristen?"

I saw Kristen a few feet away absolutely eavesdropping.

"I wasn't sure I was ready to go on a date so I asked her if she'd come along. Actually, I think you two have more in common than we do. But it was also her idea to try to make J.J. jealous."

"What?" She closed the distance between us. "That's not fair, you roped me into this mess. This craziness is all your doing."

I was relieved when Reggie laughed. He handed Kristen her drink.

"Well your diabolical plan is working," he said. "J.J. seems really jealous right now."

I looked over my shoulder at J.J. He did seem pretty mad.

"I'm sorry, Reggie. I didn't mean to drag you into this. I'm just going to go." *I'm such an asshole. What is wrong with me?* I still liked J.J. I should have never agreed to this date.

"I can help you if you want."

"What?"

"If you're trying to make him jealous, I'll play along."

Kristen squealed. "Ah, that makes this so much easier!"

"I can't make him jealous," I said. "He doesn't like me."

"He does like you. He couldn't keep his hands off you during the football game. And as soon as he heard you were here with me, he got pissed."

"Why are you helping me?"

"Um...because this is going to be fun. It'll be great, I'll act like a real asshole and hit on both of you all night long right in front of him. It's only a matter of time before he'll swoop in and save you from me. Or until he gets all self-righteous and snaps."

"Oh, fun," Kristen said. "This is third-wheeling done oh so right."

I laughed. I was already feeling slightly buzzed. Could this plan really work? I wanted my lifeguard to notice me. Me flirting with a guy who was flirting with someone else? Confusing and possibly a perfect plan.

"Besides, if I'm lucky one of you will actually like me at the end of the night. I'm a much better catch than J.J."

Kristen laughed. "I'm totally in. Here's to a fun night." She held up her glass. Reggie did the same.

"I guess we'll see where the night goes."

"Cheers to that," Reggie said. We all clinked our glasses together. Not really, because plastic doesn't clink. But it was the principle of the thing.

Reggie slung his arms over both our shoulders. I didn't feel guilty about agreeing to the date anymore. It seemed like he was having the time of his life.

"Um...how's it going over here?" J.J. asked. He looked at Reggie's arms wrapped about Kristen and me. His eyebrows pulled together. It already looked like he was going to snap.

"Great," Kristen kissed Reggie's cheek and whispered something in his ear before she stepped away from him. "You must be the infamous J.J." She put her hand out for him. "I'm Kristen."

"Ah, Kristen. I've heard a lot about you."

Kristen laughed. "Good things I hope?"

He nodded. "You've been taking up a lot of my girl's time recently."

My girl? Did he think I was his girl? If he thought that...why the hell was he letting Kristen know and not me? I downed the rest of my drink.

"Let's go dance," Reggie whispered in my ear. "Kristen said she'd join us in a minute. It's the perfect time to start our plan." He grabbed my hand and pulled me closer to the stage. He twirled me around and his hands slid to my waist. He was a really good dancer.

Out of the corner of my eye I could see J.J. glaring at us. Kristen was still talking to him, but it looked like he had stopped paying attention. He said something to her and then walked over to the blonde girl. He grabbed her hand and pulled her to the dance floor. She immediately started grinding against him.

"Yeah, you should probably dance like that with me too," Reggie whispered in my ear.

I turned around and arched my back slightly. It looked like J.J. was going to explode.

Kristen came out and joined us. "This is going well," she said as she started shaking her hips. "He's so mad, Mila. He was barely listening to anything I said." She pulled Reggie away from me and ran her fingertips down his abs. She was a much better dancer than me.

I started dancing by myself, hoping that the alcohol made me better than usual. It must have, because I noticed the way J.J. stared at me instead of the girl he was dancing with. And then he'd glance over at Reggie and Kristen and it looked like his eyes were throwing daggers. Jealous and possessive? This was totally going to work. Reggie and Kristen were freaking evil geniuses.

The DJ cut the music just when Reggie started dancing with me again.

"Okay! Who's ready for the bikini contest?!" The DJ yelled in the microphone.

Everyone started cheering.

"We still need a few more participants. So sexy ladies, make your way to the stage if you want a shot at winning the grand prize!" The music started back up.

"You should totally enter that," Reggie said.

"What?" I started laughing. "I'm not doing that."

"Really, Mila. All those guys looking at you? It's going to drive J.J. insane. You gotta enter that contest."

"I can't."

"Ah, you have to, Mila!" Kristen said. "Reggie's right, it's going to drive J.J. crazy."

I shook my head.

"Here." He grabbed my hand and Kristen's and led us over to the bar. He ordered three shots.

"Reggie..."

He lifted one up. "Come on."

I sighed. "This isn't going to make me do it." I downed my shot, but Reggie was still holding his. "You forgot to drink yours."

"I think you're going to need this one too." He handed it to me.

I downed it and looked at him. "You can get me completely drunk and I still won't enter that contest."

"This one too," Kristen said and tried to hand me hers.

"This is peer pressure."

Kristen nodded her head toward the dance floor. I turned around. J.J. had his hands all over the blonde girl. He whispered something in her ear and she started laughing.

"Okay, I'll do it," I said. I grabbed Kristen's shot and downed it too.

"Really?" Reggie asked.

"Wait, should I not?" Making J.J. jealous clearly wasn't enough. Maybe doing this competition would be the last straw. I didn't want to completely break our friendship.

"No, you should," Reggie said. "I just didn't think you'd give in that easily."

"I'm going to need one more shot."

"You got it." He ordered another round. He was smiling at me.

"What?"

"I've never convinced a girl to take her clothes off so easily."

I laughed and pushed his arm. "It's a bikini contest, not a striptease. But thanks for your help." I kissed his cheek.

"He really is the best." Kristen kissed his cheek too.

I hoped that J.J. was watching us now.

"Are you sure you want that last drink? You're awfully flirtatious when you're drunk," Kristen said. "Sometimes in a bad way."

"I know, but I need it." I lifted the glass and downed my last shot. I drummed my hands on the bar. "Okay, wish me luck, guys."

"You don't need it." Reggie smiled at me as he wrapped his arm around Kristen. She sat on his lap. She was really good at acting.

"Knock him dead!" Kristen called after me.

CHAPTER 18
Monday

I was so nervous. I had never done anything like this before. The first few girls had already walked up on stage to the cheers of the crowd. They were all much more well-endowed than me in all the right places. Kristen would have been a better fit for this contest. I was about to run in the opposite direction when I spotted my lifeguard in the crowd. He was standing with a few of his male friends, the blonde girl nowhere near him. I wondered where she went.

Kristen was standing a few feet away from J.J. She gave me two thumbs up. I gave one weak one back, hoping it didn't look like I was about to piss myself.

"You'll have to take off your shirt and shorts," a woman said to me who was standing by the stage directing the other girls. "It's a *bikini* contest. The judges need to see you in your *bikini*," she added, like I was dense. Maybe the other girls on stage needed it explained to them five times, but the idea was pretty straightforward to me. A bikini contest meant showing off your bikini.

"Right." I unbuttoned my shorts. *Can I really do this?* Any confidence I had when I came back here had suddenly disappeared. But seeing J.J. had made the flight response searing in my brain come to a halt. Sure, he'd probably just tease me about this afterward. Or maybe...he'd finally see me the way I wanted him to see me.

"Actually, do it on stage. Everyone will get a kick out of that. Like a striptease, minus the actual stripping."

I buttoned my shorts back up. *I can't pretend strip on stage! Fuck, I can't do this.* I was about to bolt when the woman grabbed my arm.

"Okay, you're up." She directed me toward the stage. It felt a little forceful, but only because I had been stepping in the opposite direction.

"I don't think I..."

"You'll do great." She lightly pushed me up the steps.

Shit. I couldn't *not* do it now. I was already halfway up the stage. I took a deep breath and walked up the last few stairs. The stage was slightly blurry. *I'm so drunk.* Or maybe I was about to blackout from nerves. I didn't even like when professors took attendance and I had to say "Here." What had I been thinking agreeing to this?

I walked toward the middle of the stage and stopped. All I could see was J.J. He smiled at me. I had finally gotten his attention. I needed this to work. I didn't have any more tricks up my sleeve. And I wasn't wearing sleeves for that matter, so this was my one and only shot.

"Take it off!" someone yelled.

J.J.'s smile faded. He turned his head toward whoever had said it.

I needed him to look at *me* again. I slowly pulled my shirt off over my head and tossed it toward him in the crowd. He looked back at me just in time to catch it. His lips were slightly parted. He was shocked by what I was doing. Was that good?

My semi-striptease had gotten a few whistles and hollers from the crowd. Even though I was still wearing my bikini top, I felt so exposed. But J.J.'s eyes were glued on me. I couldn't stop now. I unbuttoned my shorts and turned to the side. I arched my back and bent forward slightly as I let the fabric slide down my hips and to the floor. I kicked my shorts toward J.J. He had to take a few steps forward and snatch them away from some random guy.

I was glad I was wearing my nicest bikini. I twirled around during the applause. This was actually super fun. Why had I been so scared? I was a natural stripper. Well, down to my bathing suit, not my birthday suit. I'd never actually strip.

"Let's hear it again for Mila!" the announcer yelled, which caused even more applause.

I walked over to the other girls standing to the side of the stage.

"Such a good move," one of them whispered to me. "I wish I had thought of that. You're totally going to win."

I smiled to myself. I had J.J.'s attention for the rest of the competition. He didn't even look at the other girls. But I couldn't tell what he was thinking. He looked kind of...pissed.

"Okay! All the votes are in!" said the announcer. "And the runner up is Mila!"

What? Oh my God.

"You've just won a 100 dollar gift certificate to Salt Air!"

I just stood there.

"Mila, come claim your prize!"

I walked over to the announcer and grabbed the gift certificate. It was so surreal. I looked out at the crowd but

J.J. was gone. *Shit.* I didn't even listen to who the winner was as I quickly got off the stage. A bunch of guys crowded around me, blocking my path. *Fuck. Where is J.J.?*

"You were awesome up there," one of the guys said.

"Thanks." I tried to see around them, but they were all taller than me.

"So, are you seeing anyone? I'd love to take you out to dinner sometime."

"Yes, I am," I lied. "Sorry, if you'll excuse me."

But none of them moved.

"Let me at least buy you a drink," one of them said.

I'd honestly had quite enough to drink. And if I was going to do anything else tonight with anyone…it would be with my lifeguard. I tried to sidestep the guys again, but none of them moved.

"Excuse me," I said.

"Oh, come on." The one that had offered me a drink put his meaty hand on my shoulder.

I suddenly felt claustrophobic. "Get off of me."

"Don't be like that…"

"She said to stop fucking touching her." J.J. stepped through the crowd and shoved the guy who had his hand on my shoulder.

Before anyone else could react, J.J. grabbed my hand and pulled me away from them and through the crowd of people.

"J.J."

He didn't say anything. He just kept leading me away from the party.

"J.J.!"

He ignored me again.

When we were well past all the spectators, I pulled my hand away from him. "What the hell are you doing?"

He turned around. "What the hell am I doing? What the hell are you doing?!" He grabbed my hand again. "I'm taking you home. You're drunk."

"I'm not drunk!" Maybe I was, but that wasn't why I had entered the contest. I just wanted him to notice me. "You're acting like you've never seen me in a bikini before. News flash…half the people at that party were just in their bikinis."

He ignored me.

"What, you can just go around flirting with everyone, but if I do it, you get upset? You're such a hypocrite." I pulled my hand away from him again and walked past him.

"I'm not flirting with anyone else."

"You flirt with everyone, J.J.!" I yelled and turned around. "You keep leading me on and then pushing me away."

"That's not true." His blues eyes were smoldering.

"Being just friends was *your* idea. I told you I wanted more. So you don't get to be jealous if I talk to someone else!"

"You think I'm jealous that you had your hands all over Reggie? Who's a fucking prick by the way. He was clearly hitting on your friend too. And you think I'm jealous that a hundred guys were watching you do a fucking strip show on stage? I'm not jealous. I'm protective of you. There's a huge difference."

Protective. Like an older brother. I felt like he'd punched me in the gut. I couldn't do this anymore. "Goodnight, J.J."

He stepped closer to me before I could turn away from him. "What do you think would have happened if I hadn't pulled you away?"

"Nothing. There were hundreds of people around."

"Don't be so naïve, Mila. I just saved you from getting taken advantage of." He threw my clothes that he had caught during my performance at me.

I let them fall into the sand. "Taken advantage of? I can take care of myself. I don't need a knight in shining armor who doesn't even like me. If you don't like the way I act, tough luck. Deal with it. Either you want me or you don't. And obviously you don't. You don't need to take me home. Go back to the party."

He gripped my wrist. "That's not fair, Mila, and you know it."

"Life isn't fair, J.J. Look, I get it, okay. I know why you don't want to be with me." I could feel tears prickling my eyes. "I'm not like that girl you were dancing with. I get it. I'm not your type."

"I don't fucking like Jenn. I was dancing with her because you invited some other guy to this party. You should have come with me."

"You didn't invite me!"

"Because you were avoiding me."

"Because I like you, okay! I like you as more than a friend. I can't help it. And every time we hang out, I like you more and more. So do me a favor and stop talking to me. I can't do this anymore. I can't be your friend. Because it hurts like hell that you don't feel the same way."

"Damn it, Mila. You're leaving in less than two months."

"Right, there's no point in starting something. You've already told me that. So let's just stop whatever this is now and save each other the trouble. Go be with Jenn or whatever you said her name was. Go have meaningless sex, because that's what you like, right? You just want an escape from whatever it is you're so worried about with your job? I'm not stopping you. I don't want any part of that."

"That's low. I made some mistakes, but you have no fucking right to judge me. You dated some asshole for over two years just so you wouldn't be alone in California. That's pathetic. And then you came crawling back home to escape from him when things went south. You're hiding from your problems too. More than I am. And you think a new relationship will fix whatever self-doubt you have going on? Well it won't."

I wiped my tears with the back of my hand. *Shit.* "Thanks for finally telling me how you really feel about me." I shook out of his grip. "Have a nice life, asshole." I turned around and started to walk away.

"Mila. I'm sorry. I didn't mean..."

I turned back around. "I didn't want a relationship with you to fix my problems. I wanted one because I like you. I didn't want to miss out on whatever time we had to be together. But everything that's happened between us all makes a lot more sense now. I'm glad you don't want to be with me." I swallowed hard. He was looking at me so intently. No one had ever looked at me like that before. Like he wanted to devour me and strangle me at the same time.

"Mila."

I took another step back. "You don't know me at all. I'm not pathetic. I know myself better now than I did before this summer started. I'm not hiding out here. I'm figuring out what I want out of life, and there's nothing wrong with that. Maybe you should take some time to do the same."

He closed the distance between us. "You clearly don't know me as well as you think you do." He grabbed both sides of my face and kissed me hard.

Fuck. I laced my fingers in his hair as his tongue collided with mine. I should have been pushing him away instead of drawing him closer. But I had been dreaming of kissing him again for what felt like forever. And he tasted even better than I remembered. I didn't realize that anger could taste so sweet.

His hands slid down my back as he grabbed my ass and lifted my legs around him. I clung to him, hoping I could hold on to whatever momentary peace treaty this was forever. His words stung. But the thought of actually walking away from him stung a thousand times worse.

He knelt down and pushed my back against the sand. "I've wanted you ever since I first laid eyes on you." He spread my thighs and kissed one of the spots where I'd been stung.

"J.J.," I panted.

He pushed my bathing suit bottom to the side. "You've been driving me fucking crazy." He thrust a finger deep inside of me.

"Oh God." I tilted my head back.

"And now I'm going to return the favor." He curved his finger, hitting me in a spot I didn't even know existed.

I arched my back and moaned.

He pulled hard on my bathing suit bottom, making the strings on either side untie. "I've been waiting a lifetime to taste you."

Taste me? "J.J., someone's going to see us."

He bent down and placed a long, slow stroke against my aching pussy.

Holy shit! I no longer cared that there were people in the distance. I just wanted more. I wanted all of him.

He spread my thighs even farther apart and thrust his tongue deep inside of me.

I moaned again. I didn't care that we were close to the party. All I could focus on was his breath between my thighs.

His tongue swirled around my wetness, massaging me in the most intimate way. I began to climb higher and higher as his tongue continued its torturous rhythm.

I grabbed the back of his head so he'd go even deeper. He responded by rubbing his nose against my clit.

"J.J.," I moaned.

He placed one last stroke against my wetness and moved his head to my stomach.

"No," I groaned. "I'm so close."

He kissed my stomach gently, leaving a trail of kisses up between my breasts. "It's my turn to drive you crazy, Mila." He tugged on my bathing suit top and pulled it down, exposing my hard nipples. He placed his lips around my nipple and sucked hard.

I felt my back arch again. I needed him deep inside of me. "Please. Please, J.J."

I could feel him smile against my breast. He took my other nipple between his fingers and squeezed it as he continued to suck on the other one.

"J.J.," I panted.

"I love when you moan my name." His hand slid down my stomach and his fingers brushed against my clit before plunging deep inside me again.

Fuck. I turned my head, pressing my cheek into the sand.

He moved his hand fast, making me climb again. I was going to come any second. I felt myself begin to clench around him.

He quickly removed his fingers.

"J.J. Please. Please, I need you."

He looked down at me as he slid his fingers into his mouth, sucking off my juices. "I need you too."

Holy shit.

He slowly pulled off his shirt, revealing his perfectly sculpted torso. He was so sexy. I watched him unbutton his shorts and push down his boxers. His erection sprung free. He had the biggest cock I had ever seen. I wanted to know what he felt like inside of me.

"I want you," he said as he looked down at me. "I've wanted you for so long."

"I want you too." I could feel my heart racing. I couldn't believe this was actually happening.

He pulled a condom out of his wallet and slowly slid it onto his length. I could hear myself panting in anticipation. He grabbed my ass, lifted my lower back off the sand, and thrust his cock deep inside of me.

"Fuck, you're so tight," he moaned. He slowly slid his length in and out of me as he lowered my back onto the sand.

I had never felt anything so good in my life. I ran my hands down his strong back and grabbed his ass. Even his ass was muscular. "Harder," I moaned.

"You're a fucking miracle, Mila." He grabbed my thighs and thrust himself deep inside of me. He moved his hips faster and faster. "Is this what you want?"

"Yes!" I moaned. *God, yes.*

His fingers dug into my skin as he moved even faster. They burned even more than the sand against my back, in the best way possible.

I didn't want this to end. I still didn't know what he wanted between us. But I was going to come any second. I couldn't control it. Sex had never felt this amazing before. Normally I'd be analyzing every single touch. Every single groan from his mouth. But all I could think about was how right this felt. And how perfectly our bodies seemed to fit together.

A loud bang sounded in the distance. I could feel myself clench around him.

J.J. groaned in response.

Fireworks lit up the night sky.

One of J.J.'s hands slipped to my ass as he leaned down to kiss me. He squeezed my ass hard and thrust his length even deeper inside of me.

Oh God.

"Come for me, Mila." He lightly bit my lip.

And I shattered. Hard. "J.J.," I moaned. My toes curled. With each bang of the fireworks it felt like another wave of release washed over me.

J.J. groaned as he found his own release.

And then we just stared at each other, our chests rising and falling with our rapid breaths, his cock still deep inside of me. I couldn't read him at all. Was that regret in his eyes? Something else?

He reached out and tucked a loose strand of hair behind my ear, before pulling out of me and collapsing beside me in the sand. The silence stretched even longer.

"I don't want to play games anymore," he finally said.

I looked over at him. He was staring up at the fireworks in the sky. "Me either."

He turned his head to look at me again. "I'm really sorry about what I said. I was upset, I didn't mean it."

"I'm sorry too. But it led to what just happened and that was kind of…"

"Amazing."

I smiled. "Yeah. Amazing."

He slowly sat up. "We should get dressed before we get caught. He pulled on his shorts and V-neck t-shirt and then looked around for where my clothes had fallen. When he found them a few feet away, he tossed them to me. "Geez, I feel like there's sand all over me," he said.

I laughed as I retied the strings of my bikini and pulled on my clothes. "Well, we did just roll around in it."

He pulled me back down into the sand, making me laugh again. I adjusted myself so that I was sitting between his legs, my back resting against his torso. I was finally exactly where I wanted to be.

He pushed my hair to the side and kissed the back of my neck as he wrapped his arms around me. The fireworks lit up the sky.

CHAPTER 19
Tuesday

I had never woken up smiling to a hangover. But the pain in my head didn't even compare to the butterflies in my stomach. Just thinking about my lifeguard left me breathless. I ran my fingers across my lips where he had kissed me. I had never been so excited to see someone again in my life. And I couldn't even contain my excitement. "Kristen!" I yelled as I sat up. "You won't believe what happened last night!"

But there was no response. I glanced over to her empty bed. My smile couldn't possibly get any bigger. If she hadn't come back, that meant that she and Reggie had actually hit it off. Which meant...yesterday had kind of been the perfect day.

I grabbed my phone to see if she had texted me. I did have one waiting from...*crap*. Aiden. As I was staring at the unread message icon, debating whether or not to even open it, his name lit up on my screen. He was calling me. *Again*.

I dropped my phone on the bed and pulled my legs into my chest. *Shit*. I took a deep breath. The butterflies in my stomach were replaced by knots. Why was he still calling me? I closed my eyes until the buzzing stopped.

As soon as the silence returned, I opened my eyes again. I had finally given my number to J.J. and I was hoping he'd be the one calling me this morning. Part of me wanted to answer my phone when Aiden called so that I could tell him that I was seeing someone else. That would feel so satisfying. I wanted to tell him off. But I couldn't do that. My lifeguard and I hadn't talked about what we were now. All I knew was that we were more than friends. We were clearly more than friends. I smiled to myself.

My phone bleeped, letting me know I had a new unread text. I grabbed it and opened the texts from Aiden, ready to delete him out of my phone and my life.

It was just the two: "Are you up yet?" and "I really need to see you."

I deleted both messages and then found his name in my contact list. My finger hovered for a second. He wasn't allowed to need me. I wasn't his to need. He certainly hadn't needed me for the past few months. And he definitely hadn't wanted me. I was glad I was all the way across the country. If he had shown up to my dorm room, I'm sure I would have heard him out. I had been so weak for so long. I deleted him from my contacts and breathed a sigh of relief. There wasn't a doubt in my mind that I was better without him.

I jumped out of bed, grabbed two Tylenol, and downed them with a glass of water. Everything was different now. Just because Aiden didn't want me didn't mean there was anything wrong with me. He was just an asshole. The fight that my lifeguard and I had last night came back in my mind. I bit my lip. He had said I was pathetic for latching onto Aiden in the first place. Was he right? Honestly, he probably was. I left Cali for all the wrong reasons. Maybe I'd be staying in Delaware for all the right ones though. I glanced at my phone again. I hadn't heard back from admissions yet, but I still needed to call my dad and tell him to hold off on tuition. But now was not that time. I wanted to just think about J.J. and how happy I was. All the crappy men in my life like my dad and Aiden could suck it.

I opened a drawer and pulled out a sports bra and shorts. I may have been pathetic freshman year of college. But now? Hell no. And I certainly wasn't going to wait around all day for a text from J.J. to come through. I needed to make sure I didn't make the same mistakes I had when I was with Aiden. And just because Kristen was out shagging her new lifeguard, it didn't mean I couldn't go for a run.

***

Even after my scalding hot shower, my body was still sore. I had run as far as I possibly could before collapsing in the sand. The walk home had taken forever, but it was relaxing staring out at the water. I wasn't sure I had ever run so far in my life. Although, I was sore for more reasons than that. I felt my face flush, remembering last night. And I couldn't help but wonder if we'd be repeating that anytime soon. Fingers crossed we would.

I pulled my towel around myself and walked out of the bathroom to see if Kristen was back. But after a quick glance, I knew she was still missing. I thought back to when she reprimanded me for not coming home one night and leaving her wondering if I was dead in a ditch. It was a two-way street. I picked up my phone to see if she'd messaged me and smiled. There was no word from her. But there was one from an unknown number. My lifeguard had finally texted me while I was in the shower. I added his number to my phone and then clicked on his message.

"I'll be picking you up after work. And you better not be planning on pretending you're busy and running away from me. Or changing up your schedule again to try to ditch me."

I smiled. There was something sexy about him just telling me our plans instead of asking. And the fact that he didn't even say it was J.J. He was just confident enough to know that he was the only man in my life. I typed out a response as I headed back into the bathroom. "I would never. What did you have in mind for tonight?" I grabbed my hairdryer and started to blow my hair dry. For some reason I was nervous to see him. I hoped he still felt the same way he had last night. When I switched the blow dryer off, I had another message from him.

"Bring a bathing suit."

So much for drying my hair. But I didn't even care. There was no better sight in the world than J.J. in his swim trunks.

"Deal," I wrote back. "I'll see you at five." Now all that stood in between me and J.J. was a boring shift at work. I quickly put on some waterproof mascara that I hoped would withstand whatever we'd be doing tonight, and pulled on a pair of jean shorts and a tank top. After tossing a bathing suit into my bag, I was out the door in less than a minute.

The morning and afternoon did not go quite as quickly. First, I had been incredibly early for my shift because there was a pep in my step. And then I got paired up with Becca again who wouldn't stop talking. I'd excused myself an hour ago to put my bathing suit on under my clothes. I was hoping J.J. might come save me early. But I knew his shift ended around the same time as mine. So no such luck. I never thought I'd miss my previous co-worker who liked to spend her whole shift talking to her boyfriend in the storage room.

"I can't believe you got second place," Becca said. "That was so cool!"

"Mhm." I scrubbed down the counter for what felt like the millionth time.

"I tried to find you after to congratulate you, but you were gone. Did you go straight home?"

I felt my face flushing. "Yup." Just thinking about J.J.'s hands and mouth made me start to feel all sweaty. God, I wanted him again.

"So, so awesome," Becca said. "I don't know how you had the confidence to go up on that stage. I never could have done it."

I stopped scrubbing the counter and looked over at her. "Of course you could have."

She shook her head.

I finally felt like there was something we actually had in common. "The only person that can hold you back is you, Becca."

"I guess that's true."

"Trust me. I've been doing it my whole life."

"And now?"

I finally saw my lifeguard approaching. "And now I'm on team me."

She followed my gaze. "Or are you on team hot life-guard?"

I smiled. "I think they might be the same team."

"Really? You're dating *him*?"

I didn't really know what we were. But I'm sure we'd talk about it more tonight. "We haven't really had that talk yet."

"You're so lucky." It was like she hadn't even heard my response.

A month ago I felt like the unluckiest girl in the world. But now my life had done a 180. I did feel lucky.

"Hey," J.J. said as he leaned against the counter. His eyes traveled to my lips for the briefest moment. "Any chance you can skip out a few minutes early?"

"Yes!" Becca practically screamed next to me.

I glanced over at her and laughed. She was clearly as awestruck by J.J. as I was. "Thanks, Becca. Are you working tomorrow's day shift too?"

She nodded.

"I'll see you then." I pulled off my apron and left as quickly as possible so that J.J. wouldn't notice Becca drooling. But before I stepped out of the little shop, Keira and Rory walked in.

For a second I froze. I was about to skip out early and my bosses had caught me red-handed. But instead of reprimanding me, Keira just elbowed Rory in his side and then winked at me. Why was she winking at me?

"I'm sorry," I said. "I was just..."

"It's fine." She waved her hand through the air. "Just for the record...I totally predicted this. Now go have fun with your lifeguard." She winked again.

My lifeguard. I laughed. I guess there was no sense in making up some lame excuse. Keira didn't seem to care that I was leaving a few minutes earlier. She just seemed happy for me. Which made me smile. "Thanks."

As I pushed through the door, a bout of nerves hit me. Would J.J. kiss me hello? Would he hug me? Would I try to hold my hand? Would he not touch me at all?

"Hey," I said quietly as I stepped out into the sun.

He smiled brightly. Seeing his smile immediately calmed my nerves. It was proof that he had enjoyed last night as much as me. He didn't wake up regretting what had happened either.

Instead of giving myself an opportunity to do anything weird, I just started to walk. As I passed him, he immediately slipped his hand in mine. I tightened my fingers around his and swallowed all the words rolling around in my head. Especially the "I missed you" that kept threatening to spill out.

We walked in silence, hand in hand down the boardwalk. It was already pretty busy since the 4th of July crowd was mostly still in town. I was trying to look anywhere but at him when he started talking. And I swore he said he missed me, but I couldn't be certain. I looked up at him. "What did you say?"

"I said I missed you today, Jellyfish Girl. I'm used to you being at the beach with me on Tuesdays."

My heart felt like it was going to explode. He had said no more games last night. So why was I keeping what I wanted to say locked up? "I missed you too. I'd spend every second with you if I could." *Oh crap, too honest?*

But he just smiled.

God, I wanted to kiss his perfect lips again.

When we turned down the street that his apartment was on, I was relieved to get away from the crowds. But then with each step closer to his apartment, my heart started to beat faster. J.J. had told me to bring a swimsuit. Which meant we were either heading down to the beach in a bit, or his pool. He did not say we were going to have super hot sex again. But I couldn't help but think we'd be doing that too.

He didn't say a word to me as we walked into his building. Or as the elevator doors slid open. Or when we stepped on.

But soon as the doors closed, he leaned against the side of the elevator and pulled me against him. His hands trailed down my back and stopped just above my ass. "Hey," he said. His voice sounded so sexy. Maybe he had no intention of swimming or going to the beach. I could feel his erection through his swim trunks. Maybe we were just going to have mind-blowing sex all night instead.

I smiled up at him. I wasn't going to protest that at all. I closed my eyes and tilted my head up so that he'd kiss me.

Instead he ran the tip of his nose down the length of mine. For some reason it felt even more intimate than a kiss. I opened my eyes. He was staring at me so intently, our noses a fraction of an inch away from touching again. I was completely lost in his blue eyes.

"Everyone's already up at the pool," he said. "I'm glad I have a new chicken fighting partner. We're going to crush them."

It took me a second to process what he was saying. "Oh, fun." All I wanted to do was press the button to stop the elevator and jump his bones. But he had told me what he was inviting me over for. I just hadn't realized his friends would be a part of it. He lived with his friends, though. Of course they'd be here.

But they were all at the pool. Which meant his apartment was currently empty.

"Actually, I need to use the bathroom real quick," he said and pressed the button for his floor.

"Yeah, me too." I wasn't sure why I said it. I didn't have to use the restroom. But really I just wanted to be alone with him in his apartment. Apparently that was what he wanted too. Or maybe he actually had to pee.

The elevator doors opened a second later, so I didn't have time to analyze the way he was looking at me. I watched him unlock his door. I wanted to be forward. But if he actually had to take a piss, he'd make fun of me. I bit my lip and walked into his apartment. The lights were off, but the sun was streaming in through the closed curtains.

I heard the door lock behind me. I gulped. He flipped the switch and the room was flooded in light.

"I don't actually need to go to the bathroom," I said. It was easier to be bold when I wasn't staring directly at him.

J.J. wrapped his arms around me from behind and kissed the side of my neck. "Me either." And I knew he wasn't lying. I could feel his erection pressing against the small of my back now. He pushed the bottom of my tank top up, pressing his palms against my skin.

"Aren't your friends waiting for us?"

He continued to push my tank top up until his hands reached my bikini top. He massaged my breasts through the thin fabric. "Would you be mad if I told you I was just trying to get you alone?"

I laughed, but my laugh quickly turned to a moan as his fingers found my nipples.

He untied my bikini top and pushed it and my tank top up. I lifted my arms and let him trace my skin with his fingertips as he pulled them both off. They fell to the floor. Last time I had lost my top in his apartment, I had covered myself. This time, I kept my arms to my side. I wanted him to see me. And I wanted to see him.

"You could have just come to my place if you wanted to be alone with me," I said as his fingers ran down my stomach. My whole body felt alive.

"Ever since I saw you in my room, I can't stop thinking about having you naked on my bed."

I gulped.

"And I'm barely ever alone here. I wanted to take advantage of this opportunity." He undid the button on my jeans shorts and pushed them and my bathing suit bottoms down over my hips. They fell down my legs. His fingers trailed back up the insides of my thighs. One hand continued up to my breast, but the other stayed between my thighs, inching closer and closer to where I was aching for his touch.

I moaned when his fingers brushed across my wetness.

"You're so wet for me, Mila." His breath was hot against my neck. His finger encircled me, teasing me.

I moaned at his dirty words. But my moan quickly turned into a squeal when he lifted me over his shoulder and carried me to his room. There were so many things we still needed to talk about. But for just a few moments, I wanted to feel instead of think. He placed me on the edge of his bed. I wasn't sure where he'd lost his swim trunks, but he thrust deep inside of me, my name on his lips.

Maybe I'd just feel instead of think for the rest of my life.

CHAPTER 20
Tuesday

"Even better than my dreams," he whispered before placing a kiss on the top of my head. Normally I'd laugh at a comment like that. Or think it was just some line. But he sounded so sincere. Besides, I had dreamed about him too. Too many times to count. And it was better than I'd ever imagined.

I let my head rise and fall with his breath, listening to his rapid heartbeat. His bed was so much more comfortable than mine. Or maybe it was just the fact that he was in it with me. All the questions about what we were doing were still rolling around in my head, threatening to spill out. I swallowed them back down. I was not going to be the one to ruin this perfect post-sex bliss. I tried to focus on his heart racing again.

"What are you thinking?" he asked as he trailed his fingers lazily up and down my back.

That we're running out of time and I need to make the most of every second. "Nothing." I lifted my head off his chest so I could stare at him. "What are you thinking?" His answer was way more important to me.

"That we should have done this sooner." He smiled, but the brightness didn't quite reach his eyes.

Because we're running out of time. Delaware was less long distance than California. But I didn't want to tell him that I might be transferring until I at least talked to my dad about it. I'd call him soon. As soon as I got up the courage to hear his voice and not let whatever he said bother me. *Fat chance.* But I had to do it. I was thinking I could wait until I heard back from the University of New Castle, but it was taking longer than I expected. And I didn't want my dad to send the money to SMU by accident.

I was glad J.J. popped the bubble instead of me. I was even happier that he was as content as me. I smiled down at him, hoping that it looked more sincere than his. "Better late than never. Aren't your friends waiting for us at the pool?"

"Unless you'd rather stay in bed?"

I laughed and sat up. "Oh, I'd definitely rather stay here with you all night. But you promised me we'd win a chicken fight and that's what I intend to do." I slid off the bed. I really did love winning. Besides, I was a little curious about how he'd act around all those hot girls he usually hung out with now that we were dating. Or…fucking. Or…I didn't know what we were. But it felt big and important to me. The kind of important that meant I would 100 percent not be flirting with any other guys. This would at least let me know that he felt the same way. And maybe give me the extra boost of confidence I needed in order to call my dad later.

By the time we reached the pool, the chicken fighting had already begun.

"We'll join the next round," J.J. said as he pulled me toward the pool. The wonderful feeling of his hand in mine wasn't enough to distract me from looking for the blonde girl that J.J. had been dancing with yesterday. Jenn,

I think he said her name was. That was a lie…I definitely knew her name. It was seared into my brain just like the way he danced with her was. It wasn't hard to spot her. She was one of the last two people who hadn't been knocked into the water this round. And she was battling…Kristen?

"Kristen?" I called.

Kristen turned her head. The distraction was enough for Jenn to knock her backward off Reggie's shoulders.

She resurfaced in a fit of laughter. "So unfair! I demand a rematch. Mila distracted me. Are you coming in?" she asked me.

"Mhm." I was happy she was here. Just surprised that neither she nor J.J. had mentioned it. I kicked off my flip flops. "You didn't tell me Kristen was here," I said to J.J.

"I didn't know." But he wasn't focused on me or Kristen when he said it. I felt my stomach turn as I started to follow his gaze. I breathed a sigh of relief when he wasn't ogling Jenn. He was staring daggers at Reggie instead. I should have come clean right then and there about how Reggie had helped me out last night. But diving into the pool seemed a lot easier. So I chose that route instead, letting his hand slide out of mine.

J.J. splashed water all over me when I resurfaced to his cannonball.

I laughed as he pulled me into his arms. I wrapped my legs around his waist, not caring that we were surrounded by people. Apparently he didn't care that we were around other people either.

"I told you that Reggie was a dick," he said.

I sighed. I needed to tell him. Hopefully he wouldn't be too mad. I was about to open my mouth when Kristen swam over to us.

"Sorry I didn't text you last night," she said. "I stayed at the party really late and ended up crashing at Reggie's."

Crashing definitely meant banging. I wondered if she did the Thanksgiving turkey thing. Luckily that hadn't come up with J.J. yet. "That's okay." I'd lecture her later about murderers and rapists and the importance of texting your besties. Kids these days.

"I see the plan worked," Reggie said as he joined Kristen at her side.

Oh crap.

"What plan?" J.J. asked.

Before I could figure out the best way to word it, Reggie filled in the blanks.

"The getting J.J. to stop being an idiot and notice Mila plan. I pretended to flirt with Kristen and Mila all night to make you jealous. Although, my flirtations with Kristen ended up being very much real." He kissed her cheek.

I wanted to focus on how adorable they were, but I was a little preoccupied by J.J.'s face, waiting for his reaction. I was surprised when he started laughing. The breath I didn't realize I'd been holding finally escaped.

Everyone around us seemed to vanish when J.J. turned back to me, his hands drifted farther down my back. "I guess I was being an idiot, huh?"

"Just a little dense."

He smiled. "All your scheming worked then."

Technically, J.J. had claimed he wasn't jealous last night. Just protective of me. But the getting us together part? That had absolutely worked. I nodded.

"I admit that I was an idiot...but I always noticed you, Jellyfish Girl."

My heart felt like it was going to burst.

"I guess I owe you a thank you," he said to Reggie.

"No problem," he said. "It ended up working out for both of us." He pulled Kristen into his side. Her smile was so big it was contagious.

"You guys ready to play?" one of J.J.'s other friends called over to us.

"We're in!" J.J. called before turning back to Reggie. "And just because I'm thankful, it doesn't mean you two aren't going down," he said with a laugh.

"Oh, it's on," Reggie said.

J.J. went under water, maneuvering himself underneath my thighs. I laughed when he stood back up. He was so tall that in the shallow end I wasn't anywhere close to touching the water anymore. I leaned forward to try to keep my balance. He turned his head and kissed my inner thigh. "You ready?" he asked me.

I wasn't. I was super distracted by his mouth. And his wet hair that was dripping onto my legs in a way that I never knew would be so erotic. Yeah...this was not going to go well.

***

It turns out that I wasn't the best at chicken fighting even when I tried really hard to focus on the game instead of J.J. But I really did have a great night. To my delight, I don't think J.J. even looked at Jenn once. He was as smitten as me. And I wouldn't be able to get the smile off my face even if I wanted to.

"Ah, it's freezing!" I yelled when we finally got out of the pool. The breeze from the ocean was always chillier at night.

J.J. grabbed a towel and wrapped it around me. There was something sweet about that, especially because it left him shivering for longer when he had to go get another one.

"Do you want some pizza?" he asked. His friends had ordered Grottos and it had just arrived steaming hot from the boardwalk. It was late, but never too late for cheesy goodness.

"Is all you eat pizza?" I wasn't complaining, I was just curious. I picked up a slice before he even responded and took a bite. *Delicious.*

"And ice cream." He winked at me. "I really do need to learn how to make something other than cereal though."

I laughed. "I can teach you…if you want. I love cooking. Although the last time I made pizza, it didn't turn out so well. I still can't believe rentals don't have…."

"Rolling pins," he said, finishing my sentence. "Yeah, you mentioned that before. Was that one of the many nights that I was being dense and you were mad at me?"

"No…just disappointed."

He laughed. "Well, here's to not disappointing you anymore." He tapped his slice of pizza against mine.

I smiled.

"Here, you gotta see this view." He used his hand that wasn't holding a slice of pizza to guide me to the edge of the roof.

"This view is amazing. I wish we could stay here forever." But I didn't really mean at the beach. I glanced at J.J. out of the corner of my eye. I meant with him.

Time felt like it was frozen still as he turned to look at me. "Me too."

Why did it already feel like goodbye when our summer together had only just started? I cleared my throat. "What do you want to do this weekend?" Even though the weekend was still far away, it was just far enough away that he might not already have plans like this with his friends. I was hoping we could do something just us.

He wrapped his arm more securely around me as we stared down at the crashing waves. "How about something just the two of us?"

I leaned my head against his shoulder. It was like he could read my mind. "That sounds perfect. Oh." I looked up at him. "How about we go to Salt Air? I won that gift card. It can be my treat."

"Are you that sick of pizza?" he said with a laugh.

"No, but I think a night out would be fun. We can eat and drink and dance."

"You won't turn me down like you did yesterday when I asked you to dance?"

I laughed. "I wanted you to ask me because you really wanted to…not because you were being *protective*."

"You say protective like it's a bad thing."

"Is it so wrong that I wanted you to be jealous? Just a little bit?"

"People are jealous when they want something that isn't theirs. I was protective because you already possessed me. I was already yours. And you were already mine."

I turned to look up at him, the view of his blue eyes so much better than the sea itself. "You wanted to protect what's yours?" The wind from the ocean blew my hair into my face.

He pushed it back, drawing my lips up to his. But his lips stopped a fraction of an inch from mine. "I haven't stopped thinking about you ever since I first saw you on the beach. Even before I knew your name was Jellyfish Girl." He closed the distance between us. A slow kiss that took my breath away.

I'm his. And he's mine. God, his answer was simply amazing. I had been worried about asking him what he meant by protective instead of jealous. But listening to his answer made my knees weak. Everything he said was so romantic. He pulled away far too soon.

"You're a great kisser," I mumbled. I thought it was incoherent, but J.J. smiled.

"Oh, really? I could have sworn after our first kiss you said, 'It wasn't even a good kiss.' Which really shattered my confidence."

I lightly hit his arm. "I was upset. But…it wasn't technically a lie…"

He raised both his eyebrows. "Ouch. Are you trying to wound me?"

I laughed and stood up on my tiptoes. "I wasn't lying because it was a great kiss, not a good one." I wrapped my arms behind his neck and kissed him again. His hands slid to my ass, not a care in the world that his friends were nearby. Yup, my assessment was right. J.J. was a *great* kiss-er.

CHAPTER 21
Saturday

"I can spend the night at Reggie's again if you want to bring J.J. back here," Kristen said as we ran along the beach. She'd been spending most nights this week with him. Like I'd been spending most nights with J.J.

"That sounds great."

She laughed. I wasn't sure how she could laugh after running so many miles. I could barely even breathe.

"I like it," she said. "You don't hesitate anymore. You know what you want and you just go for it. I think I'm wearing off on you."

I tried to smile, but I'm sure it came out as more of a grimace because of my cramp. "Well, in that case...I'd love to turn around. The couch has my name on it. I want to make a stack of pancakes so high that the syrup drips down the sides in that picture-perfect way. And while I'm stuffing my face with sugary goodness, we can look for Swatch on Project Runway."

"Oh...yeah. Let's do that. I'm pretty sure just the thought gave me a sugar orgasm." She laughed again as we turned around. "Have you told J.J. about transferring yet?"

That was the weirdest segue ever. My mind was still stuck on syrup. "No, not yet."

"What are you waiting for?"

"I haven't heard back from admissions yet. Plus I need to talk to my dad about tuition. I've been putting it off because whenever I call him it always makes me sad. But I'm going to call him today, I swear. Right after I go into a carb coma."

"Why does calling him make you sad?"

I splashed through a wave that had come up a little higher in the sand. "Promise you won't judge me?"

"When have I ever judged you?"

"You always judge me." I gave her a hard stare.

She responded by rolling her eyes. "Never. So spill it."

"I don't know." I focused on my breathing for a minute. "He always seems so happy," I finally said.

"And that makes you sad?"

I nodded, but I wasn't sure she had seen it. "Happier than he was with me and my mom." *And he never asks how I am.* Not once. Not even after the divorce. Maybe because he knew the answer. I missed him and he didn't miss me back.

She didn't say anything. "Well, I'm happy with you. And I'm certainly not looking to replace you any time soon."

I smiled. "Thanks, Kristen."

She nudged me with her shoulder. "Race ya back to our stud Swatch and pancakes!" She took off like lightning.

Kill me now.

***

I stared down at the cracks on my cell phone screen. It was easier to look at them then the string of missed calls from an unknown number. *Probably Aiden. Definitely Aiden.* And it was easier than finding my dad in my contact list and actually going through with the call. But I had to do it. I wanted to come home. I wanted to be less than three hours away from J.J. by car. Not a six hour plane ride away. Long distance was easier when you were closer, right? That had to be a thing. I could even take the train up to New York and do homework the whole time. It would be kind of perfect.

I took a deep breath and swiped my finger across the screen. Ignoring the missed calls, I pressed on my dad's number and pulled my cell phone to my ear before I could chicken out. It rang a few times and went to voicemail.

There was no way I was leaving a message and then waiting around on pins and needles. I hung up the phone. I'd try his house phone. He'd told me before not to call their house phone. He didn't say why, but I had a pretty good hunch. His wife Nancy hated being reminded that I existed. If she had her way, I would be completely erased from the family. More so than I already had been.

The phone rang a few times. I started drumming my fingertips along my thigh. Please, someone pick up. I hoped it was either my dad or one of my half-sisters. Then I wouldn't be reprimanded for ruining Nancy's day. Right before I thought it might switch to voicemail, someone picked up.

"Hello? Wilson residence," said an overly chipper voice.

I could tell it was his wife. Every other female in the house had high-pitched children's voices. And they weren't quite as fake friendly as hers. "Um. Hi, Nancy. It's Mila. Is my dad home?"

"Oh." The chipper tone was immediately gone. "Mila. One second, I'll get Dale."

I heard her yell for my father, letting him know it was me.

"He can't talk for long though, Mila, okay? He's playing with *our* girls."

The way she said it was so snooty I wished I could reach through the phone and slap her stupid face.

"Yeah…I understand." I did. She was telling me not to cross her. I just didn't understand why talking to my father bothered her so damn much. He was mine before he was hers. And she clearly won. My dad hated me as much as she did now. I wasn't a threat to her perfect little family.

There was a muffled noise as the phone switched hands. And then I heard my father's voice. "One second, pumpkin."

I put my hand to my chest. I couldn't even remember the last time my dad called me that. But it was definitely sometime before he moved out. Maybe I'd been too hard on him. Maybe he did miss me too. I was about to say, no problem, Dad, but he started talking again.

"I'm sorry, pumpkin, but Daddy's on the phone. We can play in just a minute. It won't take long, I promise." He cleared his throat. "Hi, Mila. Sorry about that, Emma and I were in the middle of a game of Candy Land."

He hadn't been talking to me when he said pumpkin. He was talking to my youngest half-sister. "You're playing Candy Land?" I asked, trying not to sound hurt.

"Yes. It's a board game." His voice was so formal.

I knew what Candy Land was. I wasn't surprised by the game, I was just surprised that *he* was playing it. My dad had never played games like that with me growing up. He'd always wished I was a boy. He taught me how to play football, swing a baseball bat, and shoot a basket. He didn't play Candy Land. Why was he suddenly so content with having daughters? He was 21 years too late. "Oh," was the only thing I could think of to say. "How are you? How are Emma and Isabella?"

"We're all good. Nancy too."

I pressed my lips together. Of course he'd focus on the fact that I hadn't asked about Nancy. But I'd just talked to her. I could tell she was good. She was as uptight and bitchy as ever. "Great," I gritted through my teeth. "What have you been up to?" Why was small talk with him so painful?

"We just got back from vacation yesterday and are re-couping this weekend."

Recouping from a vacation? Why was that necessary? "Where did you go?"

"Down to Galveston with the whole family."

The whole family? What about me? I blinked, telling my impending tears to fuck off. "That sounds fun."

"It was."

I waited for him to ask how I was. Where I was. What I was doing. If I was going on any vacations this summer. Anything. But of course he didn't. He didn't even know I was at the beach we always came to as a family when I was younger.

"I know, pumpkin," his voice sounded a little farther away. "Just another minute, okay?"

He was trying to get rid of me. Talking to Emma the way he used to talk to me again. Didn't he realize how much that hurt me? Didn't he care at all? I gripped my phone a little tighter. The answer to my question was pretty obvious. He didn't care one ounce about me. He hadn't for years.

"I should probably go," he said. "It was nice chatting with you."

Seriously? We'd been on the phone for less than a few minutes and hadn't talked about anything. We hadn't spoken in months. Despite what he wanted, I wasn't invisible. He couldn't pretend I didn't exist the way Nancy always did. "Dad," I said before he could hang up on me. I hated the way my voice cracked when I called him Dad. "I'm trying to transfer to the University of New Castle. I haven't heard back from admissions yet, but can you hold off on sending payment through to SMU? Until I hear back?"

"SMU is a good school."

"It is. But I wasn't happy there. I want to come home." *Ask me why I wasn't happy there. Ask me if I'm okay now. Ask me anything.*

"You mean to *Delaware*, right?"

Don't worry, I don't mean home to you. "Of course. I'm actually already back in town at the beach we used to come to when I was little."

"Oh."

I waited for him to recall the good times with me. Any times with me. But he didn't.

"Well in that case, that's fine," he said. "Whatever you want. Just send me an email when you hear. It's easier that way." *AKA don't call me again.*

"Why is that easier? Because Nancy hates when I call? I tried your cell phone but you didn't pick up."

"It's off. I told you, we're recouping this weekend. Just taking some family time."

"And what am I?"

"You know what I meant," he said.

No. I didn't. Instead of saying anything at all, I just wiped under my eyes, not knowing when the tears had started to fall.

"And speaking of Nancy, the two of us had a discussion. We need to start saving for our girls' future. So this year of tuition will be the last thing we're footing the bill for. So just be aware in case you lose some credits in the transfer. And make plans accordingly for after graduation."

Our girls. The fact that I wasn't one of them was blatantly clear. He was finally cutting me off. I wasn't surprised. Right after the divorce he threw money and gifts at me, like that made up for the lack of him showing up. But it had gotten less and less over the years. The only thing he paid for now was my tuition. I figured this would happen soon anyway. And I wasn't even surprised by the way he worded it, like this was the last time he was ever going to talk to me. He was finally erasing me from his new perfect life, like I was just a bag of garbage he could toss away. "Okay." My voice sounded small. All I wanted to do was scream obscenities at him. Instead, I said okay. Nothing about this conversation was okay.

"Great," he said. "I'm glad you understand."

"Yeah, I definitely understand."

"I should be getting back."

"Go for it."

"Oh, and Mila?"

"Yes?" I let a small piece of me feel hopeful. But just a small part. Because my dad had stomped on my heart so many times I'd lost count.

"When I said we'd only pay for this last year of tuition that really did mean *just* the tuition. We'll be switching over to a new phone plan at the end of the month and we won't be transferring your number. That gives you some time to make the appropriate arrangements."

I forgot that he also paid for my shattered cell phone. *Great.* "Not a problem," I said. I could pick up a few extra shifts at Sweet Cravings. Besides, he'd always been wrong about the money and gifts. They didn't fill the void of him not being around. They made me feel cheap and unwanted. And I didn't need his fucking handouts. I didn't need him in my life at all. I was as done as he was.

"Have a good summer, Mila."

I wished he meant it. I wished his words didn't have the double meaning, because all I heard was that he didn't want to hear from me for at least the rest of the summer. But most of all, I wished my father wasn't such a dick. I think I hated him more than I hated Aiden. And that was really saying something. "You too, Dad." *I hope the rest of your life is everything you want it to be. But it won't include me anymore.* I hung up the phone. I tried to wipe my tears away, but they kept falling.

I'd wasted so many years of my life trying to be enough for him to love me. Why wasn't I enough? Why was I never enough? His new family wasn't better than me. They were just shiny and new. He'd probably get bored again in a few years and break all their hearts too. I felt a little better knowing that his assholeness had nothing to do with me and everything to do with him.

I took a deep breath and got up off my bed. I was done being a steppingstone. Anyone who didn't want me in their life? It was a two-way street. I didn't want them either. And I didn't need to wait till the end of the month to rip the Band-Aid off. There was a cell phone store at the end of the boardwalk. I'd get a new phone right now. A new number. And cut all the toxicity out of my life for good.

CHAPTER 22
Saturday

Two hours later, I was walking out into the sunshine with a brand new phone. About 30 minutes into standing around and waiting to be helped, I had considered coming back. Saturday afternoon probably wasn't the best day to go. Especially since I had Tuesdays and Thursdays off, which had to be less busy. But at that point I had already waited a while. Besides, now it was done. And two hours was a short amount of time to waste given the fact that I'd wasted 21 years on my dad. Now I was free. I wasn't even going to give him my new number. Not that he'd be missing it...he never called me anyway.

I pulled out my phone from the bag and squinted at the screen in the sun. It was an older model than the one I used to have, but it was surely just as good. It's not like I needed all the new fancy camera functions. I wasn't exactly the type that was taking selfies for Instagram nonstop like the girls I had just passed on the boardwalk.

The tech guy helping me had tried to transfer all my contacts into my new phone and I practically had to tear it out of his fingers. I didn't need all my old contacts. All I needed my phone for was communicating with three people – my mom, Kristen, and J.J. That was it. And by communicating, obviously I meant texting because calling people was the worst thing ever. Phone calls should have been un-invented years ago, if un-inventing things was a thing. *And voice mails. Don't even get me started on the demonic ways of voicemails. Anyone who leaves voicemails should be bitch-slapped into next week by the phone they used to commit such a heinous crime.*

I pulled out the piece of paper I'd scribbled my important numbers on, which had caused quite the eye roll from the tech guy, and put them into my new phone. And then I shot off three texts, letting the only three nice people in my life know how to contact me now.

Kristen responded immediately. "New phone? Exciting! But do you know what's more exciting? The package that showed up an hour ago with your name on. Get your ass home before I give in and open it myself!"

I thought about what on earth it could be as I walked down the boardwalk. But it only took me a few seconds to realize what it probably was. Well, there were two options really. Either it was anything I'd left at my dad's house that he wanted to get rid of, which may have been one book or something else small. I'd never even had my own room at his new house. Whenever I'd visited when I was younger, I was always sent to the guest room. *How fitting since that's how he views me.* I was too naïve to realize it at the time. I'd just considered the room temporarily mine since I didn't live there. For years I'd always given him the benefit of the doubt when I should have been throwing hot coffee in his face on a daily basis.

The other option for a surprise package wasn't quite as insulting. Maybe it was the stuff I'd asked Aiden to ship back to me. If that was the case, it was good news. It meant I got all my stuff back and that he was most likely done calling me nonstop. I smiled to myself. He couldn't call me anymore even if he wanted to. I had a new number. Win win all around. And if it was my stuff from his apartment, that meant I could wear that cute dress I'd left in his closet. Otherwise I'd surely be squeezed into God knows what of Kristen's. Not that she had too much time to torture me. J.J. was supposed to come pick me up in less than an hour.

I walked up the steps to my apartment. As I rummaged around in my purse for my keys, the door flung open.

"You have to see what's inside before I die!" Kristen said as she thrust the box into my hands.

It wasn't what I was expecting at all. There was no mailing or return address. And it wasn't a standard brown shipping box. It looked more like a clothing box but it was wrapped in a sparkly white wrapping paper with a pink satin bow.

"How do you even know it's for me?" I asked. I had never gotten a present wrapped so elegantly before. Not even for my sweet sixteen. Kristen was probably wrong. It was probably dropped off at the wrong house.

"Oh. That. One sec." Kristen disappeared into our apartment.

I kicked the door closed and followed her.

"It came with a note." She handed it to me.

"You read it?"

"Don't look at me like that. It's not freaking mail fraud, it didn't even come via the post office. The present was just sitting on the front step when I got back from work. So I *had* to look. How else would I have known it wasn't for me?"

Fair point. "So who is it from?"

"See for yourself."

I opened up the envelope, ignoring the broken seal from my nosy roommate. I smiled as I read the words.

You said you had nowhere to wear it. Now you do.
-Your lifeguard

Your lifeguard. I pulled the note to my chest. I had no idea what the card was referring to, but the butterflies had erupted in my stomach. I felt like I might be flown away with how fast they were flapping. J.J. was the sweetest man on the planet.

"Freaking open it!" Kristen begged.

I laughed and tugged on the satin bow. It felt so expensive between my fingers. He hadn't started his fancy new job yet, and I hoped he wasn't spending money he didn't have. I tore the wrapping paper and lifted the lid to the box.

I could feel tears welling in my eyes. It was the beautiful blue dress I'd been looking at when we'd gone shopping together. It was sexy and over the top and ridiculously expensive and...the nicest thing I would have ever worn. *You said you had nowhere to wear it. Now you do.* I blinked faster so I wouldn't start crying. He had said we were just friends when we'd gone shopping. But he remembered the dress I'd been looking at and that I said I had nothing to wear it to. He'd been paying such close attention to me and I'd been completely unaware. I ran my hand across the fabric before lifting the dress out of the box.

"Wow. That color is stunning," Kristen said.

The same color as his eyes.

"And that dress is sexy as sin. And…" her hand hesitated on the price tag. "Jesus, is he loaded?"

"No. I don't know." I shook my head. "I mean…I don't think so."

"Well, he has expensive taste." She winked at me. "It looks like there's something else in the box."

I glanced back down. It did look like there was something else beneath the tissue paper. I pushed the paper to the side and looked down at a rolling pin. *Oh my God, he really does understand me.* I smiled and picked up the second note.

You keep talking about rolling pins and I have no idea if it's some sexual innuendo I don't get or if you really want one for actual rolling pin usage. Either way, maybe you can teach me how to use it later.

-Your lifeguard

I could feel my face turning bright red.

Kristen laughed from where she was peering at the note over my shoulder. "What kind of kinky things do you like to do with rolling pins?"

"Nothing!" I slid the note back into its envelope. "I just happened to mention that we didn't have a rolling pin here. For cooking."

"It doesn't seem like that's what he heard."

I laughed. "Then he heard wrong." But my mind was going a mile a minute. I could think of a few sexy things to do with a rolling pin.

"Well I already agreed to give you two the apartment tonight. So you can test out whatever theory you have running around in your head. But..." she drew out the word in a way that I knew she was about to ask for something. And since it was Kristen, I knew it was going to be food related.

"I already made a lasagna this morning. It's in the fridge, just preheat the oven to..." I stopped talking when she scrunched her nose up. I wasn't even sure she knew how to turn on the oven.

"I have an idea," she said. "You pre-heat the oven and all that. And I'll help you get ready. You actually need to wear makeup with a dress like that. And heels! Heels are a must!" She started rummaging around in my closet before I had time to stop her.

But she was right. I didn't want the apartment to catch fire and I did want to look my best tonight. I smiled down at the dress and rolling pin. I was pretty sure that was the nicest present anyone had ever bought me.

***

I twirled around in front of the mirror. The fabric was so light and soft. There was a peephole in the front that showed off the perfect amount of cleavage to leave J.J. drooling. The dress crisscrossed at the neckline and the fabric crossed again in the back, leaving most of the back exposed. It was really sexy. Kristen even introduced me to sticky boobs. Which were basically exactly what they sounded like. A bra that just kinda sticks to your chest with tons of adhesive. They were a Godsend and I didn't know how I had lived without one for so long. Especially since my breasts had never looked better.

Kristen whistled. "You look freaking hot."

My smile was so big it practically hurt. "It's not too much?"

"All this," she waved her hands in front of me, "is perfecto. Tim Gunn would rave. Even Nina Garcia would give you two thumbs up."

"I can't imagine her doing that."

"She would…just once for this ensemble. Swatch would bark in appreciation. The other contestants would swoon."

"You really know how to build up my confidence."

She smiled. "And speaking of moving…did you call your dad?"

Kristen was great at a lot of things, but no one was worse at segues than her. I laughed. "I did."

"And?"

"He doesn't care where I go." *He doesn't care about me.* Thinking about him slashed that ego boost she had just given me. It was hard to think you were amazing when someone treated you like a literal pile of shit.

"Well…that's great! Seriously, I can't imagine going to the University of New Castle without you now."

I knew what she meant. Just thinking about not going gave me a pit in my stomach.

"So are you going to tell J.J. you applied tonight? The cherry on top of your amazing date?"

"That's the plan." We hadn't really given our relationship a label. He told me I was his. And that was wonderfully romantic. But I was his *what* exactly? Girlfriend? Greatest love? Fuck buddy? I ignored my last thought. That was definitely not what we were. Part of me wanted to ask about what would happen to us once the summer ended before I told him about possibly transferring. It would give me a better understanding of where his head was at. But I didn't want to play any more games with him. I'd give him all the information upfront. And hopefully we could agree to not just end this because the seasons changed.

Kristen smiled. "So what else did you and your dad talk about?"

God, I don't want to talk about the king of the dicks before my date. "Not much. He said he was cutting me off financially...hence the new phone."

"Oh." Her smile was gone and it looked like she physically hurt for me. "I thought you just finally bought a new one because the screen was cracked."

"Nope." The "p" in nope popped weirdly. I tried to swallow down the lump in my throat.

"I'm sorry. Don't think about him. Remember your dick diet?"

I laughed, remembering my drunken declaration of avoiding all dicks. "Right. Rule number one, no discussing dicks."

"I doubt that was rule number one, but yes, enough about him," she said. "And more about how amazing you look in that dress!"

I laughed at the same time there was a knock on the door. I rushed over, eager to see the one boy that somehow erased all the bad ones from my mind. The sight of him made the butterflies increase tenfold. He was wearing one of the new outfits we'd picked out together. He had left a few buttons open at the collar which made it look a little more casual. And he'd rolled the sleeves up like I'd shown him, showing off his muscular forearms.

"I knew that dress would look great on you." He stepped forward and kissed my cheek.

I loved the dress. But hearing him say I looked good in it made it my favorite thing ever. I smiled up at him.

"Hey, Kristen," he said over my shoulder. "I'll have her back by..." he glanced at me. "Who am I kidding. I'm hoping to have her out all night."

Kristen laughed. "No need to stay away. I'm heading to Reggie's right after I dive into this delicious lasagna Mila made me. So you'll have our apartment all to yourself tonight so you can try out that rolling pin."

J.J. smiled and looked back at me.

I could feel the heat in his gaze. "Come on," I said, pulling him to the door before Kristen could embarrass me anymore. She was worse than a parent sometimes. "Bye, Kristen!"

"If you hurt my girl, I'll kill you in your sleep," she said as we closed the door.

J.J. laughed again. "She's intense. And...not serious, right?" He touched his throat like he was actually scared she'd slice it in his sleep.

"I don't know." I shrugged and gave him what I hoped was an innocent smile. "If you don't hurt me, you don't have to find out." *Please don't hurt me.*

He caught my hand, stopping me before I could walk down the steps. "I'm not going to hurt you." His other hand moved to the back of my neck.

"Okay." The feeling of his fingers on my skin made it hard to think straight.

He tilted his face closer to mine. "Okay then."

I wasn't even sure what we had been talking about when he started kissing me. And when he finished? I wasn't sure how I was still standing.

CHAPTER 23
Saturday

"What's your poison?" J.J. asked as we made our way to the outdoor bar portion of the restaurant. The hostess was turning over our table so we had a few minutes to spare.

We were both overdressed in this little beach town, and my mind screamed wine. It was the logical choice for a sophisticated night out. But I wasn't really in the mood after downing half a box a couple weeks ago. "Oh! How about a tequila sunrise. Or a Manhattan. Or...no...a cosmopolitan."

He laughed. "Which one do you like the best?"

"I've never had any of them. I thought it might be fun to try something different."

"Well, try whatever you'd like, but I'd recommend sticking to one type of alcohol at a time. We have all summer to sample whatever cocktails you want." He leaned against the bar. "So what will it be?"

He was right. We had all summer. "I'll have a tequila sunrise."

I sat down in one of the stools and watched J.J. flag down the bartender. I was so awkward doing things like that. If he wasn't with me, I probably would have stood there for 30 minutes being ignored and then walked away with nothing.

J.J. handed me the cocktail.

"Oh, it's pretty."

"You didn't even know what it looked like?"

"How was I supposed to know? I've never had one before." I took a sip. "Mmm. It's good too. Do you want to try it?"

He leaned forward and took a sip through the tiny straw. He stuck his tongue out like he was in pain. "It's so sweet."

"Mhm." I took a bigger sip and smiled at him.

He smiled back. "So new phone, huh? I saw that your screen was cracked. What happened to it?"

I wasn't sure if he was asking how I broke it in the first place or if it finally died on me. But I wasn't going to ever not tell J.J. something just because it was uncomfortable. I wanted to have a real relationship with him, not a summer fling. Besides, the conversation with my dad was still bothering me. It was nice to have someone who wanted to talk to me about this kind of thing. "The screen was cracked because I threw it at my ex's head when I walked in on him cheating on me. I missed…it hit the wall instead."

"Bad luck."

I laughed. "Yeah. And it was still working but I needed a new number so while I was at the store it just made sense to upgrade. Well, downgrade actually. It's an older model. Phones are freaking expensive."

"I know. I lost my phone back when I was in high school right when smartphones were becoming a thing. I went to the store and they showed me these thousand-dollar phones and I couldn't even believe it. A few years before that there had been free upgrades." He laughed.

"Oh yeah, I remember those! Ugh, I wish that was still a thing."

He leaned a little closer. "So that explains the broken phone, but not the new number. Who are you ghosting?"

I swallowed hard. There was something in his eyes that I was beginning to recognize after our conversation the other night. I would have originally thought it was jealousy. But I knew it wasn't now. He was being protective. And the way he was looking at me made me feel all warm and fuzzy. He was wondering if someone was bothering me. He was trying to help. Unfortunately he couldn't protect me from my own father. I had to learn how to take care of myself around him.

"No one," I said as I took a sip of my drink to clear my head. "The added bonus of my ex not knowing my number is good. But I needed a new phone plan because my dad is cutting me off." I didn't look at him as I said it. Saying it out loud sounded stupid. It was like I was a spoiled brat with my dad cutting up my credit cards. But it wasn't like that. I worked hard for everything I had. The scholarship I'd gotten to SMU paid for more than half of tuition and on-campus housing. I hated asking either of my parents for anything. And I would have taken a hug from my dad over a check in the mail any day. That wasn't in the cards though. Regardless, it still sounded bad. Like I was an entitled asshole.

I kept talking so that J.J. couldn't fill the silence. "It's not a big deal. He has two young daughters with his new wife and apparently he needs to focus all his time and money on them." *You still sound bratty.* "Which makes sense because I'm old enough to take care of myself. They still need him, you know? And he did offer to continue to pay for my last two semesters of school, so I can't complain. I was actually more than happy to change my phone plan. I needed a new phone anyway."

J.J. put his hand on my knee. "When we first met you said he threw money at you instead of love. I could tell it was a big deal when you said it then. And it's a big deal now."

I finally met his eyes and he wasn't looking at me like I was spoiled rotten. He was looking at me like he was sorry that my father was the rotten one.

He shook his head. "And I have to wonder...if he showed love that way, how is he going to step it up now?"

"He's not. He made that pretty clear on the phone." I blinked fast, surprised at how emotional J.J. caring made me. "He does this thing whenever I call...he talks about his family like I'm not a part of it. I've fought it off for a long time, but I'm done trying. He doesn't want me in his new life. So I'm going to give him what he wants."

J.J. lowered his eyebrows like he could feel my pain. "I'm so sorry, Mila."

"It's fine. Really. Our conversation today was a long time coming."

"Anyone who doesn't want you in their life is crazy."

I smiled. "I don't know...you fought me off pretty hard."

He shook his head. "I didn't want to set myself up to get hurt again when I've been burned before. But I realized pretty quickly that you were worth that risk. You're worth any risk, Jellyfish Girl."

"About that." I was looking for the perfect opportunity to tell him I might be transferring. I leaned a little closer to him. The bar was getting more crowded as it got later, but it somehow made it more intimate. "The reason I called my dad today was to tell him to hold off on tuition to SMU. I applied to transfer to the University of New Castle. I'm still waiting to hear back, but…I'm hoping to stay in Delaware this fall."

The smile on his face was so genuine. "Delaware's a lot closer than California."

"It is."

He leaned a little closer too, his eyes dropping to my lips.

"I know we haven't really talked about what we're doing," I said. "And we only just started whatever this is. I applied for myself just as much as I did for us. I get it if you still don't want to do long distance after this summer. We don't even need to talk about it right now. I just…wanted you to know. But if you want to talk about it, I'd be happy to. I don't need to label our relationship or whatever this is. Unless you want to of course."

He took my empty glass from me and set it down on the bar. He absentmindedly spun it around in a circle as he listened to me babble, a smile on his face the whole time. His silence was infuriating.

"And I know I talked about how I needed to take this summer to better myself. And figure out what I want. But there's no reason I can't do that while we're together. It's not like we're going to be together every second. I'm rather independent. Not that I don't want to spend a lot of time with you. I do. I really, really do."

He smiled.

"But I'm in a better place now than I was at the start of this summer anyway. I feel like this weight is off my shoulders. Especially after talking to my dad. If I'd had the conversation I had with him today a few months ago, I would have fallen apart. But I'm fine. Clearly. Did I tell you I can almost run five miles? That's far for me." I heard crickets in my brain. "God, just say something and put me out of my misery."

He let go of the glass and leaned even closer to me. "Across the country would have been hard. But I thought I made my intentions pretty clear the other night."

"You said that I was yours. I don't know what that means."

A smile tugged at the corner of his mouth. "It means I'm not going to pull the plug on us just because the weather changes. I really really want to spend as much time together as we can too."

I smiled at his comment. I knew he was trying to appease me, but it wasn't as simple as time. We were running out of that. "It's more than the weather. Even if I do get into the University of New Castle we'll still be living in different states. You said you didn't do long distance."

"That was before you. And if we have to spend weekdays apart for a year, I can handle that if you can."

"Just weekdays?"

"You'll just be a train ride away. I can swing that."

"So…what does that make us?"

"You're exasperating." He pulled me into his lap, not caring that the restaurant was packed around us. "Jellyfish Girl, will you be my girlfriend?"

"Hmm." I was smiling so much it hurt. "I think I can swing that."

"You can, can you?" He tickled my side sending me into a fit of giggles.

I would have kept laughing if he didn't silence me with a kiss. Everyone around us faded away. It was just me and my lifeguard. *No...my boyfriend.*

"So what are you trying next?" he asked and tapped my glass. The kiss left me dizzy, but he still seemed perfectly composed.

"What else has tequila in it?" I asked.

"Margaritas..."

"Bad idea. I talk too much when I've had margaritas." I pressed my lips together. I hoped that wasn't a general tequila thing. Oh God, it probably was. But the bottom of my glass meant I had already committed to a night of tequila. And who cared if I had loose lips around J.J.? I had been myself around him since the start and he liked me enough to date me.

"Good to know," he said. "That sounds like the perfect drink for you." He waved at the bartender.

"No," I said with a laugh and grabbed his arm. "What else has tequila?"

"Mojitos."

"Oh perfect. Unless...what's in a piña colada?"

He laughed. "That would be rum."

"Ah. I'll just have a mojito then."

I'm pretty sure whenever I tasted tequila from now on I'd think of him.

CHAPTER 24
Saturday

Our fancy date was amazing. We sampled cocktails and talked about everything from what sports he played as a kid to what my favorite book was. But a night out on the town wasn't really us. It made sense that we wound up on the beach, albeit a little tipsier than usual. My high heels dangled from my hand and he'd rolled his pants up so they wouldn't get wet.

"The stars are so bright tonight," I said and spun in a circle. It was hard not to spin in this dress. The skirt lifted in that perfect way. And I felt so giddy and light tonight.

"Beautiful."

I looked over at him. But he wasn't looking at the stars. He was staring at me. "You're cheesy," I said. But I didn't really mean it. His compliment had me smiling so big.

"That doesn't mean you aren't beautiful." He tucked me into his side like I had always belonged there.

"Christmas or Easter?" I asked. We'd been asking each other silly questions like that all night.

"Christmas. The Easter Bunny always used to freak me out."

"Me too! What kind of creep hides out in a bunny costume and lets children sit on his lap? Talk about furries combined with pedophilia."

"Maybe the same creep that dresses up as Santa," J.J. said with a laugh. "Minus the furries thing."

"Huh. I never thought of that before." I wondered if it was the same guy that played both at the mall near my mom's house. It was hard to tell if they were even a similar height because of the big floppy ears and everything.

"I have an idea," he said and looked down at me. "Maybe we can use this game to help you choose a major."

I stared at him skeptically. "Or we can just keep staring at the ocean." I pulled him to a stop and looked out as far as I could see. The water blended with the dark blue sky in the distance. Suddenly I felt so small. Like my major barely mattered. That it didn't have to be the hardest decision in the world. It was just a small choice in the grand scheme of things. But…my mind was still blank. I didn't have a clue what I wanted to be when I grew up, which was starting to get tedious because I was already an adult.

"Accounting or finance?" he asked.

"Umm…" *Just choose. Flip a coin. Leave it to fate.*

"Marketing or econ?"

"Ugh neither."

"Philosophy or sociology?"

"No."

"Political science or whatever a teaching degree is?"

I laughed. "I don't know. Why is deciding what you're going to do for the rest of your life so freaking hard?"

He kissed my temple. "Because the rest of your life is a long time. What if you knew you'd only have to do it for five years? Then what would you choose?"

"None of the above."

J.J. laughed.

"Do you have a coin? Maybe I can just let the fates decide."

"Are you a believer in fate?"

I looked up at him. A few months ago, the answer would have been an easy no. But now? I had wound up on the other side of the country next to his lifeguard stand for a reason. It was like we needed each other. Maybe I was here to show him that long distance could work. And he was here to show me that not all men were utter garbage. If we hadn't met, would I still be hung up on Aiden? Would he still be scared of commitment? "I think when life is good, it's easy to believe in fate. But when it's bad, it's a little trickier."

"So right now?" He tucked a loose strand of hair behind my ear. It immediately blew back in my face from the light ocean breeze.

I smiled up at him. "Right now I'm a huge believer. What about you?"

"There were so many ways in which this summer could have played out differently where we never would have met. I mean, you could have stayed in Cali. I could have gone straight to New York. I'm just happy we're standing right here together."

I stood on my tiptoes and kissed him. "We were a long shot. But I'm kind of liking our odds now."

"Me too. So let's both be believers in fate. Flip a coin. What major would be heads and which one would be tails?"

"God, I can't even narrow it down to two."

He laughed.

"I know I have to figure it out. But nothing seems as glamorous as staying here." We both stared out at the water. The stars reflecting on the surface shimmered in the night.

He sighed. "Tell me about it."

"I just want to stop time and stay in our little Rehoboth bubble forever."

"Well, you said forever. So it's not a commitment issue."

I looked up at him. "No, it's not a commitment issue. I just don't know if I've tried the right major yet. And now I'm running out of time."

"Hmmm. Engineering or math?"

I laughed.

"I'll help you figure it out this summer. I promise." He pulled me closer, resting his chin on the top of my head.

I'd spent my whole life trying to figure it out. But he seemed rather sure of himself. And I believed his promises. When his arms were around me, I felt so safe and secure. I pressed the side of my face against his chest. His heartbeat was the only sound I loved more than the ocean.

We stood like that for a long time. His arms wrapped tightly around me, both of us staring out at the water.

"Is it ridiculous that I'm starving?" he asked. "The portions at that fancy restaurant were so freaking small."

I laughed. "I have the perfect thing for that." I grabbed his hand and led him back up to the boardwalk. We made our way through the Saturday night crowds.

My apartment was dark as we walked up the wooden steps. Kristen had kept her promise to spend the night out, and the thought made my heart race. I was going to be alone with J.J. all night. That was a first for us. For the past few nights I had crashed at his place, but his roommates were always around. I didn't even know if he'd want to spend the night. Maybe he preferred to sleep alone in his own bed. Or maybe he did something really weird in his sleep like yell profanities or sleepwalk naked. Honestly the last one didn't sound so bad to me. It would give me time to really study his body without him even realizing I was staring.

"It looks like your mind is going a mile a minute," he said.

"What?" I laughed as I pulled out my key. "Hardly."

He grabbed my hand before I put the key into the lock. "We can go out for dessert if you want. I wasn't expecting for your place to be empty. I just wanted to get to know you better, Jellyfish Girl."

He was acting like we hadn't already had sex. We were only going to be in the same state for another month and a half. I wasn't going to waste any time on going slow. But I loved the fact that he was a gentleman. I shook my head. "We need time to figure out that rolling pin." I felt my face flushing. Why was *that* the thing I said? I had no idea what do to with a rolling pin besides...roll it. On a counter. For baking. I quickly opened the door as he laughed.

"It smells really good in here," he said.

I flipped on the light switch. "Girly shampoos and body lotions probably." I had a love of fruity aromas. I dropped my high heels on the floor and walked toward the kitchen.

"No. It smells like an Italian restaurant."

"Oh." I laughed. "That's why we're here. To eat." I pulled the lasagna out of the fridge.

"Is it?" He walked over to me. "I could think of a few other things I'd rather do." His eyes wandered down my body.

"I forgot to thank you for my dress!" I didn't know why I was suddenly nervous around him. "It's the nicest thing anyone's ever gotten me."

"It would look even better off." He took another step forward.

Holy shit. The hunger in his eyes was palpable. And my lasagna was the most delicious thing in the apartment, not me. "Are you sure you don't want me to warm you up some lasagna? I made it this afternoon and I promise it'll be the best thing you ever put in your mouth."

He didn't respond. He just stopped right in front of me and cocked his eyebrow. Apparently he didn't believe in my cooking skills. Or else he was thinking about eating something else entirely. I was pretty sure he was looking south of my waist. I gulped.

"Do you know why I liked this dress in the store?" I asked.

He lifted his gaze back to mine.

"It's the same color as your eyes. You know, I'm not even drunk and I feel like I'm on the top of the world. I haven't felt this light and free since...God, I don't know. Since I was a kid?"

He smiled at my comment. "Why are you so nervous? You're acting like we've never been alone before." He took another step forward. I took a step back and my ass hit the side of the kitchen island.

"I'm not nervous." I was, but I had no idea why. For some reason tonight felt different between us. Better. Bigger. My heart started beating faster as my eyes wandered to his lips and then the tan skin exposed at his neck. I wondered if it would be salty like it was after he worked, or if he tasted differently when he was all dressed up. *Oh fuck.* My eyes locked back on his. Tonight felt better and bigger for a reason. *God, I'm falling in love with him.*

He reached out and ran his fingers from my jaw, down the side of my neck. I shivered under his touch.

"Tell me what you're thinking," he said.

"I don't know...I..." I tried to search his eyes to see if he was feeling as caught up in us as I was. There were a million reasons to keep my mouth shut. Every man in my life before him had treated my heart carelessly. And it was too soon to feel the way I was feeling. But I didn't want to have secrets from him. "Well, Jaime Jamison."

He laughed. "That makes it sound like I'm in trouble."

"No, I'm the one that's in trouble."

"Is that so?" He grabbed my waist and lifted me onto the counter. "Have you been a bad girl?" His fingers trailed up the insides of my thighs.

The moment to tell him was gone. He'd taken my words in a completely different direction. And it was too soon. My heart was still learning how to trust again. We needed more time together before I let myself fall for him. Besides, I kind of liked the new direction. Although I really hoped he didn't try to Thanksgiving turkey my ass. I wasn't sure it would be able to handle such a thing. "So bad," I whispered. "Are you going to punish me?" I hooked my hands behind his neck.

He groaned.

I thought for sure he'd be whipping out the rolling pin, but then he kissed me slowly. His hands were gentler than they'd been before as he slid my dress up my thighs. I hadn't said I was falling for him, but he was acting like I had said it. Maybe he felt it too.

I kissed the side of the neck and was happy that he tasted the same even when he was dressed up. He tasted like summer.

"You're so gorgeous," he said as he pushed my thong to the side with his thumb.

I moaned when he touched me where I needed him the most.

"I need you, Mila." He sounded as desperate as me. Drunk on the moment.

Maybe that was better than him saying he was falling for me. Because it had been a really long time since someone had needed me. And the words felt amazing.

I unbuttoned his shirt and he made short work of his pants. I splayed my hands on his back, drawing him closer.

Yes, him saying he needed me was wonderful. But him thrusting inside of me was better than any words.

He slowly pulled back out and then bit my earlobe as he thrust back in.

God, yes. I tightened my fingers on his shoulders.

He didn't have to say anything else, because I felt it. *I'm falling in love with you too, J.J.*

***

"Mila, you were right. This is the best thing I've ever put in my mouth."

I laughed. He was just starving. He hadn't even let me warm it up. I'd pulled it out of the fridge and he'd grabbed a fork and dove in.

"I'm serious. You should do this for a living."

"Do what? Make lasagnas?"

"Cook. I don't know. What else do you know how to make?"

I shrugged. "I love cooking all sorts of cuisine. American of course. Classic burger and fries. There's nothing better than homemade fries. And I think the ones I make are a little healthier because I bake them instead of frying them. Also I love Greek food. Japanese. Italian. French. Korean…"

"I've never even had Korean food before."

"It's good. I'll make you something with gochujang sometime. It's the perfect level of heat."

"I don't even know what you just said…but…if everything you make is this good, then I'm serious. You should start a restaurant."

I shook my head. "I can't start a restaurant."

"Why not?"

Why not? "I haven't taken any classes."

"Who cares if you're self-taught as long as it tastes good?"

I shrugged. "I don't know…probably the bank. There's no way they'd give me a loan to start a restaurant without the proper degree. Or money for that matter. Besides, you just heard how unfocused the cuisines I like are. I wouldn't be able to choose. And also…I just…restaurants are risky."

He smiled. "Do you love cooking?"

"Yeah, but…"

"No buts. I went over a lot of different majors with you and you said no to all of them. What about culinary arts?"

"I don't think they offer that at the University of New Castle."

"So finish a business degree to make sure you can handle that side of it."

"I hate all the business classes I've taken."

He shook his head. "Then go to a culinary arts school if you want a fancy degree."

"I can't start over. My dad is only paying for one more year and I'm so broke it's not even funny." I shook my head. "It doesn't matter anyway. I need to choose something more practical."

He suddenly looked sad. "Practical isn't always the best option, trust me. I think the answer is right in front of you. You just have to choose how you want to get there." He took another bite of the lasagna and groaned. "So freaking good."

I pressed my lips together. He loved my food. So did Kristen. And cooking really did make me happy. I watched the sadness melt from J.J.'s eyes as he took another bite. He chose the practical path and he wished he could go in a different direction. But how could he ask me to take such a huge risk when he hadn't? I didn't want to roll the dice on my life. Or flip a coin. But the pieces of my life weren't going to just magically fall into place. I had to make a choice.

And there was something so satisfying about a man who meant so much to me loving my food. It warmed something inside of me. Or maybe it was the fact that he believed in me when I'd found it so hard to believe in myself.

CHAPTER 25
Monday

When J.J. and I weren't soaking up the sun together and dancing the nights away, I'd been spending most of my free time thinking about what he had said three weeks ago. And cooking. So much cooking. J.J. could put away a ridiculous amount of food. His compliments made me truly believe I could do something with the one hobby I loved. The answer had been right in front of me. I'd just been too blind to see it.

I loved cooking more than any college course I had taken. I really did. A culinary arts degree was out of the question at this point. But I could suck it up and finish a business degree like he said. Then I'd have the skills to handle everything behind the scenes, from the menus to the books. Behind the scenes at a restaurant was probably where I belonged anyway. I was great at working the slow shifts at Sweet Cravings, but I avoided the busy hours like the plague. I liked things calm and peaceful. Hopefully my restaurant would have that vibe all day long. Every time I thought about it I got more and more excited, which made J.J.'s smile even brighter too.

The fact that J.J. wanted me to follow my dreams was sweet. I just wished he'd follow his own. If I could start a restaurant, then he could certainly figure out a way to live life in this town. He could find something to do during the offseason. We could make it work. *We.* I smiled to myself. Neither of us had used the love word yet, but I felt it in his gaze. In his touch. And I definitely saw it in his smile.

I wasn't falling anymore. I had already fallen. But I was still scared to say it. I was scared saying it out loud would somehow jinx it.

Especially because whenever I talked about the future, J.J. always seemed to change the subject. I knew it was hard for him to think about moving to the city at the end of summer. But I just didn't understand why he wouldn't even entertain the idea of doing something else. Like his bleak future was set in stone. Maybe I'd try to bring it up again tonight. He'd helped me figure out what I might want to do in the future. I owed him the same. And a suit and tie would never make him happy. We both knew that. I just needed to open his eyes to all the possibilities out there. Besides, it was a sin to hide his perfect body under so many clothes. Swim trunks suited him best.

My phone beeped. I lifted it up, expecting a text from J.J., but it was an email notification. I clicked on it and I was pretty sure my heart stopped beating. I read it twice because I didn't even believe it. *I got in.* I felt tears welling in my eyes. *I got accepted to the University of New Castle's business college!*

It was like I had willed the email to come today when I was thinking about committing to a business degree. If Kristen had been here I would have screamed and started jumping up and down. But it seemed weird to do alone. I jumped once anyway, because who the hell cared if I was being weird, and let the tears stream down my cheeks. *I fucking did it.*

I was coming back to the east coast for good. That dismal, empty life that I'd started in Cali was over. I let go of a breath I hadn't known I'd been holding. The thought of going back there at the end of summer had been daunting. And now...not happening. Not a chance in hell. I never had to go back. I wiped the tears out of my eyes. *I got in!*

And now I'd be a short drive away from this beach. An hour tops. If I wanted to, I could come here all the time. Not that I wanted to be here without J.J. *Oh my God, J.J.!*

I was about to call him to tell him the good news, but I paused. This was an in-person conversation. I wanted to see his face when he found out I'd only be a few hours away from him. I glanced at the time. If I left now I'd have time to stop at the beach on my way to work. I couldn't wait to see his smile. I could picture him hopping off the lifeguard stand and lifting me into his arms, twirling me around, and giving me the hottest damn congratulations kiss possible. Plus it was a perk that he'd do it in front of all those girls that tried to flirt with him every day at the beach. J.J. was mine and this acceptance email sealed the deal.

I pulled my hair into a messy bun as I slipped on my Keds. My mind was racing as I headed out the door. I couldn't even wait to tell him. And I had so much to do. I needed to let my dad know so he could send tuition. I needed to call my mom and tell her I was coming back to Delaware. I needed to figure out where I'd live and what classes to enroll in. But telling J.J. was the only thing that mattered right now. God, he was going to be so excited.

I ran down the stairs two at a time and turned so quickly that I ran straight into someone. I started to fall but he caught me.

"I'm so sorry," I said. "I wasn't watching where…" The smell of expensive cologne hit me like a ton of bricks. It was the opposite of how J.J.'s skin smelled. J.J. exuded warmth and natural summer scents. He smelled like the ocean breeze and sunscreen. My stomach churned. My nose was currently being affronted by the smell of sleazy ass. Which was a fairly generous description considering who was wearing it. I couldn't look up to confirm my suspicion. *This can't be happening.* I was supposed to be celebrating. Not…whatever the hell this was.

"That's okay," said a deep voice that was all too familiar. "I wanted you back in my arms anyway."

Fuck. I felt like I was going to be sick. I looked up at Aiden. My ex. The one that stomped on my heart, pissed all over it, and then punted it into a volcano just for fun. It was like all the good news had filled up a balloon and he'd just popped it in my face.

I pushed his arms off me and took a step back. "What the hell are you doing here?" I didn't sound nearly as angry as I should have. It was just a casual question like you'd ask an old friend. But maybe that was for a reason. Because I felt nothing when I looked at him. Nothing at all. I wanted to pinch myself. Was it possible that I was imagining him standing there? That this was some sort of nightmare?

"It's nice to see you too, Mila. You look…good. Tan. I didn't realize how much you liked the beach." His eyes trailed down my legs.

I was definitely going to be sick. I pinched myself just to be sure I wasn't in that nightmare. *Ow.* "I didn't like Santa Monica. I love Rehoboth."

"What's the difference?"

"Everything. It smells different for one."

He laughed. "Okay. I'm not so sure that's true. When are you coming back home?"

I am home. I wasn't having this conversation with him. "I have to go to work."

"Skip it. I came all this way to see you, babe."

I shook my head. "You shouldn't have." *And don't fucking call me that.*

"I told you I wanted to give us another shot."

"And I told you to go to hell." My hospitality had diminished rather quickly.

He smiled. "But we both know you didn't mean that. Come on. Invite me up." He nodded to my apartment.

I wished I could go back in time and not give him my address. Or go back in time and never date him to begin with. *Definitely that one.* I just stared at him. The books and clothes I'd left at his apartment had felt like a big deal at the beginning of summer. But now I didn't want anything that had ever been associated with him. Not that it mattered. He wasn't here to give me back my stuff. He wasn't even holding a box. He came all the way out here for…what? I just stared at him.

"We can catch up." He gave me the smile I once found so charming. But now I realized how fake it was.

"Uh, yeah…no. Like I said, I have to get to work. I'm sorry you came all this way, but we have nothing to talk about, Aiden."

"I just want you to hear me out."

I shrugged. "A few months ago, maybe I would have entertained that idea." I started walking away from him backward. "But I have better things to do with my time than waste another second listening to you." I turned around and picked up my pace.

"Mila!" He called from behind me.

But I was already turning onto the boardwalk, disappearing into the crowd. I glanced out at J.J.'s lifeguard stand down on the beach. Aiden had wasted the extra time I had before my shift. And I didn't want telling J.J. the good news to be tarnished by whatever the hell that just was. I'd tell him about my acceptance after my shift when he picked me up.

I took a deep breath and made my way to work. Aiden had impeccable timing. But I was relieved. Not that he'd come here. That was fucking stupid. I was relieved that I felt nothing when I saw him. Besides sick to my stomach. But there was no love there. Only regret for staying with a dick like him for so long. All that time I'd wasted. All the bullshit he'd fed me that I willingly believed. I wasn't the same girl that he knew. And whatever part of me that used to love him, if I ever even had, was long gone.

This summer had been about bettering myself, and I had. I'd finally decided what I wanted to do with my life. I was exercising more than ever. And my heart had mended. Originally, I thought I could do all that myself. But J.J. and Kristen were the ones that showed me the way. They were my best friends. I loved them both so much.

I bit the inside of my cheek. Kristen knew I loved her. For some reason it was easier with friends to talk about your feelings. But J.J. was more than just a friend. He was…everything. I loved him so much. And I needed to tell him. If anything, seeing Aiden had just confirmed my feelings for J.J. Maybe I'd tell him that tonight too. Just lay it all out there and see what he had to say about it.

"Hey!" Becca said as I walked up to the ice cream shop. She leaned on the counter. "And what can I get for you today? A double scoop of Flavors of Love?"

I laughed as I came in. Ever since she'd met J.J. she'd been teasing me every time we worked together. The names of flavors at this shop were absurd and there were probably at least 30 that had to do with love. I grabbed my apron and tied it on. "How about a double scoop of I just got into the University of New Castle and I'm so excited I can't even contain myself!"

"What? Ah!" She hugged me. "I didn't even know you were transferring."

Becca wasn't the first person that I wanted to tell. Mostly because although we got along fine at work we never really hung out outside of it. But I couldn't keep my news locked up for a whole shift. "Mhm. I applied last month and just heard back. I'm so freaking excited."

"Well, I'll tell Rory and Keira that we need a new flavor name. It's lengthy but at least it won't make me blush whenever a guy orders it."

I laughed. "The worst is when a little kid orders something like Wet Dream."

"I know!"

A family stopped in front of the shop, breaking up our conversation. I was focusing more on tips than I had in the past. I needed to save every dime if my restaurant was going to become a reality.

***

When there was finally a lull in orders, I pulled out my phone. It was tempting to text Kristen, but I wanted to tell her in person too. My shift was almost over. It could wait. There was one person that I needed to tell as soon as possible though. "Can you handle everything out here for a minute?" I asked Becca. "I need to tell my Dad the good news." I said it like he'd care. Not like it was a formality.

"Of course." She shooed me to the back room. "Go tell everyone. I got this."

"Thanks, Becca."

I disappeared into the storage room and clicked on my acceptance email again. I could read it a million times and still be grinning ear to ear. It would have been fun to call my dad, if we had that type of relationship. But it was better this way. Aiden was a perfect reminder that I was done surrounding myself with dickweeds. I forwarded the email to my dad and added a note about when tuition was due. No love or xoxo sign off. Simple. Formal. I was majoring in business now after all. I pressed send.

My mom would have been genuinely excited for me. She'd definitely be happy that I'd be so close to home again. I was about to call her but stopped myself. I tried to remember when she said she was going on that couple's cruise. It was definitely at the end of July. Even if she did get service, I didn't want to disrupt her vacation. I shoved my phone back in my pocket. My mental balloon still felt a little deflated. I just needed to get through this shift and then I could hand J.J. the air pump and I'd be as good as new.

I walked out of the back room and froze. *Fucking shit fuck.* What little air had been put back into my balloon by Becca's optimism and the thought that I'd be seeing J.J. any minute popped again. Aiden was standing there talking to Becca. I was about to turn back and hide in the storage room when he called my name.

I turned back around.

Becca looked so uncomfortable. "Hey, um…this guy says he's your boyfriend?" She lowered both her eyebrows, jumping to some horrible conclusion about me.

I swallowed hard. I was not going to let Aiden ruin my life here like he'd ruined my life back in Cali. "Ex-boyfriend," I said as firmly as I could. "We broke up months ago. Right, Aiden?"

"It was a misunderstanding," he said. "We're still very much together."

What the hell was he doing?

Becca looked back and forth between us. "Does J.J. know about him?"

Shit. I pressed my lips together. Everyone loved J.J. I wasn't upset that she was trying to protect him from whatever she thought was going on. But I didn't want Aiden to know I was seeing someone else. I didn't want him to know anything about my life. I didn't want him here at all. And J.J. would be coming by the shop any minute to pick me up after both our shifts were over. I needed to get rid of him.

"Who's J.J?" Aiden asked. "Are you seeing someone else?"

I cleared my throat and walked back up to the counter. I looked at Becca, trying to address her question and wishing Aiden would just disappear. "J.J. knows that Aiden and I broke up when I walked in on him cheating on me last semester. Aiden also knows this so I have no idea why he's standing here right now."

That seemed to get Becca on my side. She turned her head and glared at him.

Aiden smiled. "Like I said...a misunderstanding."

"Seeing you in bed with someone else wasn't a misunderstanding," I said.

"You never let me explain."

I'd begged him to explain. All those calls and texts that went unanswered. Just thinking about how pathetic I'd been made me cringe. "Aiden, please just go."

"Not until you at least tell me when you're coming back. If you won't talk to me here, we can set up a date when..."

"I'm not coming back."

He laughed. "Of course you are. You can't exactly do better than me."

I wasn't sure what made me madder. That he thought my comment about not coming back meant back to him, or the fact that he said that I couldn't do better. Because I was pretty sure a slimy used car salesman in his late fifties would be a better catch than him. I shook my head. The joke was on him. I had found the most generous, sweet, caring man I'd ever met. Aiden wasn't an ounce of the man that J.J. was.

I needed to shut this shit show down. "I'm transferring to the University of New Castle. I just got my acceptance letter. There is nothing left for me in Cali. And I think it's about time you went back."

He laughed. "You're seriously running away from SMU because you're mad at me? Throwing away your future over a misunderstanding?"

"God, if you use that word one more time…"

"Fine. Mistake. It was a mistake. And I already told you I'm sorry. So let's get on a plane and go home."

Becca touched my shoulder. I knew there were customers. I knew this was inappropriate. I wanted this to be over as badly as she did.

"This is my home," I said. "I don't have anything else to say to you. Please, just leave, Aiden."

"I'm not going anywhere until you talk to me one-on-one."

"Please go."

Becca tried to get my attention again.

"Now, Aiden."

He shook his head. "Not until I get…."

"She asked you to leave," J.J. said as he stepped up to the counter. His normal smile wasn't there.

Becca hadn't been concerned about the customers we were scaring off. She'd been trying to warn me that J.J. was coming. I wasn't sure I'd ever seen him look so serious. I couldn't read him at all.

"I think you should respect the lady's wishes," J.J. said and then turned back to me. "Hey, Mila."

He rarely called me by my name. Jellyfish Girl was his go-to. Or when he was being sweet he'd call me gorgeous or beautiful. Hearing him call me by my actual name made me feel even more tense. But him just being here was a relief. "Hi."

"You ready to go?" he asked, completely ignoring Aiden. He must have known who it was. He must have sensed how uncomfortable I was. He was trying to remove us from this situation as best he could. But nothing was that easy with Aiden-bitch-face.

"So this is the guy that you think is better than me?" Aiden asked. "Give me a break."

I stared at the two of them. J.J.'s skin was bronzed from the sun. He towered over Aiden. And everything about him exuded strength and charm. Aiden? He was dressed in a polo shirt tucked into khaki shorts and preppy boat shoes. The look was completed with a Rolex from his old man that he'd probably never be able to afford on his own. He was a tool. He looked like the kind of guy that deserved to be slapped before you even knew him.

J.J. didn't respond to his jab. He just stared at me, waiting calmly.

It was a few minutes before my shift ended, but we were making a scene. Customers were staying away. "I'm going to head out, okay, Becca?"

"We still have to divvy up the tips," she said.

"Hold mine for me until later. Or just keep them."

"You're not even going to look at me?" Aiden asked J.J. "You steal my girl and won't even look me in the eye like a man?" He flicked J.J.'s shoulder.

J.J. finally turned to him. "Yeah…you're not going to want to touch me again."

"Or what?"

Jesus. I untied my apron and tossed it on the counter.

"You don't want to find out," J.J. said.

Aiden laughed and shook his head. "All talk and no balls."

I ran out the door, blinking from the bright sun.

"You can say whatever you want to me," J.J. said. "But don't you dare talk about her like that."

I don't know what Aiden had said about me in the few seconds I couldn't hear their conversation. But I had never seen J.J. look so pissed. Not even at the beginning of summer when I kept trying to make him jealous.

"Just like I said. No balls." He flicked J.J.'s shoulder again.

J.J. clenched his hand in a fist and shook his head.

"Let's go," I said to J.J. "Please, let's just go." I tried to walk past Aiden as quickly as possible, but he grabbed my arm.

"I just need to talk to you for a few minutes, babe."

"Don't touch me." I pulled away but Aiden's fingers dug into my skin harder.

J.J. had let Aiden flick him. Insult him. But it was like a switch went off behind J.J.'s eyes when he saw Aiden touch me. One of the fists he'd been clenching hit Aiden's face so fast if I'd blinked I would have missed it. A sickening crunching noise echoed in my ears as Aiden's hand fell from my arm.

"Jesus Christ." Aiden grabbed his bloody nose.

"Don't you ever lay your hands on her again," J.J. said.

"She was mine first. And I'll put my hands wherever I fucking want!" He lunged at J.J.

"Stop it!" I yelled as they collided. They slammed into the ice cream shop counter and Becca screamed at the top of her lungs before they fell onto the cement. Aiden had knocked J.J. over and landed at least one punch, but he was absolutely not winning this fight. J.J. could easily annihilate him. And he did. Punch after punch after punch. "Both of you stop it!" People around us started pulling out their phones. I wasn't sure if they were filming it or calling the cops. Probably both.

I looked at Becca for help but she was just standing behind the counter with her mouth hanging open.

"J.J." I tried to pull him off Aiden. "J.J., please. Let's just go home." I wasn't sure if it was my voice or my hands on his arm, but he snapped out of his trance. He got up and ran his fingers through his shaggy hair like he hadn't just been beating the shit out of my ex-boyfriend.

Aiden got onto all fours and spit blood onto the pavement. He wiped his bloody nose with the back of his hand as he stood up. "You're fucking crazy."

I wasn't sure if he was talking to me or J.J., but it really didn't matter.

"Good luck with that meathead, Mila."

Screw it. I deserved a few punches too. I took a step forward to slap him, but J.J wrapped his arm protectively around me, keeping me by his side. "Let's go home."

Home. It wasn't my touch or my voice that had stopped J.J. from fighting with Aiden. It was the fact that I'd referred to my apartment as our home. My home with him. I leaned into him as he pulled me away from the chaos.

"Just wait until she comes crawling back to me in Cali!" Aiden yelled from behind us. "All her stuff is still in my apartment. Whatever home you two think you have here is only temporary! See you in a few weeks, babe!"

I closed my eyes and let J.J. lead me back to our home. The one I wished could be permanent.

CHAPTER 26
Monday

J.J. exhaled through his teeth as I put some peroxide on his elbow. He was already sporting the start of a black eye. Fortunately the only other injury seemed to be the cut on his elbow. He had scratched it pretty badly on the cement. All in all he was in a lot better shape than Aiden. I blotted the wound as J.J. winced again. "Sorry."

He adjusted the ice pack on his eye so he could get a better view of me.

I dropped his gaze. I wasn't even sure what I was apologizing for. The sting of the peroxide? The fact that Aiden was even in the state? All of it? I applied some Neosporin on the cut and one of the big Band-Aids I never thought I'd have a use for from the variety pack.

"What made you snap back there?" I asked.

J.J. slowly lowered the ice pack. "You know what."

I did. He'd said it weeks ago. He was protective of me. He could handle insults thrown at him or someone trying to dig under his skin. But when it came to me? He wouldn't let anyone harm me. And Aiden had put his hands on me when I'd asked him not to. "I'm sorry," I said again.

"I don't know why you're apologizing. You didn't do anything wrong."

"No?" I gestured to his black eye.

"You're not responsible for your ex-boyfriend's actions."

I knew that. But I still felt guilty. I bit my lip so I wouldn't say "I'm sorry" again. "Does it hurt?"

"It feels like someone punched me in the face." He smiled and then winced.

I took the ice pack out of his hand and held it against his eye for him. *I'm so so sorry.* Despite what J.J. said, he was hurt because of me.

"How'd he know where you worked?"

"Earlier this summer I left him a message with my address, asking him to ship all the stuff I left at his apartment. Which he never did. But I don't know how he knew about Sweet Cravings." I pressed my lips together. "I guess he followed me there…"

"From where? How long has he been here?"

"I don't know how long he's been in town. But I ran into him when I was leaving my apartment. I asked him to leave. I couldn't have been any clearer about it. And I thought I lost him on the boardwalk. I guess I was wrong."

J.J. nodded. "So today was the only day you saw him?"

"Of course."

"What were you two talking about before I came?" he asked.

I knew that J.J.'s ex had cheated on him. I knew he was already worried about long distance with me this fall. But he had nothing to worry about. "He kept saying what happened between us was a misunderstanding and that he wanted to talk." I shook my head. "I'm pretty sure he lost his mind."

"No, he just finally realized what he lost."

Maybe. I didn't want to be talking about Aiden anymore. "Good. Because he did lose me. I've moved on."

J.J. smiled but his heart wasn't in it. "He seems to still think he has a chance. If you end up moving back..." his voice trailed off. "You might think differently."

This conversation was ridiculous. I'd never ever get back together with Aiden. I was freaking in love with the man sitting in front of me. But this wasn't the moment to tell him. Not when Aiden had just been here. I didn't want J.J. to think I was saying it because I felt bad. When I did tell him, I wanted him to believe it. I wanted him to say it back.

It may not have been the moment to tell him I loved him. But it was a good moment for some other news. I lowered the ice pack from his eye. "Well, I absolutely won't be moving back." Despite the heavy conversation, I couldn't help but smile. "Because I got into the University of New Castle."

"You got in?" He didn't sound surprised, just excited.

"Mhm."

This time his smile was as real as mine. "You got in!" He grabbed me around my waist and pulled me backward onto the bed.

I laughed as he hugged me tight, like he never had to let go. "I got in!"

"I knew you would. Congrats, Jellyfish Girl."

I smiled against his neck.

"Oh my God, what happened?" Kristen asked.

I turned to look at her coming into the apartment.

"My girl got into the University of New Castle!" J.J. said.

My girl. I was pretty sure I melted into his touch even more.

Kristen squealed. She had the exact reaction I'd expected. She ran over and jumped onto the bed with us. "East coast living! Screw Cali. God, it's going to be so fun to have you on campus." She hugged both of us and then screamed again. "What the hell is freezing cold?"

I pulled the ice pack out from beneath her hip.

"Oh. Yeah," she said. "I got distracted for a second, but what I really wanted to know was what the hell happened to your face, J.J.?"

He touched his eye. "I got in a fight with Mila's ex."

"No." Kristen rolled a little away from us and propped her head up on her hand. "Aiden the dickweed? Here in little old Delaware?"

I nodded.

"What a creep," she said. "He came here to try to break up your new relationship? Low blow. Your poor face."

J.J. laughed. "You should see the other guy."

"I bet. So was that why he was here? To mess with your new life?"

I opened my mouth to respond but J.J. beat me to it. "He was trying to win her back."

Kristen raised both eyebrows. "Not a chance in hell. First, my girl doesn't play nice with cheaters. And second, she's madly in love with you, obvs."

Oh my God, Kristen.

I felt J.J.'s body tense.

"But forget about Aiden," Kristen said. She grabbed the ice pack from me and handed it back to J.J. "We need to celebrate the good news! What do you want to do, Mila? Go out for drinks? Dancing? Binge watch some Project Runway?"

All I could focus on was the fact that J.J. seemed so uncomfortable. I slowly sat up on the bed, looking anywhere but at him. What did his reaction to Kristen's comment mean? Did he not love me back? Because she wasn't wrong...I was head over heels for him. And he was as stiff as a board.

He'd been spending most nights here. We were inseparable when we weren't working. He'd just referred to my place as his home. Kristen didn't seem to mind having a third roommate. We'd become the three amigos. Although, definitely no margaritas. But J.J. and I? We'd become an us. And as an us he wasn't supposed to freak out at the mention of love. I was moving back to Delaware for him just as much as I was for myself. Didn't he see that? I hadn't told him that I was in love him, but I hadn't told Kristen that either and she saw it. Was he just hoping it wasn't true?

"Earth to Mila," Kristen said. "What's it going to be?"

I cleared my throat. "I don't know. What do you guys want to do?"

"It doesn't matter what we want to do." Kristen lightly shoved my thigh. "It's *your* night. Pick anything. Aside from streaking. I don't want you to get kicked out of your new school before you even step foot on campus." She laughed at her own joke, but I wasn't really paying attention.

J.J.'s face was hidden by the ice pack. I couldn't bear sitting on this bed with them another second. "Yeah, let's go out." I hopped off the bed. "Unless you need to ice that longer, J.J.?" I wasn't sure why I asked. It was like I was trying to give him an out. But an out from what exactly? Him and I? That was the last thing I wanted.

"I might keep the ice on for a few more minutes," he said. "How about you two go ahead though. Get us a table somewhere before it gets too crowded."

"Sounds good," said Kristen.

But I didn't think it sounded good at all. It sounded awful. I had this pit in my stomach that was growing by the second. What if I just never heard from him again? What if he was about to ghost me like Aiden had? Love was a game that I wasn't good at. And it felt like I was about to lose again.

When Kristen ran to the bathroom to check her makeup, I turned back to J.J. I needed to backtrack. I wasn't ready to lose him. "I'm sorry about what Kristen said." I swallowed hard, wishing I could muster the courage to tell him it was true though. That I was in love with him. And ask him why he was so freaked out by those words. But I held my tongue as he laughed.

"Not a big deal. We both know how she loves to exaggerate."

Right. I pressed my lips together. If he would bother to make eye contact with me, he'd be able to tell it was a big deal to me though. And that it was truer than he wanted to believe.

"Ready?" Kristen asked as she reemerged from the bathroom. She grabbed my arm and pulled me toward the door without waiting for a response. "We need to get our drink on!"

No, what I needed was to go back to tequila nights when my ex wasn't in town and J.J. hadn't freaked out at the prospect of love. What the heck had he been doing all summer if he wasn't falling in love with me back?

CHAPTER 27
Friday

I balanced my mini-golf putter between my legs so I could put my hair up. August was sweltering and every piece of me was sticky. I could feel the sweat at the base of my neck as I pulled my hair into a ponytail. *Gross.* I was going to need to start carrying a roll of paper towels around in my purse. And I was going to need a bigger purse to accommodate my paper towel needs.

"You're up!" Kristen called. She and Reggie had challenged J.J. and me to a game of mini golf. Which was a terrible mistake on their part. Between eating too much ice cream, nighttime runs on the beach, and dancing, mini-golf was one of our go-to activities. And we were freaking beasts.

J.J. smiled at me as I walked down to where my ball had landed. We had found our new normal in the past few weeks. Normal as in, we were dating and *not* in love. Well, J.J. wasn't in love. I was falling harder and harder and he was...most certainly not. Our new normal felt like slow torture to me. It was like Kristen's big reveal had never happened. Which would have been fine if it wasn't all I could think about.

I lined my putter up, trying not to focus on the nearby mini waterfall that was waiting to steal my ball, and took a swing. *Shit.* The ball hopped over the hole in the most annoying way possible and ended up farther away from it than it had been a second ago. J.J. and I both groaned. I stepped to the side so Reggie could take his shot, hoping that he'd miss too. At least I hadn't put it into the waterfall. That would have been embarrassing since I was a pro at this.

"Gotta get your head in the game, Jellyfish Girl," J.J. said and wrapped his arms around me. "What are you thinking about?"

"Nothing." *The end of summer. What will happen to us?*

"I know you too well to accept that lie." He kissed the side of my forehead as Reggie sunk his shot perfectly.

Damn it. J.J. and I were still winning, but I suddenly wanted to take my putter and throw it into the fake mini lake next to hole 16. Or the windmill that made it nearly impossible to get a hole in one at hole 17. Or just whack the fake grass beneath my feet because it was too hot to move. I was raging on the inside and trying to remain cool, calm, and collected on the outside. And failing miserably. Especially at the cool part since it was 1,000 bajillions degrees out. I pulled on the neckline of my tank top, but there was no breeze up here to help.

"Really, is there something bothering you?" he asked.

"I just really want to win."

"It's supposed to be a fun game." He leaned in a little closer to whisper in my ear. "But I agree, let's annihilate them."

I was relieved to hear a laugh come out of my mouth. A little exasperated, but a laugh just the same. And that should have counted for something when my heart felt like it was crumbling into bits. I was leaving in two weeks. J.J.

was standing there saying he knew me too well to know when I was lying. So couldn't he tell that the conversation from a few weeks ago had killed me? I knew that he had issues with long distance relationships, but I'd be less than 3 hours away. We could see each other every weekend if we wanted to. And I most certainly did want that. But as summer drew to a close, it felt like we were ending. Like there was a clock ticking down to the end of our relationship. And I was pretty sure I was seconds away from having a heart attack.

"My turn again." I ducked out of his arms and stared at the stupid little ball that I could usually sink so easily. *You are my bitch, ball. You will bend to my will.* I took a deep breath. *Go in the hole where you belong.* I squinted at the circular demon and then took my shot. "Yes!" I raised both of my hands in the air, Rocky statue-esque.

"You're acting like you two already won," Reggie said. "We still have two holes left."

Kristen laughed. "They always do this. They're both so cocky. A match made in heaven." She winked at me.

I glanced at J.J. He was staring at the next hole like he was assessing it. But I was pretty sure he was tuning out Kristen's analysis of our relationship. Yet again. I knew I was over analyzing every move he made the past few weeks. How could I not though? I wanted to believe we'd make it past the end of summer. I needed to believe it.

My phone started buzzing in my pocket. I was grateful for the distraction. The number on the screen wasn't one of my contacts. But that made sense given that most of my contacts were standing with me right now. I ran my finger across the screen. "Hello?" I said.

"Hello, is this Mila Wilson?"

"Yes, that's me. Mila. Mila Wilson." *What am I saying? She already knows my name.* I never knew what to say on the phone. It was like my brain always switched off and made me as awkward as possible. Normally phone calls made me sweat profusely too but I was already doing that. I wasn't sure if that was a pro or con.

"Hi, Mila. This is Cindy and I'm calling from the admissions office of the University of New Castle about your tuition. We're still waiting on payment. And we can't hold your seat in the classes you signed up for much longer. Is there any way you can send payment through by Tuesday? We can only guarantee to hold your seats until then."

I stepped away from my friends. "There must be some mistake. My tuition should have come through the day I got my acceptance letter, or maybe a few days after. Can you check again?"

"Oh that's great news. Let me look into that for you."

The silence stretched on too long. I walked to the edge of the miniature golf course. It was on the roof of one of the buildings on the boardwalk. But even the beautiful view of the water didn't calm my rapid heartbeat. *My dad did send in tuition...right?*

"I'm sorry," Cindy said. "We have no record of payment. Do you know if it was sent through our online portal or by mail? It's possible that the check got lost in the mail."

I breathed a sigh of relief. "That must be it. It must have gotten lost in the mail. Could you give me a few minutes to look into it? I'll sort everything out and give you a call back."

"Of course. And you have until Tuesday evening, so no rush. But our office closes at 6:30 tonight."

Okay, great, thank you." I wasn't really thankful though. They'd probably messed something up on their end. *People these days.*

"Have a nice evening," she said, and the line went dead.

Kristen jogged over to me. "We're holding people up." She gestured to the agitated family that had been behind us the whole time. They didn't understand the art of mini-golf. "What's going on?"

"There's some issue with my tuition." I pressed on my dad's cell number and pulled the phone to my ear. "Tell J.J. to take my shot for me, okay?"

She nodded and left me alone.

My dad's phone went straight to voicemail. *Son of a bitch.* The last thing I wanted to do was talk to Nancy. But I didn't really see a way around it. I wasn't waiting to figure this out on his time, especially if this was somehow his fault. The knot in my stomach was leaning toward him being the problem, not the admissions office. I hung up the phone and dialed their house number.

After a few rings Nancy answered. "Hello? Wilson residence," she said.

"Hi, Nancy. It's Mila. Is my dad there? I really need to speak to him."

"Oh." She sighed like my existence tired her. "Dale asked you not to use this number, Mila. Call his cell. Bye."

"Nancy! Wait! He didn't answer. I tried to call his cell phone first."

"That's because we're on our way out. We were just heading to dinner with our girls. Can't this wait?"

Our girls. Fuck you too. "I just need to talk to him for a minute. I won't keep him." *I never do.*

"Fine. You can talk to him for exactly one minute. But we have reservations. So don't dawdle."

I never dawdled on the phone with my dad. These conversations were as painful for me as they were for her. Regardless, I could picture her pulling out some fancy gold pocket watch and timing the conversation.

"He's a very busy man," she added.

"Can you please just put him on the phone?" I didn't mean to snap, but God she had a way of crawling under my skin. Like she was my father's keeper. And her perfect new family couldn't mingle with scum like me.

"I will not have you speak to me like that. Dale!" she called. Her words were muffled as she held the phone away from her mouth, but I could still make out what she was saying. "Dale! It's your *other* child. And you should have heard how she spoke to me. I won't tolerate this for another second. You need to figure out a way to make this stop."

Tears bit the corners of my eyes. I knew they were trying to punt me out of their lives. That was very clear from my last conversation with my father. But hearing it out loud? It still stung. I wasn't a menace that needed to be stopped. They were in the wrong here, not me.

"Mila, what did you say to Nancy?" My father sounded madder than I'd ever heard him.

"Nothing. Dad, I…"

"You will not disrespect my wife. Do you understand me? You have no business speaking ill words to my family."

His family? I was his family. Why did he always say stuff like that? Could he not hear himself speak? I wiped my cheek as a tear slowly fell. This conversation was as awful for me as it was for him. Earlier this summer I promised myself I was done with him. But here I was, trying to cater to his insanity. Letting him belittle me. "I didn't say anything rude to her. I just asked her to put you on the phone. That was it."

"Well it must have been your tone. You've always had a problem with your tone."

Did I? I wiped more tears off my cheeks. That was the first time I'd ever heard about it. But it probably was true around him and *his family.* Talking to Nancy was like talking to a Barbie doll with her head cut off. Perfect on the outside but clearly no brain because of the no head thing.

Kristen, Reggie, and J.J. were staring at me. I couldn't do this in front of them. I didn't want them to see me like this. My father made me feel weak and small. That wasn't the person I was here. I had worked hard all summer to make sure of it. And if I stood up here another second in the stifling heat, I was going to pass out. I dropped my putter and made my way back down to the crowded boardwalk.

"I'm sorry, Dad." I wasn't. Maybe my tone had been rude, but had he ever heard his wife speak to me? She was the epitome of rudeness, at least where I was concerned.

"You should be."

I rolled my eyes. *Such an asshole.* I tried to lift my shoulders. He was not going to break me in this conversation. I refused to let him. "I'm calling about tuition. There's been a problem with the payment to the University of New Castle?"

"The University of New Castle? You go to SMU."

Someone bumped into me on the boardwalk and I almost dropped my phone. "I used to. But I told you I was transferring. I forwarded you the email a few weeks ago."

"I never check my personal email. I'm a busy man, Mila."

Too busy for his own daughter? "Can you please send the payment tonight? There's an online portal…"

"I already did."

What? I really was awful on the phone. I had no idea what he was talking about. "But you said you didn't send tuition to the University of New Castle."

"Because I already sent it to SMU."

"Dad." I felt like a wave had just crashed down on top of me. "What are you talking about? I asked you not to send it." I pushed through more people until I was on the sand. Usually stepping onto the beach was relaxing but the sand was too hot tonight. The beach was too crowded. Everything felt wrong.

"I don't remember all that," he said. "You mentioned you were on vacation somewhere this summer or something. Mila, I really need to go."

"I'm not on vacation. I moved here for the summer because I hate California. I hate it there. I can't go back."

"Tuition's already been paid."

"Then un-pay it."

"That's not how it works. You'll be fine. Chin up, Mila."

Tears were currently dripping down my chin. "Chin up? Are you serious? Did you not hear a word of what I said the last time I called?"

"I was busy. I was in the middle of a game with my daughter."

"*I'm* your daughter. *Me.* Just because you left my mom doesn't mean I'm not your blood!"

"We all make mistakes. Marrying your mother was mine."

There was a double meaning to that. If marrying my mother was a mistake, that meant having me was too. My tears started falling faster. I couldn't be strong when I talked to him. He had this way of making me feel weaker than ever.

"Maybe leaving SMU would have been yours," he said. "So…you're welcome."

"I'm miserable in California, Dad. I told you all this before. I don't have a single friend. I…"

"Make friends then. If you're having trouble doing that then maybe you need to take a good look at yourself."

What the hell did that mean? "My friends are here. My life is here."

"Lives aren't built around summers. They're built around hard work and dedication."

Dedication? Who was he to say life was built on dedication? He certainly wasn't dedicated to my mom when he cheated on her. Or me when he left. "There has to be something we can do. If I call admissions…"

"I'm not going through that hassle just because you like the east coast more than the west coast. You need to grow up."

He wasn't listening to me. "I was depressed, Dad. I felt like a ghost. I couldn't eat or sleep. My grades started to slip because I couldn't focus. I've never been so miserable in my life." *Listen to me. Hear what I'm saying. Help me.*

"I'm sure you'll figure it out. I have to go…"

"The last time I was that down was when you left in the middle of the night. Do you know how much that hurt me? How much it hurt Mom?" My voice cracked on "mom." He had hurt both of us. My mom dealt with it by flitting through relationships. And me? Clearly I hadn't learned to deal with it at all. Or else I wouldn't be standing on the beach sobbing all alone.

"I'm not having this conversation with you, Mila. It's been years. Get over it."

"How am I supposed to get over it if you won't talk to me? You can't erase me, Dad. You can't undo me just because I was a mistake. For once in your life would it hurt you to care?"

"Excuse me?"

"I need you. I need you to help me figure out how to fix this mess. Please. Don't you care about me at all?"

"Go to SMU or don't. That choice is yours. But I have a reservation I'm going to be late for. And please do not call this number again, we've talked about this. Nancy is right. This needs to stop. For good this time."

"Fuck you." The words fell out of my mouth before I could stop them. But once they were out there, at least I could stand up a little taller. Despite the tears streaming down my cheeks and the sobs escaping my throat, I'd finally told my dad how I felt. I'd finally stood up to him. And seriously, he deserved it. *Fuck him.*

"I'm glad we're on the same page," he said and hung up.

I let my hand drop to my side. That was it. My relationship with my own father boiled down to two words at the end. No "I love you." Just a goodbye "fuck you." I didn't deserve that. Not from the man in my life that I was supposed to look up to. Not from anyone.

"Mila?"

I turned around to see J.J. staring at me. How much of that conversation had he heard? Did he think I was a monster from the way I spoke to my father? Would he leave me too?

But he closed the distance between us without waiting for me to say anything at all. He held me as I cried ugly tears. Snot dripping onto his shoulder ugly tears. He held me until I couldn't cry anymore.

"It's okay," he finally said as he rubbed his hand up and down my back. "We'll figure it out."

I cringed, knowing he'd pretty much heard the entire conversation. "It's not okay." I rubbed the evidence of tears and snot off my face with the back of my hand. "He sent my tuition to SMU. It's too late. I have to go back."

"Then come to New York with me. Screw California. You can start a restaurant without a degree." Those words maybe would have been enough for someone else. He believed in me. He wanted me to live in New York with him. But all I heard was that he didn't want to do long distance. And it was easy to fixate on that because I'd lived a life without love. And for once in my life I needed the words. If he wanted me to move to NYC with him, I needed to know exactly how he felt about me.

I pulled back at him and just stared into his ocean blue eyes. *Say it, J.J.* Of all people, he knew what I needed. He knew me. And yet…he didn't say anything at all. "You could come to Cali," I said. Him dropping everything and moving with me? If he couldn't say the words out loud, he could show me that he loved me. It felt like the only way.

"I have a great job lined up, Mila. I can't just drop everything and go to California with you. My life is here."

Without me. I tried not to start bawling again. I hugged him again, trying to hide my face from him. What it came down to was that he wasn't willing to change his plans for me. So why should I be willing to change my plans for him? I needed to find the strength to put myself first. For once in my life I needed to realize that I was important. I mattered. Because I was the only person capable of believing in myself. "And I can't go to New York," I said into his neck. "I have to finish school."

He didn't say anything back. He didn't have to. J.J. could do long distance if it wasn't quite that far away. Weekend train rides back and forth between Delaware and New York was as far as he was willing to go. But I was about to head back to the west coast for a whole year. With no money to visit him.

It didn't matter that he held me a little tighter as we stood there. It didn't matter that this was the best summer of my life. All that mattered was that he'd warned me right from the start. He didn't do long distance. And I was supposed to be putting myself first this summer. I just didn't realize how much it was going to hurt.

CHAPTER 28
Friday

I was supposed to leave next week for the University of New Castle. But I didn't have the luxury of waiting until the last minute to move now. I needed to find an apartment in Cali. Sign up for new classes. Start over. *Again.* I'd wanted to prolong summer until the last minute, but what was the point now? It was about to end anyway. Sticking around for an extra week would just make it that much harder to say goodbye. Ever since I had found out about the tuition mix-up, I had heard the clock ticking down in my head. The last week had felt like torture anyway, and I couldn't take it anymore.

"I can't believe you're not coming back to Newark with me." Kristen stuck her bottom lip out. "I was so excited. We would have had so much fun."

It still hurt to talk about. Everything had been right there for me. Everything I'd ever wanted. I felt gutted. And I didn't have anything left to say, so I continued packing.

"Have you said goodbye to J.J. yet?" she asked.

But she knew I hadn't. I'd spent all night with her last night, reminiscing over our summer and of course drinking margaritas. At least I'd finally learned how to hold my tequila. And I'd spent all day at my last shift at Sweet Cravings. I bowed out a little early with the excuse of needing to pack. J.J. would be stopping by here right after work.

I shook my head. "My Uber comes in thirty minutes. I told J.J. to come over…" I glanced at my phone. "Well, he should be here any minute now."

She sat down on the edge of my bed. "Does he know you're leaving early?"

"He's about to." I closed my suitcase and zipped it shut.

"Mila."

I didn't look up at her as I rummaged around in my purse to make sure I had everything I'd need to board my flight.

"Mila." She grabbed my hand. "Are you sure you're doing the right thing? You can try to take out a loan. You could postpone the University of New Castle a semester while you sort things out. There has to be a way."

Maybe. But what was the point? I had an opportunity to not start my career in debt. How would I ever get a loan for a restaurant space if I already had a pile of student loans I couldn't afford to pay back? I'd spent my whole life trying to figure out what I wanted to do. Now that I found it, I wasn't going to let it slip through my fingers because of summer like. Yes, like, not love. Because J.J. had made it clear he didn't love me. "I'm trying to think about my future."

"And J.J. fits into that how?"

I sighed because it hurt so fucking much to actually say the words out loud. "He doesn't."

"Mila."

"Are you going to sit there and tell me that Reggie is the love of your life? That you're going to get married and have babies and the whole shebang? And live happily ever after?"

"No. But that's different and you know it. Reggie and I were always going to be and were always meant to be a summer fling."

"Well, so were J.J. and I."

"You know that's not true."

"He doesn't love me back, Kristen!" I could feel my tears threatening to spill again. "His solution to my problems was that I should drop everything and just move to New York. I don't even like the city."

"Guys are dumb, but that doesn't mean he doesn't love you. Just because he hasn't said it…who cares. It's about the way he makes you feel. And the way he looks at you. I can tell he loves you even if you can't. You spent all summer trying to get the things you deserve out of life. And now you're just going to throw it all away?" It looked like she was going to start crying now. "Please don't leave."

I knew she had the best intentions. But what she was really upset about was that this was our goodbye too. "I'm sorry." I leaned down and hugged her. "But I have to."

She sniffled. "God, your dad is such a dick."

I laughed. "That he is." I leaned back. "But this isn't really goodbye. We can call each other all the time. And once I'm done with school, there's no way I'm staying in Cali."

"Promise?"

"I promise."

She took a deep breath. "I should probably give you some privacy so you can talk to J.J."

Right when she said it, there was a knock on the door. I swallowed hard. *You can do this. Be strong.*

Before I could go answer it, Kristen launched herself at me in a bear hug that was so tight I could barely breathe. "I'm going to miss you," she said.

"I'm going to miss you too."

She sniffled again as she pulled back. And without another glance she ran over to the door and opened it. "Hey," she said to J.J. She squeezed his arm and then disappeared down the steps.

It looked like he was about to ask if she was okay, but then he spotted my suitcase. And probably my face. He closed the door and walked over to me. For a second I just let myself stare at him. He'd come straight from the beach. He hadn't even bothered to put a shirt on. Tan skin, perfect six pack, and muscular shoulders. The smell of summer was all around him, drifting over to me. He pushed his sunglasses up when he reached me, showing off those perfect ocean blue eyes.

"What's going on?" he asked.

"I have to leave early. I have a lot to do before classes start."

He looked back at my suitcase like he didn't understand. "How early?"

I looked at my phone. "Fifteen minutes."

He laughed, but not his usual one that made me smile so hard it hurt. "Wait, what?"

"My flight's in a few hours and I have to get to the airport."

"You're leaving today? And you're only just telling me now? What the hell?"

I shrugged. "I thought it would be easier this way."

"Easier for who? You? It's certainly not easier for me to be blindsided. I had all these plans for our last week together. You can't leave now." He put his hands on my shoulders. "It's going to be months before I can possibly see you again."

Months? I couldn't afford to come visit him. And I knew he didn't want to come visit me. He had told me he was willing to try long distance. From Newark to NYC. But not this. We'd never talked about it at all. I knew how he felt about it though, I'd known it from the very beginning, and I gave him my heart anyway.

Someone that loved me might be up to such a long distance and long time apart. That wasn't J.J. He was scared of long distance relationships and...did not love me. I swallowed down the lump in my throat. "J.J..." I couldn't say the words. I couldn't do it.

"Stay," he said. But it sounded more like a plea.

I shook my head. "You don't do long distance relationships."

"I said I would for you."

"I don't want to make you do that. You're starting a new job in a new city. I'd just be holding you back."

"You're not making me do anything. Just because summer's ending doesn't mean we are. And you could never in a million years hold me back. I..."

What? You what? Say it! You have to say it!

He cleared his throat. "I don't want you to go. Please don't leave." He looked as deflated as I felt.

I stepped forward and hugged him, pressing the side of my face against his chest. His words weren't enough. His actions weren't enough. What we had wasn't enough. I breathed in his perfect summery scent. The salt air and sunscreen on his skin. And tried my best not to cry. "I have to go. I have to."

He held me a little tighter, like I was slipping through his fingers. "No, you're choosing to. Stay another week. Stay with me. Don't leave like this."

I didn't ever want to let go. I wanted to cling to this summer, to him. I couldn't remember a time when I'd been so happy. Maybe that's why it felt like there was a knife in my chest. I was giving up the best thing that ever happened to me. But J.J. wouldn't be happy 3,000 miles away from me. Neither of us would be. I had to end it. For both our sanities. I thought about how Kristen had described her relationship with Reggie. "I think we both have to accept what this was. A summer fling."

His arms fell from around me as he took a step back. "Seriously?" He was staring at me like I had just slapped him in the face.

The look in his eyes and the absence of his arms wrapped around me made me shiver. "You don't do long distance relationships. And I need to focus on myself."

His Adam's apple rose and then fell. "So that's it? That's all this ever was for you?"

"We knew it from the start."

He ran his hand down his face.

A car honked outside. "I have to go. Maybe I'll see you next summer?" I wasn't sure why I said it. Like I was trying to hold on to a shred of hope.

He didn't respond. He just stared at me. Because we both knew he wouldn't see me next summer. We were done. Whatever we had was over. And I was falling apart. I never thought I'd hurt more than when Aiden had dumped me. But this was worse. It was so much worse. Because I never felt this strongly for Aiden. I loved J.J. I loved him and he'd never know it. I tried to hold back my tears.

"I guess this is goodbye?" I said.

He shoved his hands into the pockets of his swim trunks. He was staring at me like he didn't even recognize me. "Have a safe flight, Jellyfish Girl."

"Good luck in New York."

He shook his head like he didn't understand anything that came out of my mouth. I didn't either. All of it hurt. But I hoped he'd eventually see that I did it for him. I turned around and opened my door.

"It was never a summer fling to me," he said from behind me. "And you know that."

I finally let my tears fall as I closed the door and walked away without looking back at him. I wanted to stay. I wanted to be with him. But I couldn't. I had to go back to school. It was a summer fling. Nothing more. *Why does it feel like so much more?*

CHAPTER 29
Friday

Time made everything easier. I knew that. It had taken me a while to get over Aiden. A lot longer to give up on ever receiving love from my father. So the pain in my chest? It would go away. Memories of J.J. would fade.

My eyes were puffy from crying the whole flight here. I was pretty sure I was dehydrated, but the tears just wouldn't stop. I'd skipped the cheap airport hotel and had come straight to the beach. I was already homesick and I thought that seeing the ocean might help. But now that I was standing here? It didn't help at all. The sun was only just rising. It should have been a magical sight. But all I could focus on was how the ocean looked cold and brutal. The air smelled different here. It didn't feel like the beach. My beach. I wanted the smell of sunscreen and sweat and salt air. *J.J.*

I sat down in the sand and I closed my eyes, remembering the way J.J.'s arms felt around me. How his lips felt against my skin. How his smile made the butterflies in my stomach multiply tenfold. And how he smelled like...home.

I opened my eyes and stared out at the Pacific Ocean. I knew my memories and feelings would fade if I gave it enough time. But what if I didn't fucking want them to?

This feeling was different than when other men in my life left me. I wasn't just sad. I felt...empty. Like a piece of myself was missing. I shook my head. What the hell was I doing in California when my heart was in Delaware? *What the actual fuck am I doing?*

I didn't want anything about this summer to fade. The realization made my tears finally dry up. I'd shed enough tears over my mistake. Because that's what leaving J.J. was. A mistake. It only took me flying across the country to realize it. And a super long layover. I was definitely sleep-deprived, but my mind had never been clearer. The sun was rising and I was not going to start a new day without being with the love of my life. Because J.J. wasn't a summer fling. He was everything.

I'd finally stood up to my dad this summer. If was like a weight had been lifted off my shoulders. But maybe this whole time I'd just needed to stand up to myself. To get over how I'd let every man in my life treat me in the past. J.J. wasn't them. And yeah, he had commitment issues. But so did I, or else I wouldn't be sitting in the sand on the wrong beach.

I left because I was scared. This whole summer was about bettering myself. And I was strong enough to face whatever life handed me. Right now it was handing me the man of my dreams. I just had to go back to Rehoboth to get him.

I stood up and brushed the sand off my ass. Fuck you California. Fuck you SMU. Fuck you fear. I was not going to run away from a good thing just because I was scared of walking away from tuition paid for by a shmuck. Not because I was scared of starting my dreams of starting a restaurant one year sooner than expected. And most certainly not because I was scared of love. I'd never give Aiden and my dad the satisfaction of making me scared of love. Not in a million years.

And so what if J.J. hadn't said those words? He'd said it in his own way. *"It was never a summer fling to me. And you know that."* That right there? *Love.* He loved me too. But I was finally going to go tell him how I felt. I'd say it first. I'd say it as many times as I had to before he said it back. I didn't care if it took him longer than me. I just needed him to know that it was true.

I wheeled my suitcase back to the street as I scheduled an Uber. There was no money left in my accounts after my flight here. But I'd max out my credit card to get back to him. Whatever it took.

My Uber driver wasn't pleased with me as I kept pressing him to go faster. When we finally pulled into the terminal, I grabbed my luggage and ran as fast as possible. I got the earliest ticket despite the long layover. And if I thought crying through a flight was bad, being eager to get to my destination was worse. Planes were supposed to be fast, but they felt impossibly slow today. I was sitting impatiently at my layover in Dallas debating whether or not to rent a car instead when I heard the most intoxicating voice losing it on an air flight attendant.

"And I'm asking what's causing the delay?" he said. "There's not a cloud in the sky. I even checked the forecast in LA and it's all clear. I'm just trying to understand what's taking so damn long."

"Sir, I'm not going to ask you again to please take a seat."

"I've been sitting here for hours waiting for a connecting flight and…"

"J.J.?"

He turned at the sound of his name. For a second we both just stared at each other. I thought I might blink and he'd disappear. But I blinked several times and he was still standing there staring at me. Of all the layover locations in the country and he was here with me. God, it was him. My heart skipped a beat. And then I ran toward him. I jumped into his waiting arms, wrapping my legs around his waist.

"I'm sorry," I said. "I didn't mean any of it. I was just scared of getting my heart broken again."

"Mila…"

"But I love you. I love you so much that it hurts."

"Mila…"

"I have a hard time trusting people. You overheard that conversation with my dad. He doesn't care about me and I've always felt so unworthy of love because of him. But all of that's in the past and I don't want it to affect us. If there even is still an us…"

"Mila…"

"Please let there still be an us. Please forget about everything that happened this afternoon. We were never just a summer fling. You're everything to me. I came back here this summer so I could be home. I thought being there would fix me. But it wasn't being there that did it. It was you. You're home to me."

"Will you let me get two words in, Jellyfish Girl?"

I laughed against his neck.

He held me a little tighter. "I never should have let you walk away," he said into my hair. "I just felt…I was shocked that you were ending it. I didn't have enough time to react. But I've had a really crappy flight and an even crappier layover to figure out what you needed to hear. And maybe a little help from Kristen too."

I laughed again.

"I love you. I love you so much it hurts. And I was scared to tell you. I was scared that we wouldn't work out and I'd get hurt. But it hurt a hell of a lot more knowing I never told you how I felt. And watching you walk away? It nearly killed me." His hot breath on the side of my neck was just as soothing as his words. "Ever since you walked away it felt like a piece of me was missing. And now that you're back in my arms, I'm never letting you go again. When I'm with you, nothing else matters."

It was everything I needed to hear and more.

"Maybe you thought we were just one summer and you were making the best of it," he said. "But I never saw it that way. I thought it was the beginning of us. I never saw the timer on our relationship. I never saw it. And if you felt it, it's gone now." He unwrapped my legs from around his waist and I let my feet slide back down to the floor.

He looked so nervous and excited at the same time that for a second I thought he was going to get down on one knee. And I loved him, but I didn't need that. This whole time I just wanted him to say that he loved me back. My heart was too full already. I couldn't handle anymore.

"Can we go back to the beach now?" I asked. It didn't matter that Rehoboth could only be until the end of summer. I'd start my restaurant anywhere with him. But I wanted to soak in as much time as possible in the place where we met.

"You're not going back to SMU?"

"I hate California. And like you said…I don't need a degree to start a restaurant. I'm already a great chef."

He smiled. "You know that business degree I thought you needed? I had a lot of time to think on the way back to you and…I already have that degree. We can start a restaurant together. I can handle that side of it and you can handle all the cooking. I think we'd make quite the team."

That was what he was excited to talk to me about. A business proposal. Not a marriage proposal. I smiled. "You want to start a restaurant with me?"

"More than anything."

"But what about your job?"

"I quit."

"You quit?" I was pretty sure I was beaming.

"We both know it wasn't exactly a good fit. Besides, I wouldn't have enough time to do both. And I was kind of hoping we could open our restaurant in Rehoboth."

The man of my dreams wanted to start a life with me in the location of my dreams. "Are you sure you want to give up your job?" I asked.

He nodded. "Are you sure you don't want to finish up school at SMU?"

God, yes. He was offering me a life at the beach. The restaurant of my dreams. And most importantly…he was offering me his heart. And I'd never give up on us again. I stared into his eyes. I used to think I got lost in them. But maybe I felt more found than anything. "I'm so sure."

"Then let's go home. After all, we still have a few more weeks of summer left."

I smiled up at him. He was right. And all those summer nights we'd shared up until this point hadn't been on a timer. They'd been the start of us. I'd wanted to find myself this summer. And I had. Because of him. He encouraged me instead of bringing me down. He believed in my goals as much as I did. And he loved me for me. Quirks and all.

I stood on my tiptoes and kissed him. It didn't matter that we were in a crowded airport. Or that neither one of us had slept last night. All that mattered was that we were together.

"I love you," he whispered against my lips.

"I love you...Jaime Jamison."

He groaned.

"My lifeguard," I corrected and ran my fingers along his scruff.

"Better, Jellyfish Girl," he said with a smile.

I smiled back and the aroma of summer that clung to his clothes hit me.

Kristen had been right about a lot of things. But mainly that a man's smell was of the utmost importance. One whiff of my lifeguard and I was a goner. And now no one would ever be able to erase the smell of summer from our skin.

EPILOGUE
9 Months Later

"I think I made too much," I said, looking down at the piles of spanakopita. "Is anyone even going to come? Who comes to Rehoboth in May?"

J.J. rubbed my back. "I have a feeling we'll at least get a few customers. Let's go open up."

"But what if we run out of Tzatziki?" I was spiraling. Opening a restaurant was the most stressful thing in the world. Now I knew how the contestants on Project Runway felt when they only had one day to design an avant garde outfit.

"It'll be fine. Come on, our hungry customers await." J.J. pulled me into the dining room of the Greek Jellyfish.

I took a deep breath and was about to flip the CLOSED sign to OPEN when someone grabbed my shoulders.

"Congrats!" yelled Kristen.

"Ah!" I screamed. "You made it!"

"Of course I made it. You think I was going to let some random person be your first customer? You must be crazy."

"But what about volleyball?" Kristen had just learned that she was going to be part of the U.S. volleyball team at the International Tournament of Athletes.

"What about it?" she asked. "Stuffing my face with gyros isn't going to make us miss out on winning gold." Kristen walked over to the counter. J.J. was standing there looking like a Greek god. Seriously. He was wearing a toga and everything. That was as close as I could get to making him wear a shirt during work.

"What can I get for you today, miss?" asked J.J.

"One gyro. And a spanakopita. And some souvlaki. Hell, just give me one of everything."

He laughed. "One Gluttonous Kristen coming right up."

"Is one of everything seriously called the Gluttonous Kristen?" asked Kristen.

J.J. pointed to the listing on the menu.

"Don't look at me," I said. "That was all J.J. He assured me that you'd order one of everything the first time you came."

"Well of course I would. But I would have preferred that you called it the Beautiful Gold Medalist. Or really anything without the word gluttonous in it. You try going through a week of volleyball practice and *not* consuming 8000 calories a day. It's literally impossible."

"Bring home a gold for the U.S. and we'll change it," said J.J.

"Deal," agreed Kristen. "Now go get my food. I have to talk to Mila in private." She shooed J.J. away.

We took a seat at one of the adorable white and blue tables I had picked out.

"God, this place is amazing," said Kristen. "I feel like I've been teleported to Santorini."

"That's exactly what I was hoping to hear. But save that for when J.J. is back. I want the juicy details on whatever you had to send him away to talk to me about. Oh my God, you have a new boyfriend, don't you?"

"I have lots of new boyfriends."

That makes sense to me.

Kristen pulled a binder out of her purse.

"Please tell me you don't actually have a binder full of men."

Kristen's face lit up. "I do. And not just any men. The *hottest* men."

"I thought you were supposed to be celibate during training?"

"I am. Which is awful, by the way. But the reward at the end will be so worth it."

"Winning gold would be pretty awesome."

"Psssh, who cares about winning gold? *These* are my rewards." She opened the binder and showed me the first page - a picture and bio for some Spanish soccer player. "In just a few weeks I'm going to be surrounded by all the hottest athletes on the planet. And I'm pretty sure they will have had the same sex ban as me. Now, help me choose my targets." She flipped through a few more pages.

"Is that a binder full of men?" asked J.J. as he approached with a platter full of food.

"It is," said Kristen. "I guess you can help me choose too."

"Looking at men isn't really my thing, but I'll tell you right now...that guy is definitely gay."

"What?" squealed Kristen. "There's no way Tim Wood is gay."

"How about Bryce Walker?" I suggested. "He kinda looks like J.J."

"Oooh, he's yummy. And speaking of yummy, this gyro is freaking fantastic."

We flipped through the rest of the athletes as Kristen finished her feast. By the end she had narrowed it down to a dozen that she was going to try to "get to know." Which definitely meant bang.

"If you two are done, we should probably open for real now," said J.J. "It's almost lunchtime."

I smiled up at him. "Okay. But first I have a surprise for you."

"You do?" he asked.

"I do. Close your eyes."

"Should I be here for this?" asked Kristen. "If it involves a Thanksgiving turkey or a rolling pin, please let me leave first."

I laughed. "That would be entirely inappropriate to do in our brand-new restaurant."

"Not to mention a potential health code violation," added J.J.

Kristen gave me a sassy look. "You mean to tell me that you two recreated Greece and dressed each other up in togas and didn't end up banging on the floor? Or better yet, in front of that mirror? What a waste."

Of course we did. I gulped as I flashed back to when J.J. had me pinned up against one of the pillars.

"Oh my God," said Kristen. "You guys did do it!"

"What? No."

"Can I open my eyes yet?" asked J.J.

"No, come with me." I led him out the front door on-to the Rehoboth boardwalk. Just as I had requested, my present had been delivered this morning. "Okay, open 'em." As he opened his eyes, I pulled the sheet off the statue I had commissioned of him wearing a toga and standing in a heroic lifeguard pose. It was everything I had hoped for and more.

"Whoa," said J.J.

"Does that mean you like it?" I asked.

"Penis!" yelled Kristen.

J.J. laughed. "Why is there such a visible outline of my penis?"

I had been focused on the face and the abs. But they were absolutely right. "I guess the shorts you were wearing in the reference photo were a little clingy."

"Well I love it," he said with a huge grin.

"Really? You're not mad about the penis?"

"No one could be mad about a penis like that. Is it for real that big?" whispered Kristen.

I shrugged. "Try not to be too jealous."

"You're going to be the jealous one after I come back from the games with Lebron James on my arm."

"He's married," said J.J.

"Fine. Bryce Walker."

"Way out of your league."

"Because he looks like you?"

J.J. nodded.

"Alright. Then definitely Tim Wood."

"Wasn't that the gay one?" I asked.

"I hate both of you."

"We love you too. Seriously, I'm sure you'll find someone perfect for you. Just like I did."

J.J. pulled me into a hug. Even though he'd been working nonstop to help me get the Greek Jellyfish open, he still smelled like saltwater. Like summer. Like my lifeguard.

ABOUT THE AUTHOR

Ivy Smoak is the international bestselling author of *The Hunted Series*. Her books have sold over 1 million copies worldwide, and her latest release, *Empire High Untouchables*, hit #10 in the entire Kindle store.

When she's not writing, you can find Ivy binge watching too many TV shows, taking long walks, playing outside, and generally refusing to act like an adult. She lives with her husband in Delaware.

Facebook: IvySmoakAuthor
Instagram: @IvySmoakAuthor
Goodreads: IvySmoak

Made in the USA
Columbia, SC
18 February 2024

31961879R00200